THE TIME MAIDENS
TELLUS TWO

(The Cold War of Vanag)

Evan F. Riley, Jr.

ISBN: 9798373841245

After their brief and sucessful missions during the pivotal year of 1968, the Time Maidens were ready to go back to planning missions at random time periods. *THE TIME: JUNE 3, 2017. THE PLACE: IRAQ-TURKEY BORDER.*

Lin and Cuca had been chosen to go on this next mission to rescue nine children from an ethnic group known as the Kurds. The Kurds were a people located in the region of Turkey, Syria, Iran and Iraq. They had no country of their own, and were caught in the middle of constant strife and warfare involving these countries. Many times they bore the brunt of persecution from these other nations.

After the 911 Attacks on September 11, 2001, the region of western Asia became the center of attention. First the United States invaded Afghanistan to destroy the safe havens for terrorists. Two years later, the Americans invaded Iraq. As a result the civilian populations in the region were turned upside down. Refugees were everywhere, including the Kurds.

On the day of this mission, the children to be rescued were attempting to cross over from Iraq to Turkey. There were a few refugee camps set up by both the Red Cross and Red Crescent. Having been displaced and separated from their families the children were seeking help. On the early morning of June 3, the children would be walking on a lone desert road.

Preparing for this quick mission, Lin and Cuca observed on the time scanner that no one else was in the vicinity. In order to fit in and appear to be someone that the children would know and trust, the two Time Maidens would be wearing black abayas. These were the cloaks, or robelike dresses that many Muslim women wear. Lin and Cuca would also wear a veil over their faces to conceal that one of them was Chinese, and the other Incan. The children may not understand or relate to these nationalities. Even though the two Time Maidens would be speaking Kurmanki, one of the many dialects used by the Kurds.

Assembling at the ring operations complex, Lin and Cuca were ready to make the time-jump into the Iraqi desert. "Are you ready, Cuca?" Lin asked. "Let's go and rescue some children from a miserable life and war zone." Cuca nodded as she made sure the veil covered most of her face. With that, both of the Time Maidens entered through the ring.

Once on the other side after the time ring materialized, it quickly vanished as planned. Lin and Cuca froze. This didn't appear to be in the Iraqi desert. It was damp and foggy, and there was green grass under their feet. The two Time Maidens thought that they heard the sound of horns. Horns coming from ships, as if a harbor were nearby. However, the fog was so thick that you could cut it with a knife. "What is going on?" Lin asked.

"Yes, what is this place?" Cuca added. "This doesn't look like a desert."

"No, it doesn't," Lin replied. "Let's have a look around."

"As Rowena would say," Cuca stated, "*GREAT SAMHAIN.*"

Lin and Cuca made their way over to what appeared to be a larger-than-life statue. At first they could hardly make out the features as it was barely morning and very foggy. Then Lin read what was written on the marble pedestal supporting the statue. In Russian it read, *VLADIMIR ILYICH LENIN. FATHER OF THE SOCIALIST COUNTRIES OF EARTH AND TELLUS TWO.* "WHAT!" Lin exclaimed.

Just then, a shadowy figure appeared out of the fog. No, two figures. It was a young mother holding a small child by the hand. The mother was wearing a waterproof hooded parka. She had long platinum-colored hair that dropped down from the sides of the hood. The woman started talking. It sounded like she said the same thing several times. But the Time Maidens did not understand what the young woman was saying. This was strange indeed. Did not all of the Time Maidens have a special Aeduian device that, when inserted into the ear, enabled them to speak and comprehend every language ever spoken on Earth? Why were they having trouble understanding this woman?

Lin and Cuca had been speaking in Aeduian to one another. "I too, saw Russian inscribed on the pedestal of the leader Lenin." Cuca stated. "But this isn't Russian that this woman is speaking. Should we attempt to speak to her in Russian?"

"I'm not sure, " Lin replied. "Is this even Russia?"

The young mother came closer to the Time Maidens. She noticed that their faces were mostly covered because of the veils. She had never seen abayas before. The woman then screamed at the top of her lungs in perfect Russian, *"SPIES. WE HAVE SPIES IN THE CITY."*

"Let's get out of here," Lin excitedly said. "Cuca, follow me." Lin then started running in the opposite direction of the screaming woman. Cuca was right behind her. Before they knew it, the two Time Maidens had kicked off their sandals, that they had assumed they would be wearing in the Iraqi desert. Their feet were now cold and wet. It was a good thing that the black abayas they were wearing were loose fitting. Lin and Cuca could at least run fast in these outfits. And run fast they did.

By now, other voices could be heard as a crowd was chasing after them. There was still that unknown tongue. Then, a man's voice shouted out in Russian, *"STOP. IN THE NAME OF THE KGB AND STATE SECURITY POLICE, STOP!"*

Lin and Cuca ran behind what appeared to be a pavillion. They were obviously in a park. The voices of the crowd were getting closer. While still running for their lives, Lin yelled into her communication bracelet. *"CONTACT. I REPEAT, CONTACT. EMERGENCY."*

A time ring appeared. Mao and Illapu were overseeing the time ring on this now confused mission. Lin and Cuca literally dived into the ring, where it instantly disappeared from wherever the two Tima Maidens had just come from. Lin and Cuca picked themselves up off the floor in the ring operations complex. They looked at each other, knowing that they were both safe and in one piece.

This was the first time in the history of the Time Maidens where an emergency was declared. As a result, an alarm went off all throughout the kingdom. Everyone had been drilled to report to the ring operations complex. The three other Time Maidens arrived first. Then Shako, followed by Justinian and Rebecca. Even Mary Collard was on her way. One of the androids from the agricultural section was flying her in via a shuttlecraft.

"*GREAT SAMHAIN!*" What happened?" Rowena excitedly stated as she approached Lin and Cuca. "What's going on?" She further asked.

"We have no idea," Lin replied, still catching her breath.

"As you all know," Cuca added, "we were supposed to be going to Iraq in 2017. But I can assure you that we weren't in Iraq. The whole mission was insane."

"Well, this has never happened before," Michaela interjected.

"Something obviously went wrong," Rowena said. "But what?"

Lin and Cuca briefly explained what had taken place. Both Time Maidens spoke rapidly as they explained their bizarre time-jump. Sensing that her fellow Time Maiden sisters, were still clearly upset, Amaresh stated, "I think that you two should get out of these clothes, go back to your palaces and get cleaned up." Everyone seemed to be nodding their heads in agreement.

"Then, let's say in about two hours we all meet in the briefing-planning room to find out what happened." Rowena suggested.

"Good idea," Michaela said. "We can look back at the video from the mission. If need be, the time scanner can help us." Lin and Cuca made their way to their respective palaces.

The other Time Maidens and assistants went to the briefing-planning room to find out what had taken place on this mission. Clearly, something went wrong, and Lin and Cuca ended up in a dangerous situation. They did indeed play back the video that recorded everything from this mission. Everything was just as Lin and Cuca related. Everyone watching this video were just as perplexed regarding the young woman speaking in a language that none of them could comprehend. But they did understand when the woman switched over to Russian.

Still, all in all, the group was just as much in the dark as Lin and Cuca. In addition, the planet-time scanner didn't have any information either. The invisible Aeduian satellite orbiting Earth recorded everything taking place on the planet down below. It had been this way since the Aeduians sent the special craft thousands of years ago. And yet, nothing beyond what Lin and Cuca had already related, could be pulled up from this latest mission.

Having freshened up, Lin and Cuca joined the other Time Maidens and assistants. They had hoped that in their absence the others had found something. But this was not the case. Lin insisted that they view the playback of the recorded mission again. This was all they had. An audio-video recording from monitors in the kingdom. Still, nothing new or revealing.

"All right," Michaela spoke up. "This is so not normal for us."

"Yes," Rowena added," do we dare plan anymore missions. Have time-jumps become erratic. Who knows where we can end up?"

"There is another thing, that strikes me as odd," Michaela stated. "And that is what is written on the pedestal of the statue of Vladimir Lenin."

"What about it?" Cuca asked.

"Yes," Lin added. "What is so odd?'

Michaela went on to explain her observation. It was a historical fact that Lenin was considered the father of the Soviet Union, and other socialist countries also praised Lenin as a hero and leader. However, there was something else engraved on the pedestal that was out of place. *Tellus Two.* "What does that mean?" Michaela now asked.

"Well, for a start, Tellus, is another name for Earth," Lin replied. "I believe the proper name is *Tellus Mater,* or *Terra Mater.*"

"That's correct, Lin," Rowena added. "Tellus is a Latin word. The ancient Romans referred to Tellus when using 'Earth Mother Goddess.'"

"Yes," Michaela said. "But where does the *Two* come in? Is there another Earth, or colony from our planet that we have somehow missed? Perhaps a Soviet-Earth colony. This may explain people speaking in Russian, and the statue of Lenin."

"We know about Texacos being an Earth colony," Amaresh now stated. "After all, we helped set it up. We had to transport the adult Confederate-Americans in order to save the children from mission thirteen."

"But another mystery regarding this Tellus Two," Cuca added, "is this: Why is there no information on the planet-time scanner? If there is another world, and it has a connection to Earth, we should be able to pull something up on it. When was this world established? When and how did the Russians leave and set up a colony?"

"Good questions, Cuca," Lin replied. "The Soviet Union collapsed in 1991. They didn't have the technology or means to find and set up a colony on an Earth-like world who knows where."

"Well," Rowena spoke up, "we are missing something and getting nowhere. There is only one source we can go to. Vix. Or should I say the Aeduians." Everyone in the room agreed with the Celtic Time Maiden's suggestion.

Next, and from this very same room, contact was made with the planet Aedui. Usually, when Vix spoke with the Time Maidens through the audio-video channel, her fellow Aeduian council members were also present. These were the only Aeduians that the young Earth women ever spoke with. For the most part, Vix would do the talking. Lin took the lead in inquiring about what went wrong on this last time-jump. After all, it was she and Cuca that ended up in running for their lives.

Vix patiently listened. One must remember that the Aeduians were humanoid, yet nearly a half-million years more advanced than Earthlings. Vix was also several hundred years old. Even if she appeared to be around the same age as the Time Maidens.

Meanwhile, the wheels were spinning inside Rowena's head. She knew that millenniums ago the Aeduians had sent out planet-time scanners to many worlds. As far as she and the other Time Maidens knew, the Aeduians had decided on Earth being the planet to rescue children from in order to keep their dying, Aeduian culture alive. *Are there other planets out there in the universe similar to Earth?* Rowena thought. *The Aeduians are humans in a way. But, are there other humanoid civilizations like us on* other *worlds as well?*

Vix declined when asked if she wished to see the video playback from the last mission. She then stated, "Time Maidens and assistants. There is no need to trouble yourselves any further. This world that Lin and Cuca somehow managed to be transported to through a time ring is indeed not your planet Earth. This Tellus Two is another planet in another galaxy similar to Earth. However, somehow, by a cosmic accident, this planet has been influenced by people from Earth.

"*WHAT!*" Rowena exclaimed as she shot up out of her seat at the conference table. "Cosmic accident. When were you going to inform us of this accident? Lin and Cuca could have been trapped or killed on this other planet."

"Rowena," Vix calmly replied, "and for that matter, all of the rest of you Time Maidens and assistants. Even we on Aedui had no idea that something like this could take place. I can assure you, though, that measures have been taken to see to it that an accident like this won't occur again."

"Vix," Michaela now asked, "are we permitted to know anything about this planet Tellus Two?"

"Yes," Cuca added. "Good question, seeing how you stated that somehow there is an Earth connection. This would explain why we heard some speaking and yelling in Russian."

"True," Rowena interjected. "How did that happen, Vix?"

"Yes," Vix replied to these questions. "You have a right to know about Tellus Two. Everything will be explained to you." The Aeduian woman then informed the Time Maidens and assistants what to expect next.

The first thing to take place was that an android from Aedui was sent through the master time ring. He was carrying a tray that contained the special ear devices that the Time Maidens had been given when first being rescued by the Aeduians. When each assistant, namely, Shako, Justinian, Rebecca and Mary Collard agreed to help the Time Maidens, they, too, had been given this ear device.

These new, additional devices would enable the Time Maidens and assistants to speak the unknown tongues spoken on Tellus Two. Each Time Maiden and assistant inserted the device into their left ear. Within seconds, the device dissolved. Like the previous ear device, they experienced a brief, yet pleasant, explosion in their minds. Instantly, everyone could understand dozens of new languages, and even dozens more dialects of these strange, unfamiliar tongues spoken on this other planet far away from Earth.

Next, the Time Maidens were informed that they now had access to the invisible planet-time scanner orbiting Tellus Two. As with Earth, the Aeduians had sent this satellite to Tellus Two thousands of years ago. Everything of the planet's history could now be retrieved. The first thing that the Time Maidens wanted to get more information on was what and where did this last time-jump that Lin and Cuca attempted to make take place?

The Time Maidens once again retrieved the video footage of when Lin and Cuca came through the time ring that was programmed to materialize in Iraq. They saw themeselves in this strange, foggy world that they now knew was not Iraq or, for that matter, Earth. However, what they really wanted to know was what this woman, an alien woman at that (as she was not an Earthling), say to them before screaming in Russian?

Now that the Time Maidens and assistants understood the languages of Tellus Two, it was clear what the woman said. She asked, "Who are you? Why are you here, and what are these strange clothes you are wearing?" Obviously , on Tellus Two, or at least in the land where they had materialized, no one had ever seen a abaya worn by Islamic women. As their faces were also partially covered, Lin and Cuca did indeed appear to the young woman to be conceling something of themselves. Thus they appeared as spies.

All of the Time Maidens and assistants could speak and comprehend Russian. They had no problem understanding the man's voice screaming about the *KGB.* Others in the crowd chasing Lin and Cuca were also speaking Russian. But now the former strange tongue, along with several dialects, could also be understood by the Time Maidens and their other associates from Earth.

This time scanner orbiting Tellus Two identified the language as *Zotovan.* And the land as *Zotova.* What was this land now influenced or even controlled by Russian-speaking people? There was so much to learn about this planet, Tellus Two.

The Time Maidens and assistants once again wanted to speak with Vix. They were at least somewhat more informed now that they had access to the time scanner orbiting Tellus Two. And they could speak and understand the languages of this "new world."

Seeing Vix through the video screen monitor to Aedui, the

Aeduian woman spoke to the group saying, "Hopefully, all of you now know a little about this other Earth-like world."

"We are somewhat out of the dark." Lin replied.

"Yes," added Michaela. "But there is so much to learn about this planet."

Vix is a woman of few words, Rowena thought. *I'm going to ask her what this is all about.* "With access and information regarding this planet, Tellus Two, what are we supposed to do with it."

"So glad you asked, Rowena," Vix answered. "For the time being, no more time-jumps should be planned on your world. Instead, what we Aeduians would like you Time Maidens and assistants to do is concentrate on research about Tellus Two. Study all of its history, peoples and cultures. And the Earth connection. The Russians were not the only ones to influence this planet. When you do your research, you will discover this."

"And just why should we get so involved studying this other world?" Rowena asked back. "Don't we have enough to do finding and relocating children from our own Earth."

"Yes, you do," Vix replied. "But we find that Tellus Two is not so different from your Earth. It holds out promise of possible future missions."

WHAT! Rowena thought. *Possible future missions. How can we cover two worlds? Do the Aeduians think that we are going to live forever?*

Now Vix didn't say for sure that there would be missions. Nor did she say who would be making these time-jumps if this did become a reality. With that, the Time Maidens and assistants concluded this meeting with Vix.

As they were instructed by the Aeduians to learn all that they could about Tellus Two, the Time Maidens and assistants set out to do just that. As a collective body, there were some great minds in the kingdom. Three groups were formed to begin this intensive study of this other planet.

The first group was made up of Cuca, Amaresh and Mary Collard. These two Time Maidens had a lot of wisdom and experience behind them. Mary Collard was a learned woman of her time, and since becoming an occasional assistant, had been brought up to speed with Aeduian technology. She was proving to be a great asset for the Time Maidens.

The second group was one Time Maiden, Rowena, along with Justinian and Rebecca. Rowena was by far the most impetuous, daring and compassionate of the Time Maidens. Yet, Rowena was sharp and also wanted to know all of the facts and background of each mission. Whether she went on it or not. The young married couple were great at research. This is mostly what they did for the Time Maidens. Justinian and Rebecca had also proved themselves as great assets whenever they went on a mission. Of all the Time Maidens, they were probably the closest to Rowena. This would be an added reason that this threesome would make a great team.

Finally, the third group consisted of Lin, Michaela and Shako. Lin was the most futuristic of the five Time Maidens. Having come from the 25th century, and on her way to another planet herself, she was familiar with technology, both good and bad. Lin was brilliant, usually calm and a deep thinker.

Michaela was the first Time Maiden, having come from Earth's distant past. The young Hebrew woman was also smart, logical, but quick on her feet.

As for Shako, the first to become a Time Maidens assistant, the former Japanese schoolteacher was a great asset in the kingdom. Although Shako had never been on a mission, her knowledge of science, history and how everything worked in the ring operations complex, childrens' complex and more made her valuable to both the Time Maidens and Aeduians. Thus, these were the three teams that were formed to find out everything that needed to be known about Tellus Two.

Using the planet time scanner above Earth, the three teams tracked what happened involving the Russians from this planet. Then, once it was discovered what took place, the other time scanner orbiting Tellus Two could be used. The Time Maidens and assistants would discover much more than they realized.

This mystery began in late January of the year 1986. One of the Soviet Union's latest nuclear-powered submarines left its arctic base in Murmansk, located in the northwest part of Russia. The military-scientific mission of this submarine was of course top secret. This submarine, *K-37* made its way to the North Atlantic Ocean and headed south. Its destination: Antarctica, or the South Pole. The bottom of the world, as it were.

In addition, though, an American submarine a couple of days later left the navy base in San Diego, California. This submarine was sailing in the opposite direction. The Arctic Circle, or North Pole. The American submarine was also on a classified mission. The submarines of both nations were made up of an assortment of personnel. Not just the usual crew. The Americans and Russians had no idea that events would change their lives forever.

A famous comet from antiquity visits planet Earth about every seventy-five years. This is of course *Halley's Comet.* The comet was last seen in the vicinity of Earth in 1910. It was due back in 1986. Halley's Comet would be closest to Earth this time on February 9. Many people from around the world were anxious to see the famous comet. A whole generation, now in their eighties, hoped to see the comet one last time. It was as if they would be getting a part of their childhood back.

Meanwhile, the two secret submarines sailed on to their destinations. On February 9, Halley's Comet did indeed reach its closest point from Earth. There are many mysteries in the universe that can never be explained. While Halley's Comet was near Earth, a similar comet was in the vicinity of the faraway planet of Tellus Two. A vortex opened up and the American and Russian submarines vanished from Earth. They both were instantly transported to Tellus Two. The American submarine was now under the North Pole of this other planet. Likewise, the Russian submarine was at the South Pole of Tellus Two.

"Great Samhain!" Rowena said to her team as they observed this from the planet-time scanner orbiting Tellus Two. "What is it with the Aeduicans and comets?"

"What do you mean?" Justinian asked.

Before Rowena could reply, Rebecca answered, "You may have forgotten, Justinian, but it was a comet that brought about the downfall of the Aeduian civilization."

"Correct, Rebecca," Rowena added. "Something in that comet rendered the Aeduians sterile."

"Oh, yes," Justinian stated. "Now I remember. This was why you Time Maidens were recruited. To rescue and send Earth children to repopulate Aedui."

These parallel comets near two worlds, in different galaxies were the reason Earth people were transported to Tellus Two. However, this was not the original name for this planet. The actual name was *Vanag*. This was why many people on this world now called Tellus Two, were known as *Vanagians*. At one time there was only one language spoken on this world. This language was also known as Vanagian. Like on Earth, other languages developed, depending on where the civilizations lived. Such as Zotovan.

The two other groups, with help from the planet-time scanner orbiting Tellus Two, also gathered the usual information.

Although working independently, the three groups agreed that it was beneficial to periodically come together and exchange information. The three teams met at Michaela's palace to compare the information gathered thus far.

By now the three groups knew how Earth people came to be on this other planet. They also knew about both Halley's Comet and another comet streaking across the skies of Earth and Tellus Two. This opened up a vortex that was responsible for transporting the American and Russian submarines to this other world. At this point, it didn't matter how. It had simply happened.

"One thing is for certain," Lin said during a meeting. "We now know that the Russians and Americans had no idea what had happened to them. Or even what world or galaxy they were now in."

"That's for sure," Michaela added. "None of the stars or new planets in this unknown solar system would look familiar to them."

"As there are so many galaxies," Rowena stated, "that only the Aeduians can keep up with them, what galaxy is this Tellus Two a part of?"

"Astronomers from Earth," Lin replied, "will officially call this galaxy *Messier 64-NGC 4826*. Or better known as the *Black Eye Galaxy*. Also known as the *Evil Eye Galaxy*. It is 17 million light years from our Milky Way Galaxy.

"Evil Eye Galaxy," Cuca said. "And Lin and me were there? This is frightening. At any rate, these Earth people won't be going back to their home planet anytime soon."

"Which raises another question," Amaresh interjected. "Why did the Aeduians allow this to happen in the first place?"

"Ah," Rowena answered. "We must remember that the Aeduians never become involved in the affairs of less-advanced civilizations. This may have been a freakish, unexplained event involving Earth and Tellus Two; but the Aeduians will not attempt to change anything.

"And yet," Lin concluded, "we Time Maidens are now involved."

This was just the tip of the iceberg for the Time Maidens and their assistants. There was so much to learn about this otherworld, Vanag, that was renamed Tellus Two by people from Earth. And what about the Americans and Russians, now that they had been transported to this faraway world in another galaxy. How much did they influence this other planet?

Using the planet-time scanner, the three groups would continue to gather information. Rowena's group would research the Americans involvement. Lin, Michaela and Shako would follow the Russians. As for Cuca, Amaresh and Mary Collard, these three would be taking an in-depth study of the planet Vanag, before it became Tellus Two.

After this brief meeting with the two other teams, Rowena, Justinian and Rebecca set out to follow the American submarine before, and then after, they were transported to a different world in another galaxy.

On February 1, 1986, a U.S. Navy Los Angeles class submarine left its base on the west coast of the United States. This was the *USS Tampa*. Its destination: The Arctic Circle. A Los Angeles class vessel usually had a crew of one hundred and thirty-three sailors. However, about a dozen or so regular members of the crew were deleted to make room for some additional personnel. These were important people. And this was a secret mission.

The USS Tampa was under the command of Captain Ronald Albritton. He was the Executive Officer, or XO. Next in command was Lt. Commander Vincent Cardova, the navigator. The Lt. Commander was a dark skinned, Puerto Rican. Another Lt. Commander, the weapons officer was Jeff Buchanan. He was a Scotsman from New England. The Senior Chief Petty Officer was Thomas Prescott, from Wildwood, New Jersey, followed by Chief Petty Officer, Douglas Mathis. This petty officer was from Idaho. A landlocked U.S. state. Chief Mathis always wanted to see the ocean. No wonder he joined the navy. All of these officers were experienced submariners. Captain Albritton had been serving in the U.S. Navy for over thirty years now. He was mostly gray, and looked like a typical submarine captain. Submarines had come a long way since then. Especially the USS Tampa.

The boat's doctor was Larry Caldwell. The doctor held the rank of a navy captain. This would make him another senior officer. But in addition to him was a female intern named Sylvia Rizzo. Sylvia had an Italian background and was from New York City. She was in her last year of schooling at a naval medical school. This young woman was a naval lieutenant. *"WHAT!"*

Rowena exclaimed as she discovered this in her research regarding this vessel. "A female doctor on a U.S. Navy submarine in 1986." All of this and more would be revealed as Rowena, Justinian and Rebecca continued on with their research. The rest of this crew in time would prove to be a cast of interesting characters. It was a secret that some of this personnel were on the USS Tampa in the first place.

By the late 1970's, and well into the 1980's, relations were strained between the superpowers. Many throughout the world feared that a nuclear war between the United States and the Soviet Union would break out at any day. This would prove to be worse than the 1962 Cuban Missle Crisis. The Americans and Soviets had ten times the nuclear weapons that they had back in 1962. For one thing, nuclear-powered and armed submarines prowled the oceans. The USS Tampa was one such submarine in the U.S. Navy.

In the event of a nuclear war, and a war could start by mistake due to human and computer error, nuclear submarines played a vital role in the navies of both of the superpowers. Land-based missile bases could be easy targets as they were stationary. Both the United States and Soviet Union knew this. However, a submarine was much more difficult to track and could change position with ease.

For instance, if the Soviet Union launched a first strike against the United States and important targets were destroyed, the Americans could strike back with devasting results. From the North Pole and Arctic Ocean area, distance for targets became smaller. Submarines such as the USS Tampa could launch their cruise missiles. From this position at the top of the world, cities such as Vladivostok, Murmansk, Leningrad, and even Moscow were in range. This was all part of *MAD (Mutual Assured Destruction.)* In other words, there were no winners in a nuclear war.

The USS Tampa was on a secret training excerise to test

new equipment and updates in case a war should occcur. But on this mission was also an intresting crew. Along with the normal personnel, was an assortment of special guests and observers. For one thing, there were a number of women on this submarine. This was unusual during this time period of the U.S. Navy. A few adjustments had to be made to fit these women on board this submarine. Who were these women? And why were they on the USS Tampa?

The intern doctor was already mentioned. The U.S. Navy was preparing to allow women doctors on their vessels. Including submarines. The days of a woman doctor assigned only on naval bases was about to change. In addition to Doctor Sylvia Rizzo, were six young women eighteen to twenty years old. They would be an E-1, or Seaman Recruit (SR.) For this mission the navy was conducting an experiment. They wanted to see how these young women would do aboard a nuclear submarine. And with a predominantly male crew.

The women were made up of two Latin-Americans, two African-Americans, and finally two Caucasians. Women aside, this was quite a diversity. But the male crew was fairly multi-national as well.

The Latino girls, both eighteen years old, were Jennifer Perez and Rosa Garcia. Jennifer was Puerto Rican from Miami, Florida. Rosa, was of Mexican descent from San Antonio, Texas. The African-American girls were Cecila Rice, nineteen years old, from Detroit, Michigan, and Leah Jordon, eighteen, from Mobile, Alabama. Finally, the two white girls were Linda Flannery, twenty years old, from Bangor, Maine, followed by Christina Salter, eighteen, from Lincoln, Nebraska.

These six young women were indeed from diverse backgrounds and regions of the country. They were all also fairly attractive, even though they had to dress down somewhat as U.S. sailors. But to all of the young males on board the USS Tampa they were a welcome sight. As this was just an experiment, most of the male crew didn't even know about these female sailors until the day of departure.

But there were even more women involved with this secret mission. There was a twenty-five-year-old journalist named Terri Eden. She represented a national woman's magazine. Miss Eden was allowed to accompany the six new female sailors. Terri was to report about life on the USS Tampa, and how the female recruits interacted with a mostly male crew.

As this mission was presently classified, the journalist was limited to what she could reveal in her magazine. She was not even permitted to name the submarine or location of its mission. And it would probably be months before her article would be seen in print. This was still an experiment as far as the U.S. Navy was concerned. Terri Eden was a native of Bethany Beach, Delaware. She received her degree in journalism from Deleware State University. As Terri was a cute redhead, heads turned on the USS Tampa.

Next came Brenda Hutt, a thirty-year-old marine biologist. She was originally from Spokane, Washington. Her speciality, though, was arctic life. Both on land and in the sea. Being allowed to come aboard a Los Angeles class submarine, such as the USS Tampa was a trip of a lifetime. Most of Professor Hutt's observations would be seen through the portal windows of the submarine and cameras. But this too could be breathtaking. The professor was a dark-haired, dark-eyed beauty. Brenda had long black hair with a very white complexion. The crew would eventually give her nicknames such as Miss Vampire or *Morticia*, a character from the television show *The Addams Family*.

Added to this was another pretty face. Miss Tampa. For the year 1986, Tiffany Ash held this title. Tiffany would be attending the University of South Florida in the fall. In the meantime, the young Tampa socialite wore her crown for various events. Having come from a wealthy family, Tiffany's father, a banker pulled some strings so that she, too, could be a part of this entourage of women on the USS Tampa. After all, Tiffany was Miss Tampa for the year. She was eighteen years old. This blue-eyed beauty queen had long blonde hair.

Last but not least would prove to be another woman that in time would have a deep impact on Tellus Two. This was twenty-four-year old Cynthia "Cindy" Henderson. Miss Henderson was from Broken Arrow, Oklahoma. She was a government intern. That is, Cindy was a state employee. She was a senator's aid. This senator from Oklahoma was a member of the Armed Service Committee. He was a right-wing, hawkish senator that believed in a strong America. Being a senator's aid, Cindy Henderson was also permitted to be one of the women to sail on this historic voyage of the USS Tampa.

In the beginning, the submarine crew thought that this Oklahoma girl was straight off the farm. Cindy also had blonde hair and blue eyes, but unlike Miss Tampa, her hair was much shorter. She wore little makeup. Cindy was given the nickname by the submarine crew, "Plain Jane." However, in the not-too-distant future, Cindy Henderson would transform into a entirely different woman. And not for the better.

Having come this far in their research regarding the Americans, Rowena stated to Justinian and Rebecca, "Now we know who the officers are in command of the USS Tampa on the eve of their being transported to this other planet."

"Not to mention how and why so many women were allowed on board this submarine," Rebecca added. "It's remarkable that they were on this vessel in the first place."

"Yes," Rowena said. "This so-called experiment with women as part of the crew was definitely ahead of its time. In addition to allowing all of these other female guests. Although, I can't help but wonder how many of these women would have changed their minds about this voyage had they known a vortex would open up and suck them out of their world forever."

"What next?" Justinian asked.

"We carry on with our research." Rowena answered. "We've only touched the tip of this iceberg. There is so much more to learn regarding the rest of this crew of the USS Tampa."

"And what happens after they end up on this other Earth-like world?" Rebecca asked. "This planet Vanag, or Tellus Two."

"I wonder what the other two teams are discovering?" Rowena concluded.

Being Time Maidens or their assistants, one would think that they had seen it all. Lin, Michaela and Shako were both amazed and disturbed at what they discovered about the Russians. And the submarine from the then-Soviet Union. The Time Maidens, when undertaking a mission, did their best not to interfere with or alter any of Earth's history. Their job was to rescue certain children on Earth who were in mortal danger and send them to Aedui. Not interfering could sometimes prove to be difficult.

However, neither the Americans nor the Russians knew anything of the Aeduian agenda. Once they were transported through a vortex to this other planet, they had no idea where they now were or what to do. Nor at first did each realize that the other was also on this other world.

By February 9, 1986, K-37 had reached its destination in Antarctica. Many Soviet submarines did not have names. But K-37 did. The boat was called *Vodyanoy.* (Water spirit in Russian.) Vodyanoy was a Delta III class, nuclear-powered submarine with unlimited range. Vodyanoy was armed with sixteen SS-N-18 missiles. Quite a lot of destructive firepower. The crew was made up of one hundred and thirty personnel. A few had been deleted to make room for other important people. Like the USS Tampa, there were special civilians on this voyage. Including women.

The crew of the Soviet submarine was as follows: The captain of Vodyanoy was Dmitri Starinov. The captain was loyal to the Soviet navy. He was an experienced submariner. Especially for long voyages. From Murmansk to the South Pole was nearly eleven thousand miles.

Next in command would be Lt. Commander Nikolai Grodno. He and the captain were both actually from Vladivostok, in the Soviet Far East. Having come from a port city, Starinov and Grodno had a love for the sea. As soon as they came of age they joined the Soviet navy and worked their way up in the ranks.

Like most submarines, there were two chiefs. One was Anatoly Poltav. He was from Kiev, in the Ukraine. The other was Matis Gaida. This chief came from a small village in Lithuania. Lithuania and Ukraine were Soviet republics. One large and the other very small. Even though most of the crew were actual Russians, these two chiefs were well-respected because of their knowledge and dedication on the Vodyanoy, and the navy in general. In addition, they could relate with other non-Russian personnel.

Next was a woman doctor. This was Yelena Ivanova. Doctor Ivanova was forty years old and from Leningrad. She was actually given the rank of lieutenant in the Soviet navy. Doctor Ivanova was a fairly attractive, dark-skinned, dark-eyed woman. The crew weren't too uncomfortable with a woman as their doctor on this voyage. Besides, she had a male assistant. His name was Pavel Tupolev. Pavel was in his late twenties from Minsk, Byelorrusia. Byelorussia was another Soviet republic. Yet, very Russian-like.

Two civilians were a married couple in their mid-thirties. This was a Jewish couple. Russian Jews made a great contribution in the Soviet Union. Especially in the medical and scientific fields. This couple was named Issac and Chaya Nimrosensky. They came from Sevastopol, in the Crimea. Issac and Chaya were both biologists. Chaya's speciality was marine biology. Issac knew all about microbes, plants, insects and many other small lifeforms.

Every ship, vessel or boat in the Soviet navy has a political officer on board. For this voyage of the Vodyanoy was a female political officer. The communist party found that in many cases women were more dedicated to the party than men. This political officer was Valeria Rostova from Moscow. Valeria was thirty years old. She had raven-colored hair, with cold-looking, chestnut eyes. Valeria was attractive but in a somewhat scary way.

As a political officer in the Soviet navy, Valeria dressed in a uniform dress that women in the navy wore. For this voyage, as she was on a submarine, Valeria dressed in a jumpsuit. Too many spiral stairs and ladders to climb. Valeria had the rank of lieutenant. However, in the event of an emergency, if the orders of the party were in jeopardy, Valeria could even assume command from the captain. And she would, if necessary.

Another young woman from the far city to the north, Arkhangelsk (Archangel), was Tatiana Semerova. She was also a reporter, like Terri Eden on the American submarine. Tatiana reported for the Soviet News Agency, *Tass.* What was Tatiana reporting on? None other than this special voyage of the Vodyanoy. However, it may be a year later before Tatiana's story appeared in *Tass.* And not at all if the navy and communist party didn't think that this mission was a complete success. And nothing would be revealed about the future, secret settlements.

Tatiana was twenty-four years old. The reporter had long blonde hair, along with green eyes that almost looked like two emeralds staring at you. Perhaps because of where she came from in the far north, Tatiana's skin was pale white. Her name in Russian means *Fairy Queen,* or princess. Tatiana almost looked like a mythical girl. Or even a character from Russian comic books. By the 1980's there were a few superhero comic books in the Soviet Union. No doubt they were copying western comic books. The difference was that Russian comic books glorified the motherland and communist system.

Two other young ladies allowed to be on Vodyanoy for this voyage were Svetlana Lebedeva and Anastasia Macagonova. Svetlana was the great-niece of a member of the politburo on her mother's side. She had a different last name from this great-uncle. No one on the Vodyanoy knew what member Svetlana was related to, so they were careful about what they said regarding any member of the politburo. People throughout the Soviet Union were careful what they said about their leaders, anyway.

Anastasia was the cousin of Svetlana, but on her father's

side. She, too, had a different last name as her mother was the sister of Svetlana's father. Svetlana and Anastasia were both twenty years old. She had long, curly brown hair. Anastasia was a cute, petite red head. Anastasia was so dainty-looking that she almost appeared child-like, or even resembled a pixie or elf. Both girls attended Moscow State University as they were Muscovites. Svetlana and Anastasia were studying to become schoolteachers. As they were ahead in their courses, the two girls were allowed to take time off to go on this voyage with other Soviet women.

There weren't as many women on Vodyanoy as there were on the American submarine. Nevertheless, as this was a special mission, a few women had been allowed on the Soviet submarine. For the time being, Lin, Michaela and Shako took an interest in knowing about the women. Like the Americans, it was unusual that they were allowed on a nuclear submarine at this time in the first place. More of the male crew would be studied later after they had been transported to the then-planet Vanag. Everyone would have a role to play in the aftermath.

Like the USS Tampa, the Soviet submarine was on a classified mission. Just what was this mission? Although a nuclear-armed submarine, Vodyanoy was actually on a peaceful mission. Again top secret. Most of the crew were used to not being informed of any mission until they were out to sea. As for the civilians, with the exception of Issac and Chaya Nimrosensky, the others were informed that they were among a privilaged few who were permitted to be on a voyage in one of the most sophisticated submarines in the Soviet navy. Details would come later.

Through the time scanner Lin, Michaela and Shako knew that the Soviet submarine was in Antarctica when Haley's Comet made its appearance. What was the purpose of Vodyanoy? The Soviet Union had several bases in Antarctica. So did the United States and other countries. Under the Antarctic Treaty there was to be no military activity at the South Pole. Only scientific research was permitted. However, nations broke treaties on a regular basis.

The Soviet Union could and would claim that the Vodyanoy was in Antarctica for scientific reasons. After all, Issac and Chaya Nimrosensky were scientists. And the other young, female civilians on Vodyanoy were somewhat involved with what was considered a peaceful mission and experiment. What was this mission, at least on the surface?

Inside the Soviet Union were many cold regions. To help get the best out of these frigid areas, the Russians were planning on constructing huge geodesic spheres. They would be made mostly out of thick glass. It may be cold in these regions, but there was still sunlight. These spheres would be greenhouses to grow large quanties of crops. They were actually farms in a controlled environment. This was also the plan for the Soviet bases in Antarctica. And this would be considered peaceful research.

However, there was more to these domed communities that would eventually be set up in Antarctica. Starting in the Soviet Research Station, Vostok, a grandiose scheme was secretly being planned. Vostok was established by the Soviet Union in 1957 on Princess Elizabeth Land, Antarctica. This was one of several bases that the Russians had set up.

The Soviet Union did plan to build geodesic domes on the surface of Antarctica. But under the ice and snow, when hitting solid ground the Soviets were going to build a half dozen or so, underground mini-cities. Up to two thousand citizens could live comfortably under the ice. For what purpose?

As tensions were high again between the United States and Soviet Union, the Soviet leadership feared that a nuclear war was inevitable between the superpowers. The Soviets desired to have some of their population spared. They reasoned that if a nuclear war should occur, Antarctica would not be affected. With these self-sufficent mini-cities, people from the Soviet Union would carry on. Some of the important leaders from the government may be living in these cities. However, no one in either the east or west had any idea that the Soviet Union would collapse in five years. The two Time Maidens and assistant found all of this quite fascinating.

Cuca, Amaresh and Mary Collard were the group that would be doing the research on the planet now known as Tellus Two. Through the planet-time scanner orbiting this planet, they knew that this world was originally called Vanag. As they began their research, the two Time Maidens and their assistant became fascinated, shocked and even spellbound by what they uncovered regarding this other world.

Starting with its formation as a planet, Vanag was millions of years old. But Cuca, Amaresh and Mary were more interested in tracing back to when the humanoids of Vanag first emerged. It only went back about eight thousand years. Vanag was indeed a very young world as far as people were concerned. When the Americans and Russians were transported to Vanag, the developing counrties were on the verge of an industrial revolution.

Vanag was the fourth world from its sun. This sun was slightly larger than Earth's sun, Sol. Vanag also had two moons. *Radu* and *Vulpe*. Both were similar to Earth's moon, but a little smaller. In this solar system were four other planets. The ancient Vanagians observed them as bright objects in the night sky and gave them mythical names. However, with the arrival of the Americans and Russians they were given new names. A lot changed after the Earth people found themselves on this faraway planet.

Excluding its fairly large polar caps, Vanag had four continents; and the Vanagians called these *Zotova, Ucella, Trozny* and *Enaim*. Zotova and Trozny were located in the northern hemisphere. Ucella, which was really three very large islands, was also in the northern hemisphere, while Enaim was located in the southern hemisphere. Enaim was about the size of Australia. Backward compared to the other continents, yet full of as yet, untapped natural resources.

Zotova and Trozny were two large landmasses, when combined were the size of Euroasia back on Earth. Separating these two landmasses was a natural strait. It was known as the *Acco Channel.*

Ucellans and Troznyans were distantly related, but through time and geographical distances became distinct in their own ways. Evidently, tribes of Troznyans in the distant past sailed from Trozny and settled in the three main islands of Ucella in the western hemisphere. Trozny and Ucella each had their own language. Besides the three main islands of Ucella were dozens of smaller islands in the area. Both Ucellans and Troznyans looked very much like the caucasoids on Earth.

The original Zotovans could be considered similar to the Ucellans and Troznyans, only a bit darker. They resembled the various races found throughout the Mediterranean also on Earth. One thousand years earlier people from Trozny migrated across the strait separating the two great landmasses and settled in parts of Zotova. At first along the coastal regions, as fishing was their way of life. Eventually, many of these people from both Trozny and Zotova intermarried. Thus, a third type of race evolved.

On Enaim was a people of a darker skin color, more like the color of what you would find on Earth's Indian subcontinent, only with saucer-shaped eyes. For the most part they did not intermarry with people from the northern hemisphere.

There were also four oceans on the planet: *Umea, Kiruna, Kovda* and *Targu.* The Umea Ocean would be considered the Arctic or North Pole Ocean. The Kiruna and Kovda Oceans divided the three northern continents. Namely Ucella, Trozny and Zotova. As for the Targu Ocean, the Vanagians concluded that as it was so large, it would be considered the ocean of the southern hemisphere.

In the southern hemisphere were many islands sprinkled across the Targu Ocean. Many uncharted and inhabited by the

Vanagians. Located to the east of Zotova was a fairly large island that was positioned in both the northern and southern hemisphere. The equator of Vanag divided this island in half. People from all four continents lived on this island called *Urishana.* In addition to Ucellans, Troznyans, Zotovans and Enaimans, were a people mixed in from all four races. They were considered the *Urishanans*, and their numbers were growing.

There were two main religions on Vanag. The *Mozdoks* and *Aelianans.* Followers of both religions could be found in all three continents in the northern hemisphere. The people of Enaim had many gods and goddesses. In the Hindu religion on Earth, there were thirty-three million deities that were worshipped. The Enaimans did not have that many deities, but there were thousands. Different tribes from the many regions of Enaim worshipped various gods and goddesses.

The Mozdoks followed the teachings of one holy man that lived over four thousand years ago. The prophet was named *Mozdok.* It was claimed that Mozdok originally came from a small village in Trozny. As noted, the other main religion were the Aelianans. This name came from the goddess *Aeliana.* She could be compared to a mother goddess on Earth. Just about every ancient civilization on Earth had a mother goddess that was worshipped. The followers of Aeliana started not long after the Mozdoks. This religion was founded by a group of women in ancient Zotova. Sad to say, like on Earth, both of these religions warred against each other down through the ages. Yet, depending on what continent they lived on, Mozdoks killed Mozdok, and Aelianans did the same.

"Well now, "Mary Collard was the first to say, "we've uncovered quite a bit about this world. It's different, yet similar to our world, Earth.

"Yes," Cuca added, "with its religions and national wars, Vanag, or now Tellus Two, bears some striking similarities to our planet."

"For good or bad," Amaresh now stated, "it appears that humans on both Earth and Tellus Two are indeed very much alike."

This then was the genesis of Vanag. Cuca, Amaresh and Mary Collard learned a lot about this planet right up to when the Americans and Russians came to Vanag through a vortex as a result of Halley's Comet. After that everything changed for this world.

The USS Tampa went totally dark under the polar cap. Twenty-eight seconds to be exact, but it seemed like hours. When the power came back online, lights were blinking and alarms sounding. Panic struck the crew. From officers and enlisted personnal to the civilians onboard this nuclear submarine.

"Damange reports," Captain Albritton, the XO, calmly, yet nervously, said through the intercom. "All departments report." Within a few minutes all department heads on duty reported to the XO. Everything on the vessel appeared to be in order. Or so the crew thought. Some instruments were spinning or blinking out of control. All wristwatches mechanical or digital, were also spinning or had just plain stopped. "Communications," the XO added, "Contact *ALCOM* (Alaskan Command) to report and find out if they know what just happened to the Tampa."

"Aye, Aye, Sir," came a voice on the intercom.

"All department heads," Captain Albritton stated. "Meet me in the wardroom in twenty minutes."

When the submariners of the USS Tampa met up in the cabin-compartment room for officers only, everyone was full of questions. Basically, what had just happened? The newest nuclear submarine of the Los Angeles class was supposed to have a backup system for backup systems. Yet, the Tampa went dark or dead for nearly half a minute. Why?

"All right, everybody calm down," Captain Albritton said to all those seated around a table. "Let's take a deep breath, and one-by-one discuss what's happened. For now focus on what we know. Not on what we don't."

"Well, for now," Lt. Commander Cardoza stated, "all personnel and civilian guests appear to be safe. Although the civilians seemed a bit shook up."

"We really didn't need these civilians on the sub to begin with," Chief Prescott chimed in. "Just more pressure and a headache having them here. Why, that Miss Tampa, Tiffany, whatever her last name is, came running out of her quarters screaming at the top of her lungs, *"GET ME OUT OF THIS TIN CAN."*

"Well, they're here now," the captain said. "It was beyond our control as to whether or not it was convenient for them to be allowed aboard the Tampa. This decision came all the way from the Pentagon." Speaking into an intercom located on the long table, the XO asked, "Communications. Have you reached Alcom yet?"

"No, sir, Captain," came a young sailor's voice over the speaker. We've tried Anchorage, Fairbanks, Juneau and even Seattle. Nothing. Not even static. Just plain dead silence."

"Keep trying, sailor," the captain concluded.

The captain, Lt. Commanders and petty officers now began to discuss the possibility that the Soviets had launched a first strike against the United States. Nuclear missiles could very well have taken out *ALCOM*, Anchorage, Seattle and even Washington, D.C. The purpose of the Tampa and other nuclear submarines was to launch a counterstrike against the Soviet Union in the event of a first strike. "Captain," Chief Petty Officer Mathis asked, "Could the fact that we went dark for half a minute be the result of an *EMP*? (Electromagnetic Pulse) If the Soviets hit one of the cities in Alaska, could this be the effect that we felt?"

"Anything is possible, Chief, "the captain replied. "But once our instruments came back online, if seismic activity had been recorded, we would know. We may be under the North Pole's icecap, but we would have felt something more than we just experienced."

"What's next then, Captain?" Lt. Buchanan asked. "We need to make a statement soon. The crew and civilians are anxious to know something."

"For a start," the captain replied, "let's recheck all equipment again on the Tampa. We will have all departments report back in thirty minutes. In the meantime, move about the boat and reassure everyone that we're trying to get to the bottom of what happened."

The executine officers and chiefs did as Captain Albritton ordered. Terri Eden, the journalist, was full of questions. *Just what we need,* Lt. Cardoza thought. *A reporter full of questions.* Miss Tampa, Tiffany Ash, had somewhat called down. Linda Flannery, one of the young women, an E-1 or seaman recruit, or really a seawoman, took the beauty queen under her care.

Cynthia Henderson was also very inquisitive. Working for a senator of the Armed Forces Committee, Miss Henderson imagined herself as someone important. She attempted to follow behind Chief Prescott, with a pen and notebook in hand, asking questions. The chief politely blew her off by saying, "In due course, the Captain will make a statement." The crew of the Tampa were well-trained and carried on with their duties. The civilians eventually calmed down and stayed out of the way.

As planned, the officers and chiefs met with the captain again in thirty minutes. Doctor Caldwell was present, too. Everyone concluded that a first strike against the United States was unlikely. But why the total radio silence? Communications onboard the Tampa even attempted to pick up radio signals elsewhere. Vladivostok, Tokyo, Seoul, even Moscow. From the North Pole, the submarine should be able to pick something up from these cities. Even under the ice.

"That does it," the captain said. "We are going to break through the ice and surface."

"I agree, Sir," Lt. Mathis added, "Maybe we can find out something from the surface. Even if we are at the top of the world."

"Let's give the order to surface," the XO stated.

"May I make a suggestion, Captain?" Doctor Caldwell asked.

"Sure, Doc," the captain replied.

"If it's safe," the doctor went on, "Why not let some of the crew, and any civilians that wish to, get some fresh air and see the sky. A few at a time should be able to go out for a look on the sail." (Conning tower.) The captain agreed.

The USS Tampa surfaced in an area where the ice was the thinnest. Even though the snow and ice was over two feet thick, the power of the submarine broke right through it. Captain Albritton and Lt. Commander Buchanan were the first to exit outside the top of the submarine and make their observation on the conning tower. They both were wearing heavy, navy-blue, fur-lined coats with hoods.

"Just another cold day in the arctic," the captain stated. He briefly looked through the binoculars hanging around his neck. "I suppose everything appears normal. The sky is clear, and thank God there aren't any mushroom or dust clouds present. If Anchorage, Tokyo or even Vladivostok were nuked, by now we would see something from even way up here."

"I don't know, Sir," Lt. Buchanan said, "something just doesn't feel or seem right."

"What do you mean, Lieutenant Commander?" The captain asked.

"It's something in the air, Captain," The Lt. Commander said. "And look at the sun. It looks different to me."

"Look Jeff," the XO replied, "We've been up to the pole before. From this position, the sun, moon and even stars appear different. We are at the top of the world. We'll get some answers soon."

"I hope so, Sir," the Lt. Commander stated.

"I'm going back below," the XO said. "I think it's important that the crew sees me while I check on all the departments. Meanwhile, I'll send some of the crew up. A few at a time. Let them get some fresh air. And some of the civilians, too. That Miss Tampa is itching to get out of the sub."

"A Florida girl wanting to take in the sights of the arctic," Lt. Buchanan added. "Well, let's not keep her waiting."

Within a few minutes, Miss Tampa and her new friend, Seawoman Flannery, climbed up to the conning tower. Both young women were wearing the standard-issue fur-lined coats. With the hoods covering their heads and faces it was hard to tell that they were females. After looking around for a moment at what some would call an arctic wasteland, Miss Tampa asked the Lt. Commander, "How far is the nearest city?"

"Well, Miss Ash," the Lt. Commander replied, "Fairbanks, Alaska is about two hundred miles away."

"Geez," the beauty queen stated. "I don't even want to know how far we are away from Tampa." Miss Tampa and the female sailor then went back down below.

Several from the crew also made their way up to the top of the submarine for some fresh air. With the Lt. Commander's permission, a few of the submariners climbed off of the Tampa and walked around on the ice. There was no danger, as this area of the icecap was several feet thick. A few from the crew passed a football back and forth.

By now it was almost dusk. Some stars were visible. Two bright ones appeared to be close enough to touch. But then, heavenly bodies did appear closer at the North Pole. Lt. Commander Buchanan had returned below to the submarine.

The other Lt. Commander of the Tampa, Cardoza took his place on the conning tower.

Brenda Hutt, the marine biologist, was also begging to go up to the surface. She had been to other areas of the arctic circle, such as Alaska and Scandinavia. But Brenda, or Professor Hutt, had never been this close to the top of the world. Captain Albritton had given the biologist permission to get down off of the submarine and venture out perhaps fifty yards or so.

Two seaman escorted the professor. They climbed down from the submarine which was several feet above the ice. The biologist observed a few fairly large black boulders on the surface. They stood out in the white snow. Perhaps some type of arctic lifeforms could be found underneath one of the smaller nearby rocks. Algae, fungus or a lichen. Professor Hutt had brought along a small specimen jar and even a polaroid camera. After turning over a couple of rocks, the biologist discovered the remains of a runner from an underground sheaf of a tiny plant. It may have been the remains of a perperennial plant. She gently pulled up the runner or root and placed it in the jar.

Something else caught Brenda's eye. A few foorprints. They were now frozen in the ice. But they were originally made in an earlier fresh snowfall. They must have been over eighteen inches long. *A polar bear? No way,* Brenda thought. *These footprints are way too big, and from a biped. Wow! What do we have here?* The bilogist further pondered.

"Professor Hutt," one of the seaman called out. "Time to return to the sub." Brenda quickly took out her camera and snaped several photos of the footprints. There were only a few before they disappeared behind a larger rock. At least the biologist had something to study back on the Tampa.

Two more of the civilian women wanted to come up to the tower. Terri Eden the journalist and Cindy Henderson, the senator's aid. Miss Eden, who was covering the story of the six women sailors on the Tampa, also brought her camera. She wasn't sure what pictures would be permitted to be part of her story, but she wanted a picture of the North Pole. If anything, just a picture for herself to say that she had been there.

Cindy Henderson just wanted some fresh air or to feel like she was important, too. It was now dark. A half-moon appeared above. The moon was becoming visible right before nightfall. As everyone's watches were now working again, it showed that the time was a little before four PM. Daylight was much shorter at the poles. "The moon appears to look strange," Cindy commented.

"According to the crew," Terri added, "the sun, moon and stars all appear different up here at the North Pole."

As the moon rose a little higher, another light appeared to be coming up from the ground. Or top of the world as it were. Northern lights? Then, there it was. A second moon. Also in half phase. But this other moon looked so close it appeared as if you could touch it. *"OH, MY GOD!"* Cindy Henderson cried out from the tower. "Where in the hell are we?" She and the red-haired journalist stood there with their mouths wide open.

Lt. Cordoza immediately had a seaman take the two young women below and quickly. The Lt. Commander then contacted the captain from a large handheld radio. Lt. Cardoza explained to the XO what they were seeing. "Calm down, Lieutenant," the XO said. "Don't allow anymore civilians up to the tower. I'm sending up Seaman Hartford. One of his many talents is amateur astronomer."

David Hartford was somewhat of a self-taught astronomer. Being from Prescott, Arizona, he had plenty of opportunities to gaze up into the clear night skies. As a young boy, all of his science fair projects involved astronomy. David had several good-sized telescopes back at the home of his parents in Arizona. The seaman had a compact-sized telescope with him on the Tampa. And his star charts. While out at sea, the desert boy, now a submariner, would stargaze as often as he could. David had been to the North Pole before, so he knew the sky was excellent for astronomy.

As it sounded like an emergency, Hartford didn't have time to grab his telescope. He would have to haul it up the ladder leading up to the top of the submarine. And then set it up. Captain Albritton explained to the seaman what the two girls and Lt. Commander had observed: Two moons. The captain reasoned that possibly because of an aurora, or northern lights, this was all just an optical illusion. Thus, a double reflection of the moon.

Seaman Hartford did bring his camera, though, that was equiped with a zoom lens. And he asked another sailor, Tony Miller, to accompany him with a camcorder that they had aboard the Tampa. Many times the crew on any U.S. Navy ship or submarine would film parts of their mission on *VHS* tape. Especially Russians ships.

Reaching the top outside of the sub, Hartford did indeed see the dual moons. All that he could say was, "Wow!" The closest moon was a shade darker than the moon that appeared first. Perhaps being closer to the sun it was reflecting its rays.

"Well, Hartford, " Lt. Commander Cordoza asked, "what do you make of this?"

"Bizarre, Lieutenant," Hartford replied. "Bizarre. That's all I can say. Let me get some pictures. Tony, get some footage with the camcorder of both moons. Then scan the sky and take in some of these brighter stars."

"Got it," the other seaman replied. "Some of these stars are so close that it feels like you can touch them."

Two of these bright objects appear to be planets, Hartford thought. *Only they don't look like Venus, Mars or Jupiter. Especially for this time of year.* He then began taking pictures himself of the moons and other heavenly bodies. "All right, Lieutenant," Hartford said, "I think that we have enough to analyze for now."

"Copy that," the Lt. Commander stated. "Let's close up for the night. It's dark and the temperature is dropping."

As the Lt. Commander and two seaman were preparing to head back down into the sub, they heard a howl from some kind of creature coming from this cold, dark and now-windy night. "My God, what was that?" Tony Miller asked. "That doesn't sound like anything I've ever heard before." Miller was an African-American from Toledo, Ohio. He didn't like anything strange or out of the ordinary.

"Come on, sailors," Lieutenant Cardoza emphasized, "Let's get down below."

Captain Albritton called for another meeting in the cabin-compartment again with all of the department heads. The captain concluded that it was time to leave the pole and head south during the night. The USS Tampa would submerge and go through the Bering Strait. At least what the Americans hoped was the strait. This strait separates Alaska and the Soviet Union. Perhaps by morning they could pick up something on radio. No one wanted to discuss just yet what was observed above by the two young women and some of the crew.

Brenda Hutt was too anxious to go to bed just yet. In the tiny, makeshift lab that had been provided for her on the sub, the biologist wanted to get a closer look at the remains of the plant that she had gathered. Brenda brought her small, yet powerful, microscope with her on this voyage. As for the two developed polaroid pictures that she took of the strange footprints, with the aid of a magnifying glass, perhaps she could identify the species.

Being a bookworm, and studying biology since a pre-teen, Brenda's eyes had been overworked for over a decade. Although only thirty, Brenda switched back and forth from contacts to thick glasses. Maybe the young biologist's eyes were tired up on the surface. The white glare can play tricks on even someone with good eyesight. And she had been in a submarine with artificial lighting for days now.

Seaman Hartford went to the library reading room on the sub. He could get the pictures that he took developed on the Tampa tomorrow. As he had taken other pictures eariler, even before this voyage, the roll was almost used up. The submarine had quite a library. Even diskettes, floopy disks that could be used on the *IBM* computer, also in the library. Hartford pulled out a star guide book published in the late 1970's. The seaman pretty much had a photographic memory when it came to the stars.

Nothing that Hartford had observed tonight matched what should be visible for this time of year in the Northern Hemisphere. He then placed the *VHS* tape that Tony Miller filmed into one of the library's *VCR's.* Hartford put the tape on slow speed to get a better look. The two closer bright objects in the sky were indeed not stars, but planets. And the dual moons were not optical illusions.

"Holy Moses," as we used to say back in Charleston," Rebecca stated, "these Americans have no idea where they are." Rowena, Justinian and Rebecca followed all of this from the time scanner.

"No, they sure don't," Rowena added. "And when they do, it will be the shock of their lives."

On that eventful day of February 9, 1986, the Soviet submarine in Antarctica experienced the same thing as the American submarine 12, 500 miles away at the North Pole. The Russian submarine also went dark and offline for twenty-eight seconds.

The Vodyanoy was at periscope depth as the submarine had reached its destination: The coast of Antarctica. It was about 11:00 AM at this region of the continent. When the power was restored on Vodyanoy, there was some panic, as expected among the crew. When a submarine went dark it could be a frightful experience even among well-trained submariners.

"Calm down, and restore order," Captain Starinov, calmly, yet firmly stated over the intercom. "Stay vigilant at your posts or stations." He then ordered officers and chiefs to the control room.

In a few minutes, the captain, Lt. Commander Grodno, the two chiefs, along with the political officer Valeria Rostova, assembled in the control room. Doctor Ivanov was there as well, also being an officer. The control room was the nucleus of activity on any submarine.

"What happened, Captain?" The female doctor asked.

"I have no idea, Comrade Doctor," the captain replied. "We're less than twenty miles from our destination, Mirny Station. (This science station was the first Russian station established in 1956 on the Queen Mary Land region of Antarctica.)

"Was there some type of nuclear accident on the Vodyanoy?" Lt. Rostova, the female political officer, had to ask.

"Let's not jump to conclusions, Comrade Rostova," Lt. Commander Grodno stated. "But I doubt it."

"We're running a systems check now," Captain Starinov affirmed. "We should know in a moment if all systems are functioning." As the Vodyanoy attempted to communicate with Mirny Station, they discovered the same thing as the American submarine. Total silence. No static. Simply nothing.

"This is odd," remarked the captain. "Yesterday we were in radio contact with the *Shelikhov* and *Golovin*." The Shelikhov was an icebreaker, and Golovin a freighter. These two vessels left several days after the Soviet submarine. The Shelikhov was loaded with supplies and building materials to begin the future settlements in Antarctica. Radio contact had been lost with the two ships.

"Captain," Chief Gaida said, "we are at Mirny Station now. Certainly we can hear them, and let them know of our arrival."

"I would think so," Captain Starinov replied.

"Then I suggest you contact them now," Rostova, the political officer, stated. "Fleet and Moscow will not like us being out of contact."

"Nor do we, Comrade Rostova," Lt. Grodno replied.

The Vodyanoy attempted several times from underwater to reach Mirny Station. Still silence. Nothing. "Let's surface," the captain commanded. "We're at the station's backyard now. Perhaps their radios are out." The powerful submarine broke through the ice.

The captain then peered through the periscope. The station had several domed complexes and tall communication towers. Captain Starinov was puzzled from offshore, he should be able to see these structures. It was very clear outside at the moment. And it wasn't snowing.

"What do you see, Captain?" Chief Gaida asked.

"Nothing," the captain replied. "We're in the right place for Mirny Station. Yet, nothing is out there."

"Well, now, Captain," Valeria Rostova stated, "did our settlement just vanish?" Most crews on any Soviet submarine or ship had little use for political officers.

"Perhaps it did vanish," the captain calmly replied as he pulled down on the periscope. "Mirny Station is not where it should be. Just snow, ice and emptiness."

"Would you like to take a small escort to see for yourself, Comrade Rostova?" Chief Gaida asked.

"If need be, I will, Chief," the political officer replied. "Meanwhile, all of this will be going into my report."

"I'm sure it will, Comrade Rostova," the captain said. "For now, let's all report to the galley to consider this dilemna."

In a few moments the senior officers and chiefs met in the galley for some privacy. Captain Starinov had asked the husband and wife biologist team, the Nimrosenskys, to join them. Although they were not in the military, they seemed to be professional and logical. They were all confused and slightly worried of what was taking place. And the crew obviously was, too, even though at present they appeared calm.

"Comrade Captain," Valeria asked. "Do you think that there has been a nuclear war?" The political officer was the first to break the silence. Everyone in the room was thinking that this could be a possibility.

"It's possible, Comrade Rostova," the captain replied, "but let's not jump to that conclusion just yet." The other officers in the galley debated this briefly.

The biologist couple had little knowledge of military matters. However, they were scientists and something didn't add up. "Comrade Captain," Professor Nimrosensky spoke up, saying, "A nuclear war may explain the radio silence. But not the disappearance of Mirny Station. We certainly don't see any evidence of a nuclear strike down here in Antarctica. Is there any evidence of radiation?"

"No, Comrade Professor," the captain replied.

"Are we sure that the submarine is in the area of the station?" The professor now asked. "Could your instruments be off?"

"The instruments appear to be in working order," the captain answered. "As for the base, we were twenty miles away from the station when everyting went dark and crazy. And right now we're twenty miles further. The station should be in this area."

"Did anything look familiar, Captain, when you looked through the periscope?" The political officer asked. "Any familiar landmarks along the coast?"

"You can't be seriois, Lt. Rostova," Chief Gaida remarked. "This is the Antarctic. Ice shelfs break off and disappear. And there is fresh snow and ice all of the time. There are no landmarks other than our stations, flag and radio tower. We are at the white abyss."

"The orders for now," Captain Starinov stated, "are for us to remain on the surface for the rest of the day. We will keep attempting radio contact with any of our bases and stations on the continent. Our range should be able to pick up any station. I don't care if we make contact with any base, be it the United States, New Zealand, Argentina, whoever."

"Captain, from our position we should be able to pick up radio signals from Chile and Argentina," Lt. Commander Grodno interjected. "Yet, all is silent. Dead, as it were."

"Well, let's keep trying,' the captain said. The captain then suggested that the crew and others take turns going outside the tower for some fresh air. They could even take a walk on top of the Vodyanoy, as the submarine was stationary at present.

It had been a long voyage so most of the crew were anxious to get out of the submarine. For the smokers it was great to light up in the fresh air. Even if it was freezing.

As the afternoon wore on, communications desperately attempted to make contact with someone in the South Pole. Some of the crew could speak English, so they spoke in this language hoping that an English-speaking base would respond.

At one point the political officer approached Captain Starinov, complaining, "I don't think that it's a good idea to be broadcasting in English where we are, or reaching out to rival bases. After all, we're on a classified mission."

"Let me remind you, Comrade Rostova," the captain replied, "all of the Soviet navy's missions are classified. We're allowed to visit our own stations and resupply our people. The Americans, or for that matter, anyone else have no idea why we are here. Futhermore, there are other Soviet submarines in and around Antarctica. Fleet also has regular patrols of our submarines in the lower regions of the South Pacific and Atlantic Oceans."

"Have you tried to contact our submarines in these other waters, Captain?" the political officer asked.

"Indeed we have, Comrade Rostova," the captain replied. "The sailors from communications are tirelessly working as we speak."

Like the USS Tampa at the North Pole, the crew took turns coming out on top of the Vodyanoy. After being submerged for nearly ten days, it was refreshing to take in some fresh air and light.

Also, like the Americans at the arctic, as the sun went down and it became dark, the Russians were in for a rude awakening. What they figured was Earth's moon appeared. Within a short time, though, the second moon appeared. Once again, this moon looked much closer. A dozen Russian sailors witnessed this bizarre happening. They did indeed feel as if they could touch this moon. The snow and ice all around them lit up as a result of the moonlight. The sailors were frantic. One called out from a handheld radio to the control room down below.

"All hands back down below," Captain Starinov ordered through the intercom that everyone could hear. When all hands were accounted for, the captain and Lt. Commander Grodno went up to the tower to see what all of the commotion was about. Captain Starinov asked Professor Nimrosensky to join them. Lt. Rostov insisted on coming up as well. As a political officer she wanted to know everything.

Outside the tower it didn't take long to see what had alarmed the other sailors that had been out on top of the submarine. It was not snowing, so the now-dark sky was clear. Two moons were clearly visible.

"What is this Comrade Captain?" The Lt. Commander asked.

"Great Marx," the political officer stated. She then put her hand over her mouth. Valeria Rostova was usually a stern, in-control woman. But even in the fur-lined coat provided for her by the Soviet navy, she was clearly shaking. Not from the extreme cold, but out of fear.

"Professor Nimrosensky," the captain asked, "What do you make of this? Two moons down here at the bottom of the world."

"I'm not an astronomer, Captain Starinov," the professor replied. "But clearly something has changed."

"I think we've seen enough," the captain said. "Let's get back down below. We need to have another meeting with all senior personnel."

Within an hour, the officers, chiefs, Lt. Rostova, and the Nimrosenskys were meeting again in the galley. There was much speculation as to what had happened. The subject of a nuclear war kept coming up. But what did the presence of dual moons have to do with that? Finally, Professor Nimrosensky stated,

"Captain, comrades, we have to accept the possibility that when the Vodyanoy briefly lost power, we went through some type of vortex. If this is what took place, then we are someplace else." No one really wanted to think about that possibility. Nor could most comprehend it.

"Is this really possible, Comrade Professor?" The political officer asked. The professor only nodded his head."

"There is only one way to find out," Captain Starinov said. "We must leave this area and head back out to sea." The captain explained that once leaving the South Pole, that perhaps they could make radio contact with the Shelikhov or Golovin. Or other Soviet submarines. In fact, if contact could be made with anybody, this would be a relief. As for being "someplace else"like the professor theorized, the captain could only hope that this wasn't the case.

Lin, Michaela and Shako had still been monitoring the crew of the Vodyanoy. "The Russians are just as much in the dark as the Americans are at the opposite pole." Michaela stated.

"They sure are," Lin added. "And when both sides realize that they are no longer on Earth, this is going to be interesting how they react."

Rowena, Justinian and Rebecca continued to follow the USS Tampa once it left the North Pole. That is, the North Pole on Vanag. There was of course no Alaska or Bering Strait. Nor a Canadian or Pacific Northwest American coast as the submarine headed south, then east. It was still just ocean.

After about three days the USS Tampa observed small islands, or atolls. Going up to periscope level, the submarine would have a better view. The two Lt. Commanders took turns looking through the periscope. All of a sudden, Lt. Buchanan observed a ship near an atoll. It was a fairly large fishing vessel, but wooden. Like something from the mid-1800's. "I don't believe this," the Lt. Commander stated. But before alerting Captain Albritton, who was sleeping, the Lt. Commander thought that he would scout around some more. Besides, the periscope was equipped with a camera. He took several pictures.

The USS Tampa cruised on, but at periscope depth. Then, Lt. Buchanan spotted another ship. This time, though, the vessel appeared to be a steamer. The smoke stack was clearly visible. "Someone tell Lt. Cardoza to come to the conn," Buchanan ordered.

When the other Lt. Commander came to the conn, Buchanan said, "Take a look through the scope." Cardoza did so.

"I don't get it," Cardoza said as he took his eyes off the periscope. "What is this antique doing out there?"

"Good question," Buchanan replied. Then lowered the periscope. "Let's go to my cabin." Buchanan then had Chief Petty Officer Prescott take over command of the conn while the Tampa maintained a southeasterly course.

"You watch," Rowena said as she and her assistants followed events on the time scanner. "These two American naval officers are going to start trying to make some sense of their dilemma."

Once inside Buchanan's tiny cabin, they could talk more freely. They didn't want to awaken the captain yet, or alarm the crew on the conn, that they had no idea what was going on. The two Lt. Commanders discussed what these two older vessels could be. A small fishing vessel company that couldn't afford a modern boat? Was the steamer part of a nostalgic cruise? Something for a movie set? Interesting theories, but no conclusive answers.

"There is still one possibility that we have to consider," Cardoza stated. "Has a nuclear war taken place? Maybe these old ships are the only vessels that any survivors could get their hands on." Possibly, yes. But there was still no trace of radiation. It had only been less than five days since the USS Tampa had lost contact with command or anyone else. A nuclear strike and its aftermath would be clearly evident. After getting the two developed pictures that Buchanan had taken through the periscope, it was time to wake up the captain.

After the captain was awake, the two Lt. Commanders joined him in his cabin. Buchanan presented the XO with the photos of the fishing vessel and steamer. "This in itself doesn't prove anything unusual," the captain stated, "but it does add to the other unusual events, such as two moons and a total communication blackout."

Buchanan and Cardoza agreed. They also expressed their concerns that the landmasses south of the North Pole were nowhere to be found. Namely Alaska, Canada and the American coastline. Right now, they were still submerged and crusing below an ocean. "Can we even state that this North Pole where we were, is even our North Pole. And what is this ocean we are under?"

The three officers admitted for the first time that perhaps they were no longer on Earth. Or at least their Earth. "I'm not a science fiction fan like some of the young guys in the crew," the captain stated, "but maybe we are somehow now on a parallel world. Not our Earth as we know it. This would explain a lot. The two moons again and unfamilar sea and missing landmasses." The captain and Lt. Commanders still thought it best to keep this to themselves for now. And to stay on the course they had set. Wherever that was.

"The Americans are traveling under the Umea Ocean," Rebecca spoke up saying, "yet have no idea about this body of water."

Meanwhile, David Hartford had stayed up most of the night studying and comparing photos, charts and video footage taken that first night up at the North Pole. *This isn't Earth,* the young seaman concluded to himself. Hartford was both worried and restless. He finally concluded that he needed to see and speak with the captain. One deck above Hartford was where Brenda Hutt slept and worked. The biologist had also made some startling discoveries. She, too, needed to see Captain Albritton.

The captain agreed to see both Seaman Hartford and Professor Hutt at the same time. They met in the library. The seaman presented his findings regarding the star charts and the video footage taken at the North Pole. Nothing from a view on Earth, and what they observed in the night sky at the pole added up. Hartford explained to the captain that in the video, the two visible brighter lights were indeed planets, but not any planets in their solar system. Hartford may have only been an amateur astronomer, but he could identify and position planets. At least the planets he knew about. "And the appearance of two moons," Hartford concluded, "proves that this is not our solar system or world."

"Thank you, Seaman," the XO replied. "It appears that you know your stars." The captain was even more convinced that this place wasn't their world. "And what did you come up with in your findings, Professor Hutt?" The captain asked the biologist.

Brenda Hutt proceeded to present the captain several discoveries. First of all, the plant she found under a rock was unknown to her. Being an expert on lifeforms in both the Arctic and Antarctica, she confessed to the captain, "The remains of this plant under a microscope are nothing like anything I've seen before."

The biologist then informed Captain Albritton that through the portals inside the Tampa she was able to take several close-up photographs of fish. At first glance, these fish may have appeared to be a familiar species found on Earth. But at a closer look it appeared that the fish were a new or different species altogether. And several at that.

And finally, the footprints left in the snow. They were from no mammal found in the arctic, or anywhere else on Earth for that matter. "Captain," Brenda Hutt stated, "these footprints found in the ice and snow are not from a polar bear." She then handed the captain a picture she had taken. "Futhermore, these tracks are from a biped. And whatever this creature is, it probably weighs over five hundred pounds and is perhaps about ten foot tall."

Great, the captain thought as he studied the photo. *Dual moons, new species of fish and now a snow beasts. What next?* "Thank you, Professor Hutt. Your findings are most revealing." Captain Albritton then left the library. After summoning his officers and chiefs, they discussed a few matters. Those ships sighted at sea had to come from somewhere. It was time to find out where, and what kind of people or beings ruled this planet. It was obvious that the Americans were not on their planet. Or the planet they once knew.

The USS Tampa surfaced and sailed on to the course the captain had set: Southeast. At this point, the Americans were no longer hiding under the waves. Anyone out in the ocean could now see the submarine. In fact, the crew of the Tampa wanted to be seen.

Several small islands were now visible. From the tower, Captain Albritton, Lt. Commander Buchanan and Chief Mathis focused in on some of these islands with their binoculars. Small dwellings, such as cottages, could be observed on these islands. And a few people. "People," Chief Mathis stated. "These are the first people we've seen outside the sub since we left port nearly two weeks ago."

Next, a couple of small boats came into view. Mostly men were in the boats, but also a few women. The clothing appeared strange to the American sailors. Old-fashioned, as it were, but yet a unique, unknown style. Several waved at the officers on the sub, but they also appeared to be in a state of awe, and perhaps a bit afraid. They obviously had never seen a nuclear submarine. "Well, at least the natives appear friendly," Lt. Buchanan commented.

"Yes, it appears so," the captain added. "However, I wonder if these people have an army or navy. How friendly will they be then?"

The Americans were about to find out. From the long range information that they could gather, some of the crew on the Tampa concluded that a large island or landmass was not too far away. They could tell by the uderwater rock formations of this sea or ocean. As the submarine sailed on, it passed near a much larger wooden vessel.

A few of the women guests below begged to come up to the tower. Perhaps they were tired of being cooped up in a submarine and wanted some fresh air. Or just curious about what was unfolding up on the surface. The captain finally allowed the young redhead, Terri Eden, to come up to the tower. After all, she was a reporter. But Captain Albritton instructed the young lady, "No pictures, Miss Eden. We can provide you with photos taken from the periscope." Terri had a camera hanging from her neck. If they got close enough to another ship, the "natives" may misunderstand what the reporter was doing.

And soon enough, the USS Tampa did indeed get close to a ship. A fairly large ship. "Would you take a look at this ship?" Chief Mathis stated. "It looks similar to an American or British Man-Of-War from the 1800's. Cannons and all." The sailors, many of whom were now on deck, were dressed in a type of jersey-light blue shirt, along with gray pants. This, obviously, was a uniform. Most of the sailors had beards and mustaches. "What is this? A blast from the past?" The chief added. The sailors on the large three-decked wooden ship just stared at the Tampa.

What are they thinking? The Captain wondered. *Are they going to open fire on us?* As most of the submarine was still below water, the ship appeared to be taller, as all three decks were visible, along with the three masts and four large sails. "I think you had better go below deck, Miss Eden," the captain said. But his requests fell on deaf ears. The young redhead stood on the tower with her mouth wide open while starring at the ship with now big, green eyes.

On the main sail was what appeared to be a fearsome bird of prey. But again, nothing like the ones from Earth. Was this creature real or mythical? Like the plant, fish and footprints that Brenda Hutt had discovered, perhaps this image on the sail of the warship was also a real, yet different, species than anything the Americans were familiar with.

The officers on the tower had concluded that a port was nearby. Perhaps even a harbor town. From the tower, Captain Albritton sounded the alarm for general quarters or battle stations. The Americans had no way of telling whether they would encounter friend or foe. The crew of the USS Tampa were well-trained. Everything fell into place.

The captain then ordered up thirty seaman armed with *M-16* automatic rifles. No one wanted to go in with guns blazing, yet they had better be prepared. For the time being, the captain had the submariners line up in formation on top of the Tampa. They appeared more like an honor guard for someone special.

But whom? At any rate, this Los Angeles class nuclear submarine was one of the most powerful war machines on planet Earth. And now somewhere else as well. Again, wherever that was.

In about twenty minutes a port and town began to come into view. There was actually thick smoke in the air. Smoke stacks were also visible. This smoke was coming from both factories and homes. The scene looked like a European or American city at the dawn of the Industrial Revolution.

The USS Tampa was going to find a place to dock. By now hundreds, if not a thousand, people were crowding the seawall leading up to the dock. To them, the American submarine appeared as a giant sea monster. As the Tampa came to a slow stop at the large dock, around two hundred soldiers lined up on the seawall. They were dressed in baggy red trousers and light blue shirts. Their footwear were black boots. As for their red caps, it appeared like something from the American Civil War. In addition, all of the soldiers were armed with muskets.

From the conference room back in the kingdom, Rowena, Justinian and Rebecca had been following all of this. The blonde Time Maiden then stood up, and proclaimed, *"BEHOLD, AMERICANS! UCELLA."*

When the Vodyanoy first left what the crew believed was the South Pole, the submarine was submerged. But by the next day the vessel surfaced, and continued to sail north. The Vodyanoy still could not make radio contact. This silence proved to be eerie for the crew.

For a time it appeared that this area was nothing more than a vast polar cap ocean. But small atolls began to come into view. Lt. Commander Grodno and Chief Gaida were outside on the tower. Different members of the crew would join them a few at a time. It wasn't as cold as it was back at the pole, yet very windy. If their course made any sense, the Vodyanoy should come upon the tip of South America, where Chile and Argentina border each other, almost at the bottom of the world. But right now nothing made sense.

Then, all of a sudden, there was a ship on the horizon. Signs of civilization. Perhaps the vessel was from a South American country. If something out of the ordinary had taken place, maybe these people knew. As the Vodyanoy got closer and the Lt. Commander and chief focused in on the ship with binoculars, they could see that this vessel was a fairly large wooden ship. But not like the Man-of-War that the Americans came upon during their journey. This ship looked more like a cargo ship. And something from the 1800's as well. "What is this?" Lt. Commander Grodno remarked.

Captain Starinov was notified and quickly appeared outside the tower. The captain also peered through the binoculars. On the main sail of the ship was the image of a three-headed serpent. Yet, the heads didn't resemble any serpent that the captain had ever seen. The ship figurehead was elaborately carved. This head, too, resembled some type of mythical creature. Also not like anything the Russians outside the tower had ever seen.

As the Vodyanoy sailed closer to this strange ship of unknown origins, Lt. Grodno asked, "Captain, do you think that this ship is from some kind of motion picture? Many of our movies featured replics of Peter the Great's navy."

"I have no idea, Comrade Grodno," the captain replied. "Not unless it's from a science fiction film. I've never seen creatures like the ones on that sail. And what does the figurehead of that ship represent?"

As the submarine got closer, the Russians could see that, although this ship looked like a throwback of over one hundred years, it appeared to be fairly new. As if it was built recently. The Russians had decided that they should make contact. They had to know what was going on in the world. But first they needed to discuss this with the other officers and chiefs, and of course the political officer, Comrade Rostova. The captain and Lt. Commander went down below deck.

A quick meeting was held in the captain's quarters to see what the next move would be. The unusual ship that the Vodyanoy encountered appeared to drop anchor. They were just as curious about the Russians, as the Russians were about them. The Russians of course didn't know it, but these unknown sailors had never seen a huge submarine before. To them, the Vodyanoy may as well have come from another world, which it did.

The officers, chiefs, the Nimrosenskys and the political officer, Lieutenant Rostova, were present. It was decided that a liferaft from the submarine could be launched to make contact with the wooden vessel. Possibly the captain, a chief and two crewman could ask for permission to come aboard the ship. They could even display a white flag to show that their intentions were peaceful. (As the Russians had no idea yet that they were on a different world, who knows what a white flag could mean.)

However, Valeria Rostova had other ideas. "Captain Starinov," the political officer stated, "the Soviet navy is one of the most powerful navies in the world. Its hardly fitting that we approach another vessel waving a white flag. We will appear weak."

"Comrade Rostova," Lt. Commander Grodno stated before the captain could reply, "anyone with a brain in their head can see that the Vodyanoy is a powerful vessel without us firing over the bow of any ship."

"That will be enough, Lt. Commander," the captain now said, "as a political officer Comrade Rostova has a right to her say."

"Thank you, Captain," the political officer replied. "Please just let me explain our position." The political officer realized that this ship out in the middle of the ocean was the first sight of civiization that they had encountered since the strange events of nearly two days ago. Yes, it was imperative that the crew find out what was taking place. Especially the missing Soviet base in Antarctica and the radio silence. But they needed to proceed with caution. Who or what was this ship? What is their origin?

"Here is a suggestion, Captain," Lt. Rostova went on to explain. A liferaft would be used to approach the ship. As the captain felt that it was his responsibility to attempt to board the vessel, the political officer felt that she should, too. Perhaps one of the chiefs should accompany them as well. And another sailor to help paddle the raft. And Valeria Rostova had the perfect sailor in mind.

So far, the Russians still believed, or hoped, that they were heading to the tip of South America. And that this strange-looking ship had a Spanish crew. Everyone was still trying not to think about the dual moons that they had observed two nights ago.

"Captain," the political officer said, "the sailor I had in mind to accompany us to the ship is Borya Petrov. His file shows that he speaks six languages: German, Polish and Armenian to name a few. But also Spanish, as he was stationed in Cuba several times.

If these people speak Spanish, then Petrov can perhaps find out what's going on."

Captain Starinov thought that this was a good idea, but the political officer had another suggestion. In order to flex some muscle, hopefully without firing a shot, she recommended that twenty-four from the crew line up on top of the submarine armed with *AK-47*'s. If anything were to go wrong, these sailors with automatic rifles could do some serious harm to anyone posing a threat. The captain, Lt. Commander and chiefs reluctantly agreed. Professor Nimrosensky asked to be permitted to go aboard this ship as well. His request was denied, and his wife was relieved.

Within a half an hour, a liferaft was inflated and lowered into the water from the Vodyanoy. The raft could hold up to fourteen people. Yet, there would only be four. The captain, Chief Poltav, Valeria Rostova and the young sailor Borya Petrov. They wore life vests and the officers had sidearms. Once in the raft, all four paddled towards the ship.

On the top deck of the ship, it appeared that about fifty men were assembled. They were watching as the raft came closer. Many didn't have a shirt on. Yet, it was still a cool, windy day. As the Russians paddled closer, they could tell that these people were dark-skinned.

Petrov stopped paddling and took out a bullhorn from a canvas bag. Speaking into the bullhorn in Spanish, Petrov yelled, *AHOY, WHO IS YOUR CAPTAIN? PERMISSION TO COME ABOARD."* The crew of this ship just stared and looked dumbfounded. Petrov repeated the request. He then stated, "Captain. I don't think that they comprehend Spanish. Shall I try another language? Perhaps English." Petrov tried again now in English. Still nothing. Then, a rope ladder was lowered from the ship.

"Well," the captain responded, "it appears that we have an invitation to come aboard."

"Go easy, Comrade Captain," the political officer said. "And keep a hand on your sidearm just in case."

"Let's hope it doesn't come to that, Comrade Rostova," Chief Poltav added.

The three submariners and political officer climbed up the ladder and stood at the top deck. There were quite a few from the crew of this ship on deck. This was indeed a cargo ship. Most of the goods were covered with tarps. However, there were a number of baskets containing what looked like fruit. It was as if the fruit was exposed so as to ripen. But what kind of fruit was this? Grapefruit? Oranges? Pears? The Russians weren't sure what kind of fruit they were looking at.

The crew backed away so as to give their new boarders some space. Many of the men were eyeing Valeria Rostova. The political officer was an attractive woman. Even though she was dressed in a jumpsuit and had her dark hair pulled back, one could tell that she was a shapely woman.

Two other men now appeared. They looked as if they were in charge. These people did resemble the Indians from the sub-continent. Yet, unique in their own way. One man said something and most of the others on deck went back to what they had been doing. Back to work as it were. Was this an order? Is this man the captain?

"Comrade Petrov,' the captain asked, "see if you can find out what language these people speak."

Petrov spoke in Spanish first, thinking that perhaps because they were on a raft the first time he attempted to address these people, they couldn't hear him. And the bullhorn may have muffled his voice. No response. He tried English again. Still nothing. Then Petrov tried in the other languages that he was fluent in. The men gathered near them and still just stared.

Next, Petrov used several phrases or greetings in some other languages that he had picked up. The men shook their heads and shrugged their shoulders. Finally, the lead man, probably the captain, said something. Petrov had no idea either of what he was saying.

"Can you understand anything this man is saying, Petrov?" The captain asked. "Anything at all."

"No, Comrade Captain,' Petrov repled. "This tongue is unlike anything I've ever heard."

"Can someone, somehow find out who these people are?" Valeria now asked. "We must try to find out something."

Captain Starinov glanced around the deck of the ship. Then something caught his attention. "I have an idea," he said to his comrades. "Wait here."

The captain had observed a young boy with a type of sketch pad. He was actually sketching the Vodyanoy. And doing a great job of drawing the submarine. The boy had what appeared to be a wooden box of what may have been something similar to chalk in various colors. The young artist was fast, too. No sooner had he drawn the vessel that to him was strange-looking, the boy then started drawing on another piece of paper. Now the boy was working on one of the Soviet sailors standing on the submarine with the *AK-47* in his hand.

Captain Starinov smiled and nodded to the boy. He then motioned for a piece of paper. The boy seemed to understand what the captain wanted and handed him a piece of paper. The captain then reached into the wooden box and took out a red piece of chalk. He smiled again at the boy.

Captain Starinov then placed the paper down on one of the crates. As best as he could, the captain drew a map of both Americas and the South Pole. The captain now attempted to communicate with the other captain. He handed him a map and asked, "Does this look familiar to you?" Of course the other captain didn't understand a word he said, but he did study what the Russian captain had drawn.

This other captain then said something to one of his crewman in whatever language he spoke. The crewman disappeared and went down below deck. In a few minutes he returned and handed his captain what resembled a leather scroll. The captain unrolled this scroll and flattend it on the same crate where Captain Starinov had made his drawing. The other captain motioned for the Russians to gather around. It was none other than a map. It was well-painted and very detailed.

However, to the captain, chief, political officer and Petrov the map looked like something out of a fairytale land. Nothing looked familiar or made any sense. Yet, there were two great landmasses in the northern hemisphere, a large one south of the equator, many islands sprinkled in the oceans and two polar caps. "Just what is this?" Chief Poltav had to ask.

"Let me see if this captain can show us something on this map," Captain Starinov said. "Maybe exactly where we are." Starinov motioned for the other captain to come over and join them.

Back in the kingdom, Lin, Michaela and Shako observed all of this from the time scanner. "This ship the Russians stumbled upon," Lin commented, "is of course from the continent Enaim."

"And," Michaela added, "it appears that they are about two hundred miles away from Enaim out in the Targu Ocean."

"It would seem that these people must be Enaimans,' Shako stated, "and are some type of merchant sailors. Trading and delivering goods to many smaller islands in the southern hemisphere." The two Time Maidens with their assistant continued to look in with great interest on this encounter involving Earth people and Vanagians.

The Russians were still confused as to where they were. Captain Starinov kept pointing down at the map so as to say: *Where are we?* Finally, the Enaiman captain pointed to an area out in an ocean. He pointed with his index finger several times.

Somehow these people knew exactly where they were without any instruments or stars, as it was daylight.

Now it was Valeria Rostova's turn to ask a question. She pointed at the Enaiman captain several times and then down at the map and asked, "Where are you from?" The captain speaking in an unknown tongue understood. He then pointed to a large landmass west of their position in the ocean. Written on the map of this large continent-island was a name in a language that the Russians couldn't comprehend. This was of course Enaim.

There was still a lot of confusion. But at least the Russians now knew where they were positionwise, and the origin of this ship. "I don't know," Valeria muttered as she scratched her head.

Valeria Rostova wasn't through, by any means. She now obtained a piece of paper and began to draw something. It was two crescent moons. Valeria then held up her drawing to the Enaiman captain, pointed up in the sky and asked, "Moons. Are there two moons?"

The captain of this ship gave the political officer a strange look. It was if he were thinking, *Of course there are two moons. What's wrong with you, woman?* First the Enaiman captain shook his head in disbelief, but then nodded yes as he pointed up to the sky, held up two fingers and stated something. He most likely said, "Yes. Two moons."

Captain Starinov and the chief had to hold back their laughter. Valeria Rostova was a beautiful woman but very uptight. This other captain responded to her as if she had a few loose screws. It was well worth it to see Comrade Rostova now perplexed over her inquiry with the Enaiman captain, but it would sink in later with all of the Russians that the two moons were indeed real. So then, what is this world that they are all now a part of?

The Enaiman captain appeared to be a good soul. He probably realized that this metal boat shaped like a sea monster and the sailors standing on deck with strange weapons could blast his ship out of the water. After all, the Enaim ship was just a cargo vessel. The Enaiman captain gave orders in his unknown tongue for some of his men to gather up baskets of fruits and vegetables from his inventory. Some of his sailors even went down below deck and returned with four crates of what looked like bottles of wine.

"That's nice of these people to give us this food and wine,' Chief Poltav stated. "Maybe we should give them something in return."

"That's a great idea, Anatoly," Captain Starinov replied. "I'm going to contact the sub and tell them to send over another raft. There are quite a few baskets and crates of goods they are giving us." Within about twenty minutes another raft was on its way with two sailors paddling.

Onboard the Vodyanoy was an ample suppy of vodka. Including vodka that the crew made. Officially, this was prohibited. But long voyages under the sea could be hard on a crew. When not on duty, a couple of shots of this spirit helped with the isolation. In the galley were plenty of potatoes to set up vats to distill vodka. The captain had two cases sent over on the raft. One distilled in Moscow, and the other homemade.

Once the vodka was delivered on the Enaiman ship, Captain Starinov had the baskets of fruit and wine lowered down to the other raft. The two Soviet sailors then paddled back to the submarine with these gifts from whoever these people were.

Wooden drinking cups were brought out. Captain Starinov and Chief Poltav then began to pour the vodka. The Enaiman captain and some of his men accepted and gulped down the spirit. The Russians began to raise a toast, then another, and several more. A toast to new friends, good health, prosperity, the ships and even a toast to the two moons. Needless to say, both the Russians and Enaimans were feeling a bit light-headed. Even Valeria Rostova was feeling good and enjoying herself.

Captain Starinov then proceeded to roll up the map belonging to the other captain. After getting the Enaiman captain's attention, he held up the map and then pointed to himslf, as to ask, *May I take this map?* The Enaiman captain smiled, and then nodded his head so as to say yes. The two captains then drank another toast. The sailors on this cargo ship seemed to take a liking to Russian vodka.

The Russians were about to say their farewells to these helpful new acquaintances when they received yet another surprise. From below the deck two exotic-looking women appeared. But these girls did not have a dark complexion like the men on this ship. One was a fair-skinned blonde, while the other had light brown hair. Their eyes and features also appeared different from those of the sailors on the cargo ship. They were obviously from a different race. They pointed to themselves and kept repeating the same thing. Most likely their names. But the Russians couldn't comprehend what they were saying.

These two women were also wearing the shortest, tightest pair of black shorts that the Russians had ever seen. Both women were very shapely to say the least. Valeria Rostova was beginning to snap out of being a bit high from all of the vodka toast. She stopped drinking the spirit after about the fifth toast. *Who and what are these girls?* The political officer thought. *Are they sex slaves, or comfort girls?* She further pondered. Yet, these two women also appeared to be in charge, having some authority. They spoke to the Enaiman captain telling him something. But what?

The blonde went down below deck, but shortly returned with what looked like two knapsacks. The blonde then handed one of the knapsacks to her companion. Captain Starinov, the chief and Petrov stared in amazement at these exotic-looking and energetic young women. The two women then proceeded to walk over to the side deck to the rope ladder that led down to the raft used by the Russians to climb aboard the cargo ship. The blonde woman motioned for the Russians to climb back down the ladder. She had a big, beautiful smile on her face. It looked as if the woman was saying, *Time to leave. And we are going with you.*

"Captain," Chief Poltav said, "I think that these girls want to go with us."

"I don't think that this is a good idea," Valeria added. "It wouldn't be wise to take these two honey bears back with us to the Vodyanoy. They could be a major distraction for the crew."

Rostova is just jealous of these beautiful girls, the chief thought, then stated, "Here's something to consider, Captain. We don't know the language here. These two girls do. Perhaps they could help us with the map as well."

"You're right, Chief," the captain replied. "It would seem that these two girls know what they're doing and have this captain's blessing. Let's get back to the sub. Comrade Rostova, Petrov, we're going back to the Vodyanoy. And these girls will be joining us." Petrov was all smiles, while the political officer was not.

Petrov climbed down to the raft first, followed by the girls. They both climbed down like acrobatics. These girls were in great shape. They could have performed in the 1980 Moscow Olympics. Valeria Rostova then climbed down herself. As she did so, Chief Poltav remarked to the captain, "It's a pity we can't leave Rostova here on this ship. An even trade. We get the two girls, while this ship can keep Rostova."

The captain chuckled. "Just what this ship needs. A political officer." The captain and chief then also climbed down to the raft. Once in the raft, Captain Starinov waved to the captain of the cargo ship.

The new girls each grabbed a paddle and helped in getting back to the submarine. "They certainly are industrious, Captain," the chief said.

"That they are, Chief," the captain replied. "Something tells me that they carried their own weight back on that cargo ship."

"Chief, Chief," the brunette stated as she smiled at Chief Poltav.

"By the way, Comrade Rostova," the captain said. "I'm putting these two girls in your care."

"*WHAT!*" Valeria exclaimed. "I can't communicate with these two wild women."

"You will figure something out," the captain replied. If anything, these two girls would keep the political officer occupied, and perhaps out of their hair.

"Great," Valeria mumbled, "just great. Well, I'm not even going to try and learn their names. I'll give them new names. You," as Valeria pointed to the blonde, "Your new name is Baba Yaga." Then pointing to the brunette said, "Your name is Kikimora. Baba Yaga and Kikimora. Say it." The two girls did as the political officer demanded, and then laughed.

By now, the raft was at the Vodyanoy. Several crewman helped everyone onto the submarine. Naturally, the Soviet sailors couldn't take their eyes off of these new arrivals.

Once aboard the submarine, Captain Starinov set a course to the north. Actually where, he wasn't sure yet. Valeria saw to it that "Baba Yaga" and "Kikimora" were given jumpsuits to wear. The political officer couldn't have them running around in the outfits that they had on. The crew would't be able to stay focused. Even in the jumpsuits it was hard not to stare at these beautifil girls.

The new girls were of course amazed at being on the Vodyanoy. At first, they thought that they were in some kind of powerful monster. They were also spellbound by the instruments and blinking lights. The girls wanted to see it all, and all of the crew wanted to show them around. But the political officer wouldn't allow it. She kept them both on a short leash. The two chiefs, Poltav and Gaida shared a cabin. They let the girls stay there. For the time being, the chiefs would bunk with the crew.

Captain Starinov called for a meeting. He asked for his Lt. Commander, chiefs, Doctor Ivanova, the political officer and the Nimrosenskys to be present. The captain had come to respect the scientists couple. The captain also requested for Valeria Rostova to bring the two girls. They met in a recreation area for the crew. The captain simply rolled out the map on a table that the captain of the cargo ship had given him. Captain Starinov then said to the new guests, "Girls, I know you have no idea what I'm asking, but where should we go as he pointed down at the map?"

Both girls came closer to the table. The brunette, the one Valeria called Kikimora had a gleem in her eyes as she smiled. The girl said something that of course no one could understand. Kikimora pointed down at the two large landmasses in the Northern Hemisphere, and a channel that separated the two continents. This was the Acco Channel. And the landmasses were none other than Trozny and Zotova.

"So be it, the captain stated, "Lt. Commander Grodno, it shouldn't be too difficult using this map to set a course for this channel."

"I'll see to it, Captain,' Lt. Commander Grodno affirmed.

"Excuse me, Captain," the political officer said, "but you're taking the word of this young barbarian girl as to where we should set a course. It could be a trap."

"Do you have a better idea, Comrade Rostova?" The captain asked.

"Yes, do you, Comrade Political Officer?" Chief Poltav added.

"No," Valeria replied. After pausing added, "I suppose that I don't."

"'Great Samhain', as Rowena would say," Michaela stated. Lin, Michaela and Shako were still taking all of this in on the time scanner.

"It appears that the Russians are about to discover a new world as it were," Lin said. "And I mean a literal new world."

"Yes, as in another planet," Shako added. "But I'm curious about these two Vanagian girls. The ones given the names Kikimora and Baba Yaga."

"Yes, Shako," Michaela said, "me, too. Let's use the time scanner to find out more about these barbarians, as Valeria Rostova called them."

The two girls on this planet Vanag were from Trozny. This would make them Trozyans. And they spoke several languages. Their own as well as Zotovan, and some of the dialects of Enaim. This made the girls a great asset. Kikimora and Baba Yaga were from the same village in Trozny. They were basically peasants, farmer girls. But these girls wanted more in life than to follow in the footsteps of their mothers and grandmothers.

Trozny was ruled by a monarch. At present, this was King Agopia. However, he was more of a figurehead. The twenty-six provinces in this vast land were controlled by a type of governor. Yet, they were all loyal to the king.

The Troznyan girls were the same age, being in their early twenties. When they were only fifteen years old, Kikimora and Baba Yaga left their village. They took a boat across the Acco Channel to Zotova. The girls worked on a fishing boat and picked up Zotovan and some Enaiman very quickly. For this reason they came to be in demand and were protected by many sea captains. Next, Kikimora and Baba Yaga sailed on merchant-cargo ships to Enaim and many islands. This is when they learned the other dialects from these other places.

Kikimora and Baba Yaga were attractive girls, yet never settled down. They traveled from ship to ship and port to port.

The girls were traveling the world of Vanag as it were. Because of their language skills they would interpert to negotiate trade deals for many merchants. And now, here these two girls were on a Soviet submarine. Kikimora was a shrewd, mischievous girl, while Baba Yaga was a little more laid-back. Eventually, the Yaga was dropped from this part of her new name given to her by Valeria Rostova. Both of these names came from Slavic mythology. And Kikimora could also represent an evil creature.

Lin, Michaela and Shako followed the lives of these two Troznyan girls for a while. They had seen enough for now. One thing was for certain. Kikomora and now Baba would play an important role in helping the Russians on this new planet. Valeria Rostova may not have known it at the time, but Kikimora would become a close ally and asset for the political officer. But for what purpose?

"Well, now," Rowena stated. "It has been three months since the Americans sailed into Torama, the capital of North Ucella." Rowena, Justinian and Rebecca were viewing the time scanner. They moved ahead several months to observe what was now unfolding. "It appears that some of the Americans are adjusting quite well. While others are not."

"True," Justinian added, "and they even changed the calendar, as it were."

"I guess they would have to," Rebecca said, "otherwise they would lose what sanity they had left."

The seasons were about the same on Vanag as they were on Earth. Whether they still wanted to admit it or not, the Americans knew that they were no longer on Earth. And they came to realize that the passing of Halley"s Comet, while they were at the North Pole, most likely had something to do with the great changes they were now experiencing. Thus, the term "After The Comet" became a new way of life for the Americans. But the Americans were still trying to comprehend this bizarre transformation beyond their planet.

"From what I can see," Rowena said, "about half of the Americans on the USS Tampa have accepted that they are no longer on their planet. While the other half, while going through the motions that their lives have changed, are still in denial. They think, or hope that this is all a bad dream. Somehow, they hope to wake up and find themselves back on planet Earth.

Fortunately, the American sailors and this unknown army at Torama did not clash. Thus, a bloodbath was avoided. Perhaps the soldiers in the North Ucellan army could sense that these "foreigners" in this large metal boat were much more powerful than they were.

Captain Albritton had concluded that the less of the crew that went ashore for the first time in Torama, the better. The captain, of course, would go, taking the lead in representing the United States of America. Lt. Commander Buchanan would also accompany him. The captain was taking a chance, but two of the women on the Tampa were more than eager to visit this new, strange city. Terri Eden, of course. The inquisitive reporter. And Slyvia Rizzo, the intern for the submarine's doctor, Larry Caldwell.

With that, Captain Albritton stated, "Here goes nothing," as the two men and two women stepped off of the submarine onto a long wooden dock. Several soldiers then motioned for the Americans to accompany them. No one from the two groups could understand one another. Once leaving the dock and pier, a carriage was waiting for them. The carriage was pulled by two animals that resembled horses. Like the fish that Brenda Hutt had observed through a window on the submarine, these horses were similar to the ones found on Earth, yet different.

Looking back, it was like a fog that day when the four Americans met some North Ucellans for the first time. The city of Torama did indeed resemble a city from North America or Europe during the days of the Industrial Revolution. Because of buring coal and the close homes of the factory workers, living conditions were deplorable and unsanitary. The majority of the children were not in very good health. When later asked by many of the crew back on the USS Tampa what Torama was like, the redheaded reporter replied, "It reminded me of a city out of a Charles Dickens novel."

The American visitors were taken to a rather large, well-kept home. They would eventually figure out that a man in his fifties was the current leader of North Ucella. His name was simply, Benatta. No one had last names on the planet Vanag. This new land for the Americans was by no means a democracy, nor a dictatorship. Basically, if a wealthy, influential man did the best that he could to govern, then he could be the main leader as long as he chose to do so in this country. This was the case with Benatta.

There was no electricity on this world yet. The streets did have gas lights. Inside homes, light came from either small gas lamps or candles. Benatta greeted his guests from a land unknown to him, in this governmental/residential house. Benatta's wife was present as well. Her name was Kureyri.

Kureyri, appeared to be much younger than her husband. Terri Eden had once again been told by Captain Albritton not to use her camera to take pictures. However, being the good reporter that she was, Terri was making plenty of mental notes. One of the things she focused on was the manner in which Kureyri was dressed. The North Ucellan woman was wearing a rather loose-fitting lavender dress. The length of the dress came down halfway pass her knees before reaching the woman's ankles. Kureyri was also wearing white ankle-boots. *Interesting fashion,* Terri thought.

While the captain and Lt. Commander were attempting to exchange formalities, and even drinking some type of liquor with Benatta, something caught Sylvia Rizzo's attention. A horrible cough was coming from a nearby room. Almost being a doctor, Sylvia, also a lieutenant in the navy, quietly left the room where the others were and went to investigate.

In another room down the hall, Sylvia stumbled upon a young woman cuddling a small child. A girl. This horrible cough was coming from the child. Sylvia knew right away that this child was seriously ill. The woman holding the little girl was evidently some type of nanny. To Sylvia, this condition resembled whooping cough. Very deadly for children. The intern immediately joined the others in the large room. She explained to the captain, Lt. Commander, and reporter what she had just seen.

No one was quite sure how they did it, but they were able to convince Benatta and Kureyri that their daughter, named

Messina, was in grave danger. They convinced the North Ucellan couple to allow them to take Messina with them to the Tampa to treat her. They agreed. No doubt Benatta had already been informed about the huge metal vessel docked in his city. Possibly, the leader reasoned that if these people had a vessel like the Tampa, then they also possessed superior medicine. Or so they hoped.

Another carriage was provided to transport the nanny and sick child. Sylvia Rizzo also rode in this carriage. The four Americans, along with their two guests, made their way back to the Tampa. The ill little girl was immediately taken to the sick bay where Doctor Caldwell and Sylvia could hopefully treat Messina.

The doctor and intern did discuss briefly whether they should attempt to use their medicine on this child from another world. After all, they knew nothing about these people. But Doctor Caldwell stated, "If we don't try something, this young girl will probably die anyway." The doctor and intern knew that they had the means to develop a vaccine to cure this ailment.

The next day, Captain Albritton had concluded that some of the crew could venture into Torama. The citizens appeared to be friendly and even welcomed the Americans. Brenda Hutt and Terri Eden were allowed to go into the city as well, but had to be escorted by two sailors for each woman. This was for their own protection. The sailors of course, enjoyed this duty. Who knows how the men of the city would react when catching sight of these two attractice women? For one, in the case of Terri Eden, red hair was extremely rare on this world. As the captain wasn't present, Terri began to take pictures. But very discreetly. She still had quite a few few rolls of new film back on the Tampa.

Everyone that ventured into the city fanned out in different directions to see what they could find out. Brenda Hutt, escorted by two sailors, also had two young Ucellan women accompanying her. They had difficulty communicating, but appeared to be becoming friends. Brenda wished to visit a museum in the city. Why? So she could learn more about the animal life on this planet. The museum was similar to what one would be like on Earth during the late 1800's, but there were plenty of stuffed creatures and others preserved in some type of fluid, as well as many books and countless drawings and paintings of these creatures. In great detail at that.

The marine biologist could spend weeks in this museum. Brenda was happy to say the least. She discovered and learned a lot about lifeforms on this new world. Brenda would be making many visits to this main science center in Torama.

There was actually an observatory in this city. David Hartford, the amateur astronomer, made it a point to go there. An old man was the caretaker/stargazer at this observatory. Like the museum, this center would be the equivalent to what an observatory back in the 1800's on Earth would look like, but the main telescope was somewhat impressive. And there were drawings of the other planets in this solar system and of the two moons along with star charts. Hartford, too, made extensive notes. Like the marine biologist at the museum, Hartford knew that he would return to the observatory. The old man was very helpful even though the seaman had no idea what he was telling him.

A sidekick and friend of Davia Hartford was a fellow sailor named Tim Spivey. He was nicknamed Sci-Fi Guy. Tim was quite the reader of science-fiction novels, and loved old and new movies on the subject. Sci-Fi Guy also collected comic books and was a good artist of these characters. Spivey accompanied Hartford to the observatory. Naturally, they found two pretty young women their age that showed them around Torama. The Ucellan girls even took the two American sailors to their homes to meet their families. No one could speak each others's language, but everyone was friendly and hospitable.

Many of the people from North Ucella resembled Scandinavians back on Earth. These two girls were fair-skinned blondes. Their names were Palas and Alya. These Ucellan girls were fascinated with the two young Americans. And the feeling was mutual for Hartford and Spivey. The two seamen were trying to conduct themselves as gentlemen. However, Palas and Alya were followers of the Aelianan religion. The morals of this religion on this planet were quite different from most of those on Earth.

Over the course of several days, the members of the crew and civilians on the Tampa that ventured into the city, reported back to Captan Albritton and Lt. Commander Cardoza. This was a requirement if anyone visited Torama. So far there had been no incidents. The "natives did appear to be friendly." And, in fact, helpful, despite the language barrier. The captain and Lt. Commander recorded all of the findings. With all of these fresh eyes, the information coming back was both interesting and informative.

Brenda Hutt had learned a lot about the animal life on this world. But she could spend the rest of her life finding out more. David Hartford was obtaining as much information as he could, learning about this new solar system that the planet they were now a part of. Sylvia Rizzo, the intern for Doctor Caldwell, reported back to the captain that many of the children in this city were extremely ill. She did learn about some of the medicine available in the city from the local doctors. Some of it was promising, but needed a booster, as it were.

On a good note, after a few days, Messina did recover from the strain of whooping cough. The vaccination worked. This was great news. The little girl went home to join her parents, Benatta and Kureyri. They were forever grateful for these people "from beyond" for saving their daughter. More vaccines could be made and hopefully distributed to the many sick and dying children of Torama and North Ucella. This new vaccination, though, would have to be taken orally. The current civilization on Vanag wasn't advanced enough yet to manufacture medical needles. And the Americans only had a limited supply on the Tampa.

David Hartford and Tim Spivey reported back to the captain and Lt. Commander what they learned about how the people of Torama lived. That is, their dwellings and living conditions. The two seamen also told their superiors about their new North Ucellan "girlfriends." Both officers cautioned the young sailors about not taking advantage of these girls. After all, this was a different race, from another world, and over a hundred years behind Earth.

Both seamen looked at each other, then nodded at the two officers. But David Hartford thought, *Right Captain. You need not worry about Sci-Fi Guy and me. It's these two girls that are all over us.* This was true. Palas and Alya, when alone with the two young Americans were like octopuses. The Vanagian girls literally wrapped themselves around the Earth boys. Hartford was dismissed to study more of his findings about this other solar system. Lt. Commander Cardoza had other duties to tend to. But Tim Spivey asked to converse a little more with the captain.

Tim Spivey was not as knowledgeable about astronomy as David Hartford, but did have a logical mind. The problem, though, for most people was that Spivey was obsessed with fantasy and science fiction. Spivey talked and even wrote about life on other worlds and traveling to other planets. And now, here he was on another planet.

As a young boy, Spivey collected and read hundreds of pulp science-fiction books and comics. He had quite the collection. While on leave before going on this last mission aboard the USS Tampa, Spivey briefly went home. This was in Akron, Ohio. His mother complained about him having too much "stuff." Meaning his books and comics. He promised to weed a few out. He took quite a bit of his collection back with him to the submarine. Spivey got away with bringing all of these publications with him by donating them to the submarine's library. There appeared to be plenty of space in this reading room.

Sci-Fi Guy then began to relate to Captain Albritton about a book by H.G Wells and a movie based on a novel by Jules Verne. Spivey had a photographic memory, so could relate about many books and movies. He could also remember every science-fiction movie and television show. Even the TV commercials sponsoring the shows. Spivey knew the names of every actor, actress, director, and anythings else relating to a movie or series.

Spivey began to explain to the captain about a book and movie that may have had a connection to the recent passing of Halley's Comet back on Earth. The 1961 movie was based on a Jules Verne novel. It was called *Valley Of The Dragons*. Two dueling men attempt to return to Earth after being swept away on a comet to a prehistoric world. They hope that the comet when it returns in seven years will get them back to Earth.

The other book Sci-Fi Guy talked about was by H.G. Wells. This novel was written in 1906. This book was *In The Days Of The Comet.* This story features that when a comet passes near Earth, an unknown gas that replaces oxygen, changes mankind for the better. Happiness and peace on Earth prevails on a planet with a history of misery and turmoil.

Captain Albritton was indeed listening to Tim Spivey. But he then pondered, *Why am I listening to this young kid, a science fiction buff?* The captain then rationialized that this was good therapy for the young sailor. He then thanked Sci-Fi Guy for his input and dismissed him. However, the captain later went to the library. He hadn't read a book for a while. The captain decided to read one of Spivey's books. *In The Days Of The Comet.* "Mankind had changed for the better." At least in the story on Earth.

Rowena, Justinian and Rebecca continued to track and document the Americans. "Will mankind change for the better on Vanag, or Tellus Two?" Rowena asked. "Time will tell."

Nine days after the Vodyanoy had an interesting encounter with an Enaim ship out in the middle of the Targu Ocean, the Russian submarine, now submerged cruised to the Northern Hemisphere. The colorful map that the Enaiman captain had given the Russians proved to be informative and valuable.

The two Troznyan girls, now known as Kikimora and Baba Yaga, were also a great asset. As these girls had a gift for speaking several Vanagian languages, it didn't take them long to pick up much of the Russian language. They were obviously fast learners. The captain and political officer were amazed. Kikomora and Baba were constantly in close contact with as many young Russian seamen as they could be around. That is, until Valeria Rostova broke up these friendly encounters. But this was how the two exotic, energetic girls were picking up this Earth language.

Lin, Michaela and Shako, with the aid of the planet-time scanner, looked on with great interest. "These Troznyan girls are something else." Lin remarked.

"Yes," Michaela added. "They are very smart, but a bit on the wild side."

"That's for sure," Shako stated. "They also appear to be devious and crafty. Especially the one now called Kikimora. You can see it in her eyes."

At the suggestion of Kikimora and Baba, the Vodyanoy's first port of call was a city by the name of Tellovaci. This city was located on the shore of the Acco Channel. On the side of Trozny. Like the Bosphorus Strait back on Earth that separated the continents of Europe and Asia, the Acco Channel did a similar thing. This channel of eleven Earth miles separated the two Vanagian continents of Trozny and Zotova.

Naturally, like with the Americans at Torama, North Ucella, the people of Tellovaci were spellbound at the sight of the Vodyanoy. To this city of about one hundred and twenty-five thousand, the submarine appeared as a huge gray sea monster with a bright, red star. There were two huge Soviet red stars on each side of the conning tower.

Kikimora and Baba both desired to go to this city in their homeland. But Valeria Rostova didn't think it was a good idea for both girls to ventue into the city. The political officer didn't want to admit it, but she knew that the crew needed and now depended on these girls. If something happened to one, or if one girl ran away, the Russians would still have the other girl. Valeria didn't know it, but the two Troznyan girls had no desire to run away. They had a good thing going, now being a part of the crew on this futuristic vessel. Besides, Kikimora and Baba loved all of the attention that they were getting from the young submariners.

Against his wishes, it was decided that Captain Starinov also remain on the submarine, as he was too important. So, one of the chiefs would go into the city with the political officer and two armed crewman. This would be Chief Poltav. No one on the Vodyanoy liked Valeria Rostova, even if she was fairly attractive.

Before departing ashore, Chief Poltav whispered to the captain, "Maybe some bandits from this city will abduct Comrade Rostova. Then we will be rid of the political officer for good." The captain, of course laughed.

The four Russians led by Kikimora ventured to the dock area of the Port of Tellovaci. They got quite a few stares, as everyone knew that these people were the strangers that came out of the mysterious-looking vessel. And they had never seen anything like the form-fitting jumpsuits that Valeria Rostova and Kikimora were wearing. As mentioned, Trozny was ruled by King Agopia. One of the king's governors ruled in his behalf in the province where Tellovaci was located. This governor was not available, so one of his deputies was sent to inquire about these new visitors.

The deputy and his small entourage talked briefly with the chief and political officer with Kikomora acting as the translator. The *AK-47*'s of the two seamen were clearly visible. The deputy and others with him had never seen weapons such as these automatic assault rifles. And with the huge metal vessel in clear view, these Troznyans concluded that these visitors were a force to be reckoned with. But where did these people come from? Was there another land that most of the Vanagians didn't know about? Much more advanced than the rest of the planet?

After some pleasant small talk, the deputy invited the visitors to return when the governor was available. The Russians thanked the deputy, but, with Kikimora's recommendation, decided to return to the Vodyanoy and sail on. At least the chief and political officer could report back that there were no unfriendly incidents. Once again, Kikimora proved her worth.

As the Russians and Troznyan girl were heading back to the submarine, there was quite a large crowd staring at them and the Vodyanoy. Sitting on the dock wall, though, were a dozen young children, mostly boys, drawing. Drawing what? Like the young boy on the Enaiman ship, they were drawing the submarine. Red star and all. And all of them were quite good and fast. Much like reporter-artists back on Earth during the 1800's. Before photography was invented. One boy, though, as the Russians walked by them, began to rapidly sketch Valeria Rostova in her jumpsuit. He wasn't sure what it meant but he even sketched in on the dark blue jumpsuit the letters, *CCCP* over one of the pockets

“Good Goliath,” Michaela stated from back in the kingdom while viewing the time scanner. “This young boy is good.”

"He sure is," Lin added. "Before technology back on Earth, people were more gifted in the arts. It appears to be the same on Vanag. Their talents come to full bloom without the distractions of technology."

"I wonder what this boy is going to do with this drawing of the Russian Earth woman?" Shako had to consider. "Or for that matter, all of these other drawings of the submarine?"

"Perhaps, they sell them," Michaela concluded.

Later it would be revealed what would become of some of these drawings. That night, the young boy would return to his humble family home and work further on his drawing. Recreate what he had drawn with paint on a canvas.

The boy painted the striking woman he saw dressed in strange clothes with a red star over one pocket and the letters *CCCP* over the other. It became a very detailed portrait. Valeria Rostova looked so real in this painting. She was featured with her shoulder length, raven-colored hair and chestnut eyes. The young boy-artist was truly quite remarkable. Valeria was depicted as the beautiful woman that she was, with a mysterious look. Not smiling, stern as she usually was, yet with unusual sad eyes. The next day, this young Trozyan artist would build a frame for his masterpiece, then hoped to sell it at one of the many marketplaces in Tellovaci.

After the small party returned to the Vodyanoy, Capain Starinov called for a brief meeting with his senior staff. Kikimora urged the Russians to leave the Acco Channel and head to Zotova. She suggested they set sail for Tannsisi, the somewhat official capital of this large country. According to the Enaiman map, the directions from Kikomora, and their own calculations, the Russians should arrive in this Zotovan city in eighteen hours.

Every time the two Trozyan girls were part of the conversation, it was apparent that they had pretty much mastered the Russian language. There was little that the Russians couldn't comprehend as the girls explained matters to them. While en route to their destination, the Troznyan girls explained a few things regarding Zotova to the captain, chiefs and political officer. This huge land was in a somewhat chaotic state, and had been for many years. The capital, Tannsisi, wasn't even really a safe, stable city.

Most of Zotova was a cross between the wild west back in the early days of the American southwest and corrupt cities. The main cities were in the control of crime bosses. They changed hands often as a more powerful crime boss came to power with his own private gangster army. In the interior, small armies set up by rival warlords were in control. Peasent farmers toiled the land and paid tribute to the warlords. Kikimora and Baba further explained that in the cities, most of the girls and young women their age worked in brothels or did dirty work for the crime bosses. Kikimora and Baba probably wouldn't have come to Tannsisi by themselves. After all, they both were attractive girls. Young boys in the cities and frontier towns were forced to serve in the many private armies. Many died young.

The wheels were spinning inside Valeria Rostova's head. *Soviet socialism will put an end to this decadent rulership,* she pondered.

Before they knew it, the Vodyanoy, was at another Vanagian port. The Port of Tannsisi. In view of what the Troznyan girls had told the Russians, the officers felt that eight seamen armed with *AK-47*'s should accompany the political officer and Chief Poltav again. The captain felt better with the chief keeping an eye on Valeria Rostova. Who knows what she may try to pull off? Valeria and the chief also each had a sidearm strapped to their hip. This pistol was the Makarov 9mm. This time Baba would go ashore and be the translator. Kikimora pleaded several times to be the one to go again. The political officer kept telling her, "Nyet, Nyet." As the Troznyan girls had become so valuable, to the Russians, there was no way both could go ashore. Especially in this notorious Zotovan city.

By the time the Vodyanoy sailed into the port, like in Tellovaci, there was quite a crowd waiting for them. But this time the civilians were kept back at a great distance. There appeared to be around fifty men armed with muskets closer to the dock where the submarine had come to a halt. Behind them, though, not too far back, were several hundred more of this army. It was obviously a private army as the men were not in uniform.

The chief, political officer and Baba walked closer to the men. The eight seamen stood in a row about ten feet behind the three-person delegation. Baba held up her right hand and was about to say something in Zotovan, but then, four men raised their muskets and fired. A musket ball whisked past Valeria's left ear. Baba was shot in what appeared to be her upper chest. The Troznyan girl screamed and fell to her knees. One Soviet seamen was shot dead and fell to the ground.

The chief and political officer simultaneously pulled out their pistols and began firing at the group of armed men. Several dropped dead. Chief Poltav picked up Baba and threw her across his shoulder while still firing his pistol. Valeria did likewise. They then fell back behind the now seven seamen. *"FIRE."* The political officer yelled out. She had the authority to give such an order.

RAT-A-TAT-TAT, the *AK-47*'s fired a barrage of bullets at this army now on the run. They had never experienced a burst of gunfire such as this. A dozen and a half dropped dead or were severly wounded. The political officer and the chief, who was still carrying Baba, ran back to the submarine. The captain, Kikimora, and a few others witnessed this bloodbath from the conning tower. There were an additional twenty Russian sailors also armed with assault rifles standing outside on the Vodyanoy. Before the captain could say anything, Valeria ordered as she yelled out again, *"BACK UP YOUR COMRADES! GO IN HOT PURSUIT AND SHOOT AS MANY AS THOSE ARMED VERMIN AS*

YOU CAN!" The seamen did as ordered and ran down the dock and began firing as they got closer to the fleeing gangster army. Most of the civilians had already fled.

This was not what Captain Starinov wanted. After having a peaceful encounter with an Enaiman ship and at the Port of Tellovaci, this was not what he expected. But this army did fire on his people first. Valeria Rostova had a right to give the order to fire and counterattack. Baba, was taken below and treated. The Troznyan girl would recover. Doctor Ivanova and her assistant removed the musket ball, and with the right medicine were able to stablize the girl.

At the end of the dock was a large warehouse into which the gangster army had retreated. With now close to thirty Russian sailors firing their burst of fire from the *AK-47's*, the opposing army scattered and ran into the city. The thugs were like cockroaches that disappeared when the light was turned on.

Back on the Vodyanoy, Valeria Rostova was incensed. As was Kikimora. After all, these Zotovan thugs almost killed her friend. As soon as the warehouse was secured, the political officer suggested to the other officers that a perimeter of defense be established. This would keep anyone else from getting near the submarine in the event of an counterattack. Captain Starinov agreed.

In a short time Valeria Rostova, Lt. Commander Grodno and Chief Gaida went to the warehouse and set up a command center. Kikimora joined them. It was hoped that they could talk to some Zotovans. They would need Kikimora to translate. A few young children actually approached the warehouse and were allowed to gain entry. Kikimora asked some questions and got a few answers. But more intel was needed.

About an hour later, a lone man appeared waving a truce flag. He looked to be in his fifties. Perhaps the young children were sent first as part of a fact-finding mission. The man identified himself as Tefano. Speaking through Kikomora, Tefano said that he, too, had a somewhat small army. He was obviously a lesser, rival crime boss. Tefano claimed that he knew the location of the main crime boss's headquarters in Tannsisi. It was in a Mozdak temple. Many of the priests of this religion allied themselves with the various crime bosses throughout Zotova. Tefano stated that with a little fire power from the Russians, he could take out the current crime boss and that he would then rule the city in behalf of the Russians.

What a great idea, Valeria Rostova thought. *Why not let these bandits slaughter each other and then we will pick up the pieces.* Back on Earth, the Soviet Union in their proxy wars did this all of the time. Valeria, the Lt. Commander and chief talked this over. They then passed this information on to the captain on the Vodyanoy. Captain Starinov really didn't want to become involved in a private little war. But this was the lesser of two evils. Why risk anymore Russian lives. With this plan and decision events were about to unfold rapidly. This move would eventually affect Zotova and the planet Vanag for many years to come.

Part of the crew on the Vodyanoy, were made up of a half-dozen Soviet marines. Special forces as it were. Valeria wanted them involved in this operation to take out this gangster threat. Two of these special Soviet operatives would be armed with *RPG-7V's.* (Rocket Projectile Gernade.) The political officer had taken control of this operation, and she meant business.

Finding their way to the Mozdok temple, Tefano, the rival crime boss, accompanied by over one hundred men from his private army, along with six Russian special forces, took up their positions. Tefano's men began firing at the rival army stationed around the temple. They were drawing them out into the open. After several clashes involving these two armies with musket fire, the Russians knew when to hit the opposing army. While both armies were reloading their muskets, one Russian fired his *RPG* through the front door of the temple. Even though the large door was made of thick wood, it was blown to pieces by the *RPG*. A huge explosion was heard, followed by screams from the inside. This was followed by another explosion as the second *RPG* was launched into a side window. As it was night, the building lit up with the explosion.

With Tefano's army leading the way, four Russian special forces followed. Once inside, they let out a barrage of fire from their *AK-47*'s. Within a minute, everything was silent. Bodies of the rival army were lying everywhere, along with the former main crime boss of Tannsisi, and several Mozdok priests. Tefano came to power that night with the backing of the Russians. Word about this change of leadership would spread quickly throughout the city.

There was another meeting on the Vodyanoy with the senior staff to discuss this latest development. But in the days that followed, more was to come. Once again, events were happening quite rapidly for the Russians. "I suppose, then," Captain Starinov stated, "that this Tefano comrade with our help, is now the new boss of this city."

"Party Boss, Comrade Captain," Valeria Rostova said. "This man owes us. We now own him and his private army. Tefano will become the first commissar on this world representing the Soviet Union. He and his army will become indoctrinated in the principles of Marxism-Leninism." Although none of the others in the meeting said anything, they all realized that the political officer was right. All present knew that they needed to be in control of Tannsisi.

"What next then?" Lt. Commander Grodno asked.

"I'll tell you what's next, Lt. Commander," Valeria replied. "We need to make some interrogations. We may be in control of this city, but we're at war with an unknown enemy. According to Kikimora, the crime boss that we took out tonight is one of many throughout this vast continent. As political officer representing the Soviet Union, we must stay one step ahead of this coalition of thugs." Valeria Rostova, was now in a frenzy, and drunk with power, to say the least.

The next day the interrogations would begin. Tefano had set up his new "administraton" at a stately home in the middle of the city. Valeria, along with the six Soviet special forces that were involved with the overthrow of the previous crime boss, paid Tefano a visit. Using Kikimora as her interpreter, Valeria laid down a few rules for this new commissar. Namely, that he now worked for the Russians and was to follow their orders. After witnessing what the Russians could do, there would be no argument.

Next, Tefano, his family, and all that worked under him, would be required to learn Russian. Starting today. Valeria brought along the perfect people for this task. Svetlana Lebedeva, Anastasia Macagonova and Tatiana Semenova. Svetlana was, of course, the great-niece of the member of the Soviet politburo. Antastasia was her cousin. This was why they had been allowed to come on this misssion of the Vodyanoy back on Earth. Both girls were almost schoolteachers, so this would be the perfect job for them. Like the American, Terri Eden, Antastasia, with her red hair, would stand out. Especially in Zotova. The three Russian girls would always have several armed seamen from the submarine accompany them for protection.

Tatiana Semenova, the reporter for Tass would also assist in teaching Russian to this first group of Zotovans. She could make notes in her journal and would eventually help in setting up a newspaper. There were a few papers and printing presses in Tannsisi and other major cities across Vanag. This newspaper would be called *New Pravda.* Pravda means truth. *This will make some story when I get back to Russia and Earth,* Tatiana thought. *If I get back to Earth.*

Later that day, back at the warehouse near the Vodyanoy , the interrogations did begin. With Valeria Rostova taking the lead. Kikimora stayed busy for the rest of the day and into the night translating for both the Russians and Zotovans. The Trozyan girl appeared to love this new role, as she was now considered a part of the Vodyanoy crew.

Tefano helped round up and turn over any of the loyal followers of the previous crime boss. With any men that were interrogated, Valeria's approach was simple and direct. "Tell me what I need to know, or die." The political officer even put her pistol up to their heads as she said this. They all talked. A battery operated cassette tape recorder was used during the interrogations. Kikimora would later go back and make sure everything was heard and translated correctly.

As for the wives and older children of these men who were followers of the former crime boss, Valeria used a different approach. She would tell them that if they also cooperated, they would be rewarded. As most of the cities in Zotova were in chaos, there were food shortages. But now that the Russians were in control of Tannsisi, they had control of the food distribution. The wives and children told Valeria through Kikimora what they knew. And as promised, they were rewarded. All of these tactics were straight out of the *KGB* manual, that the political officer knew by heart. Valeria Rostova had what she needed. Now, back to the captain and other officers on the Vodyanoy.

The information that Valeria had obtained through Kikimora was as follows: Zotova was similar to Afghanistan back on Earth, in which the Soviet Union was still fighting a quagmire war with. Like the tribal leaders in Afghanistan, the crime bosses and warlords in Zotova were made up of many rival factions. However, if there arose a common enemy or threat, the various factions in Zotova would unite for the time being.

Some of the cities and towns in Zotova had a type of telegraph system used back on Earth during the late 19th and early 20th centuries. And through horseback, word of the latest developments could be spread. Through the interrogations it was pretty much established that the many factions throughout

Zotova knew what had happened in Tannsisi with the arrival of the Russians.

In the middle of the interior of Zotova was a frontier city known as Zelessio. This is where the many rival factions would meet to form a confederation. For what purpose? To plan a counterattack against these new invaders that had control of Tannsisi. It was acceptable for Zotovans to slaughter one another. But how dare an outside army shed Zotovan blood? That was the thinking in this land.

The political officer had a plan. Take out this now-rebel city with one blow. Especially now that the new enemies of the Russians were making their next move. Take Zelessio out! How? Valeria Rostova, as the political officer on the Vodyanoy, had a full security clearance. She knew everything about this special submarine. Including the weapons system. Besides, the sixteen *SS-N-18* nuclear missiles, and the four *S33* mm torpedo tubes, were another secret prototype weapon.

This was the Burya II cruise missile. This weapon carried a low-yield nuclear warhead. In the event of a crisis, rather than using the more powerful *SS-N-18* missiles, this cruise missile could be used against an enemy target. Perhaps a military installation away from the center of a civilian population. Or a carrier task force out at sea. Rather than starting a full-scale nuclear war, the Burya cruise missile could be launched as a show of force weapon until cooler heads prevailed. At least this was the thinking of the Soviets. This tactic was still quite a gamble.

However, the Russians were no longer on Earth. According to Valeria, this was the perfect weapon to use against their new enemy on Vanag. Especially on a city out in the middle of nowhere where the rebel Zotovans had gathered. This would be a quick and easy strike with mimimal radiation. After the strike, the radiation would dissipate after several days. At least this was the theory.

The rest of the senior staff appeared shocked that the political officer would even suggest this plan. But the young political officer was adamant. You could see the flames in her chestnut-colored eyes. "Well, comrades, what do you think?" Valeria asked.

"Comrade Rostova," Captain Starinov replied, "you want us to launch a nuclear missile on this new world?"

"Low-yield nuclear missile, Comrade Captain," Valeria answered. "And yes, this is our only hope in gaining control of this land."

"Comrade political officer," Chief Poltav now said. "the Soviet Union never used nuclear weapons against an enemy even on Earth."

"We're not on Earth, Chief," Valeria replied. "Do any of you have a better idea on how to take out this superior force against us?" No one said anything.

Valeria added that they only had only so many magazine clips left for the *AK-47*'s on hand, and only a small amount of rocket grenades left for the *RPG's.* In short, before long, with continued fighting the Russians would be out of ammo, and would be reduced to firing musket rifles that had been confiscated throughout the city they now controlled. This was more reason for a nuclear strike at this rebel base in the city of Zelessio.

At one point, the scientist couple, the Nimrosenskys, left the room. The thought of a nuclear weapon being used by their government was too much for the Jewish couple to contemplate. But the political officer was undaunted. She next had Kikimora explain a few things about these now renegade Zotovans. Kikimora's Russian was now quite remarkable. She told the Russian senior staff what to expect from these Zotovans. Again, as photography did not exist yet on Vanag, the Troznyan girl had drawings obtained from a nearby museum and newspaper office.

The drawings depicted fellow Zotovans being hanged, flayed and decapitated.

Kikimora also told the Russians about young girls and women being raped or killed by rival Zotovan crime bosses or warlords whenever they were victotious over a rival. Young boys were then forced to fight in private armies. And, many Troznyan women were abducted from coastal cities by Zotovan pirates. For what purpose? To become sex slaves.

Doctor Yelena Ivanova finally spoke up saying, "This is appalling."

"Need I say more, comrades," Valeria Rostova paused. "We must strike against these rebels today. Destroy Zelessio. This is what the Soviet Union would expect us to do. Then we can build a socialist paradise in this great land of Zotova." The meeting then concluded.

Later that evening, as the Vodyanoy was already on the surface in the Port of Tannsisi, the Burya II cruise missile was launched from a torpedo tube. This missile had to be fired while the submarine was on the surface. The target city, Zelessio, was four hundred miles away from Tannsisi. The cruise missile would reach its target in eight minutes. Burya, in Russian, means "storm," and when the missile hit, Zelessio did indeed turn into a firestorm. A mushroom cloud ascended into the Vanagian sky. This missile was equilvent to one of the atomic bombs dropped on Japan in 1945 back on Earth. The United States may have been the first to use nuclear wepons on Earth, but the Soviet Union was the first to use one on Vanag.

The population of Zelessio, including the crime bosses, warlords and their armies, was around ninety thousand. The majority of these people perished in the nuclear blast. The rest would die of radiation posioning in a few days. This era of Zotova ended with the destruction of this interior city. A new era had begun. Within a few short years a red flag with a hammer sickle would fly over every city and town in Zotova. This land would become another Soviet Union.

"I can't believe the Russians did this," Shako Aomori commented. The former Japanese schoolteacher was clearly shaken and upset. After all, Shako had almost become a victim of a nuclear bomb herself. If it hadn't been for the Time Maidens, namely Lin, she would have been vaporized when the United States dropped an atomic bomb on Hiroshima in 1945.

"Good Goliath," Michaela added as the three women continued to view the time scanner. "This is horrible. Wait until Rowena sees this. The Cold War from Earth has now moved to another planet. What next?"

"People from Earth have now unleashed a nuclear weapon beyond their own world," Lin said. "And between the Russians and Americans they have plenty more. Oh, my."

Out in the middle of the Targu Ocean, Kikimora had observed the tactics and moves of the Russians since coming onboard the Vodyanoy. Becoming a translator for the Russians, she was quickly brought up to speed with 20th century technology. She was treated with respect and given the rank of lieutenant in the Soviet navy. Kikimora really was now a member of the crew.

The Troznyan girl was an opportunist and wanted to be on the winning side. She saw her new friends, the Russians, as the now-most powerful force on her planet. Or so she thought. Whether Kikimora would ever come to be a true believer of Marxism-Leninism, only she knew the answer to that. But one thing was certain: Zotova would gradually be transformed into a new Soviet Union. Kikomora would be a part of this and given a lot of power. And power was what this young Troznyan woman wanted. More than anything.

On the other side of the planet Vanag, in the harbor of Torama, North Ucella, the USS Tampa remained docked. The

Americans were still working with and helping the people on this large island-nation. It was in the middle of the night and Seaman Kyle Whiteside was one of a few on duty in the comm room. Watching a radar screen he saw a flash appear. *What was that?* The seaman thought. With the video playback, he could review what he just observed. *There it is again,* Whiteside thought.

Chief Prescott was in charge of the submarine tonight as all the other senior officers were asleep. Seaman Whiteside summonded for the chief. When he came to the comm, the seaman played back the image from the radar screen. It was indeed a flash from the other side of this world. But what was it? "Play it back again, Seaman," the chief asked. "I think that we had better wake up the captain," the chief concluded.

Although mission forty-one was the first time two Time Maidens stepped foot on the planet Vanag, it actually was not a mission. Lin and Cuca had planned a time-jump for Iraq in the year 2017. But by accident, they came to this other world.

However, the Time Maidens were actually planning a mission one on Vanag. While viewing the Russians launching a nuclear missile on the Zotovan city of Zelessio, they saw an opportunity to rescue two hunded and fourteen children minutes before the missile strike. How would the Time Maidens accomplish this?

Justinian, Rebecca, Shako and Mary Collard returned to their other duties as Time Maidens' assistants. Amaresh and Cuca joined the other three Time Maidens as they continued to follow the Americans and Russians on the planet Vanag. Mission one on this new world would be quick, or "in and out," as Rowena stated about some of the missions during the year 1968. Using some of the tactics and tools from previous missions, this first mission would be successful.

"As we know," Lin opened up by saying, "like the invisible, Aeduian satellite-time scanner orbiting our world, we have access to the one orbiting the planet Vanag."

"I think I know where you're going heading with this, Lin," Rowena interjected. "The invisible force field like we deployed in missions twelve and twenty six."

"Correct, Rowena," Lin replied.

"On some missions," Michaela added, "we used more than one time ring. I think that it would be wise to use more than one ring in view of what will happen to this city in the short time that we have."

"Excellent point, Israelite girl," Rowena replied.

"How many time rings, then?" Amaresh asked.

"Five," Lin replied.

"*FIVE!*" Cuca exclaimed. "How many of us are going on this first mission?"

"All of us," Lin replied again.

The five Time Maidens then prepared for the time-jump. During the briefing it was revealed that these children to be rescued were not just Zotovan, but also Troznyan. It appeared that the cunning, opportunist Kikimora, now working for the Russians, was right. Of the two hundred and fourteen children, twenty-five were young Troznyan girls that were abducted by Zotovan pirates. Most would become sex slaves or domestic slaves for the Zotovan crime bosses and warlords.

Right before the nuclear strike on Zelessio, all of these Troznyans would be in a tent compound in this wild, outlaw city. The Time Maidens knew when to make this time-jump. With no adult guards present, the invisible force field could be emitted down from the Aeduian satellite. As noted, this method had worked before on Earth.

The Time Maidens first went to the wardrobe-accessory complex to determine what to wear for this mission. They all decided on wearing purple jumpsuits, along with a black cape and matching boots. This outfit was both striking and otherworldly. And the Time Maidens were otherworldly. They were from Earth, not Vanag.

All five Time Maidens then assembled in the ring operations complex. Each android assistant for the Earth girls would send and recover a time ring. As the rings were activated, Michaela stated, "This is a special day, my sisters. This will be our first official mission on this new planet."

"Yes, indeed, Michaela," Rowena said. "To Aedui and the Vanagian children," as she raised her right fist up. In that instant the Aeduian satellite projected the invisible force field around the perimeter of the children's camp. With that, all five Time Maidens entered their particular time ring.

Instantly, they were now on the planet Vanag. The force field was projected in a circular pattern around the camp, and the five time rings also materialized in this pattern. Out of each ring a Time Maiden jumped. Any adult soldiers that observed these five Earth women from the other side of the force field in their purple jumpsuits, black capes and boots were startled to say the least. The Time Maidens didn't care if the Zotovan army saw them or the time rings. These people would be vaporized in a few minutes.

"CHILDREN, COME WITH US," Lin yelled out in both the Zotovan and Troznyan languages.

"DO NOT BE AFRAID," Rowena added.

"WE ARE HERE TO SAVE YOU," Michaela now proclaimed.

"DON'T BRING ANYTHING WITH YOU," Amaresh instructed. "JUST COME QUICKLY."

"YOU WILL BE SAFE WITH US," Cuca also added. "AND YOU HAVE NOTHING TO FEAR."

The Time Maidens said this several times in these two Vanagian languages. If these children thought these huge, glowing rings were unusual, or that the five women in their midst wore strange clothing, they didn't show it. They began to do as instructed and gathered in small groups near the various time rings. After all, anyplace was better than these awful camps they had been living in.

Each Time Maiden began ushering children through a time ring, then called out for more children to come forward. In a short time it appeared that all of the Vanagian children had gone through a ring. Lin had a special device that could scan inside the force field to make sure that no children were still present. All were accounted for. They were safely back in the kingdom. "That's it, Rowena," Lin said. "Let's go. The sky is about to light up here. See you back in the kingdom." Lin went through the time ring and then it vanished.

This now left just Rowena and one time ring. The Celtic Time Maiden looked around. By now the invisible force field was surrounded by Zotovan thugs, bandits and so-called soldiers. They were shouting, shaking their fists and even banging on the shield with the backs of their muskets. One soldier even leaned back and fired his musket. The musket ball ricochet off of the force field, hitting the soldier right in the forehead. *What a fool,* Rowena thought. *But I suppose that this is a better death for this slug than what is about to rain down on this city.*

Rowena then raised her right arm with a clenched fist into the air. With a smirk she definitely proclaimed, *"FAREWELL, LOSERS."* Even though no one could get to her on the outside of the force field, the Zotovans knew that this strangely dressed woman was antagonizing them. And it made the Celtic Time Maiden feel good.

As Rowena made her way back to the lone time ring, she saw a Zotovan musket lying on the ground. One of the Zotovan soldiers must have left it there before the force field went up. Rowena picked the alien weapon up and said, "My first trophy from the planet Vanag." The Time Maiden then went through the ring. Then the ring disappeared. Forty-eight seconds later the Russian cruise missile hit Zelessio.

By going back in time for this first mission on Vanag, the Time Maidens were able to save over two hundred Zotovan and Troznyan children from perishing in a nuclear holocaust. What a successful time-jump this proved to be. Justinian, Rebecca, Shako and Mary Collard were all on hand to escort the Vanagian children to the master time ring. It was best to send them to Aedui right away. Once on Aedui, these non-Earth childen would be cared for. In the meantime, the Time Maidens were elated with the results of this first mission. Would there be more?

"I can't believe that Earth people inhaled this deadly plant into their bodies for centuries," Michaela stated as she and the other Time Maidens viewed the planet-time scanner on a large console. "I'm so glad that my people didn't have this dangerous plant in ancient Israel."

"I concur, Israelite girl," Rowena added. "Celtic Britain didn't have tobacco plants either."

"Nor in Africa," Amaresh said, "That is until many centuries later."

"I guess that we can blame the Americas," Cuca now stated. "Tobacco was a native plant from Mesoamerica and South America. But eventually found its way all over the world."

"By my time," Lin interjected, "humanity realized that smoking nicotine was harmful to your health, and learned to live without it."

More than half of the crew on both the USS Tampa and Vodyanoy were smokers. During the 1980's, for both the Americans and Russians serving in the military, it was "cool" to smoke. Mostly cigarettes, but a few such as Captain Albritton and Captain Starinov, smoked a pipe. The Nimrosenskys were both chain smokers. But finding themselves no longer on Earth, and with their tobacco products dwindling, what would the Americans and Russians do?

For a start, the Vanagians did have a type of cigarette. However, it wasn't from a tobacco-nicotine plant. It was actually a type of dry seaweed. Kikimora and Baba smoked these Vanagian cigarettes. They, in turn, introduced them to the Russians when first coming aboard the Vodyanoy. When the American sailors began to run out of their cigarettes, the North Ucellans gave them these seaweed-cigarettes as well. It took a little getting used to these Vanagian cigarettes, but it was better than nothing. The Americans nicknamed this product "sea sticks," while the Russians called them "sea smokes."

The Russians actually had a few tobacco plants on the submarine. For what purpose? As Issac and Chaya Nimrosensky were both biologists, they brought several plants and many packets of seeds from Earth with them. Recall that the Soviet Union had planned to set up geodesic spheres, or greenhouses, at their bases in Antarctica. Tobacco plants were a necessity for the Russians in these settlements. Eventually, from these plants, tobacco would become available for both the former Earth people and Vanagians. How? More about that later.

Doctor Caldwell of the Americans, along with his Russian counterpart, Doctor Ivanova, couldn't determine just yet if the Vanagian cigarettes were harmful to a human's health. The problem was that at this point in time of Vanag's history, all of the major cities burned a sedmentary rock similar to coal like on Earth for most of their energy needs. This was especially true in the northern hemisphere. Thus, it was hard to determine how many Vanagians did have lung problems. And if so, was it from the industrial pollution, or from smoking the dried plant that grew in the sea?

As the Time Maidens made their observations regarding the Americans and Russians on Vanag through the time scanner, they decided to keep looking into the future. Events were continuing to unfold with this influence from Earth.

"It is interesting," Lin concluded, "how the tobacco plant from Earth, took root on Vanag."

As the Americans kept trying to integrate into the North Ucellan population of Torama, it became apparent that there continued to be a language barrier. The Ucellan language was difficult to learn. Alya and Palas, the attractive blondes that were fascinated with David Hartford and Time Spivey, attempted to teach them Ucellan. The two sailors were having a hard time with this tongue from another world. In fact, the two Ucellan girls were doing a better job learning English.

On the other side of the world, the Russians fared a little better. They had Kikimora and Baba Yaga, who quickly learned Russian. And the two Troznyan girls knew several other languages and dialects. To the Russians it was a great asset to have the young women as interpreters. But the Russians were still limited when it came to the masses in Tannsisi and the rest of Zotova. The Americans were still stumbling around in the dark because of this language barrier. However, the former Earth people came to the conclusion that the Vanagians were also pretty much human. Thus, they could learn a new language. That is, English or Russian.

The Vanagians in North Ucella, and the Zotovans in Tannsisi, knew that the Americans and Russians were much more powerful than them, especially in view of their weapons and submarines. They reasoned that it was best to cooperate and get on the good side of these "strangers from beyond." And the Zotovans had witnessed firsthand the power of the Russians in Tannsisi. Word had also spread throughout Zotova of the "fireball" weapon that destroyed Zelessio. To the Earth people it would make more sense for the Vanagians in their midst, and later to influence them to learn their language, than for the Americans and Russians to learn a Vanagian tongue.

It was actually the young people from both crews of the USS Tampa and Vodyanoy that devised a plan to teach the North

Ucellans and Zotovans their Earth language. How was this to be accomplished? Several factors were involved.

As in any culture, young people and children are usually quicker to learn a new language. This would also prove to be true regarding Vanag. The children of Torama and Tannsisi usually flocked around the Americans and Russians whenever they came to town. The young Vanagains were already learning the Earth peoples language.

David Hartford, Sci-Fi Guy-Tim Spivey, had an idea. Why not teach English through the use of comicbooks. Sci-Fi Guy and another crewman, Robert Newell had a large collection. They donated quite a few for the library on the Tampa. You were never too old for comicbooks. On the submarine were several copy machines. With the proper care and being inventive regarding parts, the copiers should last for years. There was a newspaper company in Torama. The American seamen were able to obtain paper, cut it down to the copiers size, and with Vanagian ink keep the copiers going.

Robert Newell, was from Kansas City, Missouri. He was quite the comicbook artist. Seamen Newell could draw anything. He could then take them to the newspaper printing plant and distribute hundreds of copies. For now though, the comicbooks were in black and white. But it would serve the purpose that the young seamen had in mind. To teach the young North Ucellans English.

Every young boy at one time wanted to become a superhero, or create their own. This is what Hartford, Spivey and Newell did. This was all new for the young people of Torama. But most importantly these children and young people were learning English, and fast. The three seamen broke the young people down into groups of about thirty. They were able to obtain several large blackboards from schools in the city.

Each group found a place to meet and got busy drawing characters and learning English. The Toraman children would then return home or to school only to draw and speak English. In time, several of the young, female sailors on the USS Tampa also joined the seamen in this new teaching adventure. This included Cecila Rice, Christine Salter and Rosa Garcia. Rosa always wanted to be a schoolteacher. For now she was one.

The three American sailors created their own comicbook hereos. For instance, one was called *Metaman.* Meta, is a small town in Robert Newell's native Missouri. His grandparents had a farm there. Newell had good memories of the place. Another was *Akronman.* Tim Spivey's hometown in Ohio. The North Ucellan kids loved them, and continued to improve in their English.

David Hartford and Tim Spivey also came up with other concepts, especially for the Ucellan girls. This was inspired from the two Toraman girls, Alya and Palas. These characters were know as *The Rhea Girls.* Rhea was a Titan goddess from Greek mythology. And one of the moons of the planet Saturn was named Rhea. Rhea sounded like a great outer space name for these comicbook characters. It didn't matter that nobody on Vanag knew about Greek mythology or this moon. These two, cute Vanagian girls in their animated form would save the day from evil. They were mostly dressed in red and silver, and could of course fly. *The Rhea Girls* even ventured to the two Vanagian moons and outer space. The Americans were the first to walk on Earth's moon, so why not interest the Ucellan-Vanagian youth in their moons and space.

"Oh, my," Michaela remarked as all of the Time Maidens viewed this segement of the Americans on Vanag. "the Americans brought a whole new culture to the youth of this alien world. But very clever."

"Yes," Rowena added, "we have the ability to speak and comprehend every langauge ever spoken on Earth, and now on Vanag. The Americans reasoned that it would be easier for the

Vanagians in this land to learn English. And they discovered an interesting way to accomplish this starting with the young."

This little endeavor to teach English to young Ucellans would eventually evolve into a great business venture. David Hartford, Tim Spivey and Robert Newell would in time become wealthy. Even kids from another planet, over one hundred years behind Earth, took a liking to comicbook hereos, and the merchandise that went along with it. In what way?

At first crude action figures and dolls were made. But as Ucellan manufacturing improved with help from the Americans, the toys improved. Costumes of the new superheroes came next. *Metaman*, *Akronman* and *The Rhea Girls* continued to gain popularity on all three of the Ucellan islands, and even to faraway Trozny as trade and shipping increased.

As the Time Maidens viewed other influences from both the Americans and Russians, they saw how in a few short years that television and movie theaters would also be found on Vanag. Any technology that existed on Earth up to the year 1986, the Earth people intended to duplicate on Vanag. Some of the first television shows produced with help from the Americans were animated features. Yes, these comicbook characters would be featured on the big screen and piped into most homes via small television sets.

In 1970 back on Earth, the first international Comic-Con was held in San Diego, California. An organization similar to this would find its way on Vanag as well. The Russians would even participate. But more about that later. For right now, during this viewing by the Time Maidens, the Americans and Russians had no idea that the other was on this alien planet. Many years later both Alya and Palas would attend these Vanagian comicbook conventions. After all, they were the original *Rhea Girls.*

Captain Albritton was pleased with the work of these young sailors and their ambition. Their plan worked. Toraman children were learning English at a rapid pace. They, in turn, taught their parents this new "alien language." To the Ucellans, the Americans were aliens. And vice versa for the Americans. The crew from the USS Tampa often brought young people from the city for a tour on the submarine. The young Ucellans were in awe. The senior staff on the submarine were also amazed at the young people speaking almost perfect English.

However, can two people or groups come up with a great idea at the same time? What were the Russians up to in Tannsisi, Zotova? Great minds do think alike. Comicbooks were also popular in the Soviet Union. Except they focused mostly on real historical people or featured the country's scientific achievements. Such as Sputnik, Laika, the first dog in space, then the first man and woman in space.

Valeria Rostova has assigned Tatiana Semenova, Svetlana Lebedeva and Anastasia Macagonova to teach Russian to the new Zotovan officials along with their families in Tannsisi. Tatiana was taking the lead. The three young Russian women were making progress, yet more Zotovanas needed to learn the language spoken by the new rulers of Zotova. This is where the comicbooks would also come in handy in this part of the world. Tatiana, along with several Russian submariners would spearhead this project. Some of these sailors were also great artists.

Some of the characters in the Soviet-Zotovan comicbooks were men and women heroes from the Soviet Union during World War II, or the Great Patriotic War as the Russians called the conflict. There were copies of these comics on the Vodyanoy's library.

One group of real-life characters were called *The Snipers*. Again, both men and women. When the Nazis invaded the Soviet Union in 1941, many Russian partisans stayed behind the conquered territory and continued on with guerrilla warfare. Some of these snipers, were young people that grew up on farms and were good with a rifle. Countless German soldiers were picked off by these snipers. In many of these comicbooks, the life stories and bravery of these snipers during the war were featured.

One female sniper was Lyudmila Mikhailovna Pavilichenko. She was credited with three hundred and nine confirmed kills. But these new Russian creators and artists for the comicbooks they were now drawing and writing on Vanag, embellished a bit with these characters. Lyudmilla would live on to be a sniper during the U.S.-Vietnam War. Now our heroine back on Earth, is picking off American soldiers in the jungle. Of course this never happened.

Nevertheless, Zotovan children and young people would see and learn about brave Russian soldiers fighting off their enemies with much more modern rifles than the muskets used on Vanag. These Russian rifles would evolve to become the *AK-47* assult rifle. Many people in Tannsisi had seen or heard about these powerful rifles. Yet, the Russians now in control of this Zotovan city, could not let on that they were almost out of ammo for these weapons. They needed to figure out a way to manufacture these ammo magazines. And they would.

More comicbook heroines were what was known as *The Night Witches* These were Russian female pilots that flew bombing missions, mostly at night, once again against the invading Nazis during World War II. Most of these young women were in their late teens and early twenties. The Nazis gave them the name Night Witches, as the women pilots kept them awake at night and wrecked havoc on the Germans from up above. Tatiana Semenova and her artists friends thought that this would also be a great concept for the youth of Zotova. Especially the young Zotovan girls. They would be learning Russian and exposing the youth of this land to Soviet airplanes.

Like The Snipers, the creators of the comicbook projected *The Night Witches* beyond World War II. As the female pilots were so young, many went on to fly and fight in the *MIG-15* during the Korean War, and *MIG-23* in the Vietnam War. *The Night Witches* outflew and shot down many American pilots. This, of course, was not true, either. Just a fabricated storyline to keep the concept going. But many young Zotovan girls saw themselves as the Night Witches and flying jets. In the not too distant future, *MIG's* would be flying over the skies of Vanag.

The young Russian sailor-artists also created a mythical-political heroine based on a real Russian girl. This was none other than Tatiana Semenova herself, the main comicbook editor. The artist creators called this character *Red Queen.* Tatiana's name means *Queen of Fairies,* and her nickname was *Fairy Queen.* And, as already noted, Tatiana with her long, blonde hair and pale skin, looked like a mythical girl from Russian folklore. Thus, *Red Queen* would be a great fantasy character for Tatiana Semenova.

Red Queen as a character heroine was a type of communist superhero. The charcater advocated and proclaimed Soviet communism on both Earth, and now Vanag. But in a cute and interesting way. *Red Queen* could fly. She was dressed in either a yellow jumpsuit with red boots, or a yellow skirt and tights, also with red boots. In either outfit *Red Queen* had a red cape and a large red star on her chest. She would fly across the worlds of Earth and Vanag putting down greed, corruption or anything else that stood in the way of socialism. At Red Queen's disposal were myriads of powerful, flying robots that came from an unknown realm.

This concept was also targeted for the many Zotovan girls that had long been surpressed by the previous rulers of Zotova before their new liberators, the Russians, arrived. They, too, could learn to become good communists.

When Titiana saw some of the artwork depicting her as *Red Queen,* she remarked, "I don't know comrades," as she scratched her head and studied the pictures more, "The Soviet Union and socialism doesn't usually promote a monarchy. And yet you have me as a queen."

"Ah," one of the young artist replied, "but a Red Queen. Red as in our main communist color. The queen is just a mythical, story-telling role. Red Queen is a champion of socialism, and she upholds its principles along with standing up for the proletariat. Especially here on this new planet for us."

"Well, all right," Tatiana added, "We will have to see about this Red Queen." Once the concept took off, it went well. *Red Queen* became very popular. All of the young Zotovan girls wanted to be just like her, while the boys wanted to find a girl just like this character. That is a girl that looked like Tatiana Semenova.

Tatiana, did set up and become the editor of *New Pravda*, the official communist newspaper in now Soviet-Zotova. But as her character of *Red Queen* became more popular, the girl from Arkangelsk (Archangel) found herself in great demand. Tatiana became a national symbol and a very busy person. She, too, would have to go on tours promoting this otherworldy character. Eventually, there would be merchandise of *Red Queen*. Dolls, action figures of the robots, and like *The Rhea Girls* back in North Ucella, costumes for young girls, and also animated cartoons of this new Soviet-Zotovan heroine. Movies and television would also become a way of life in Zotova.

Yet, the Russian creators of these comicbooks felt that another role model was needed for young Zotovan boys. They would of course feature Yuri Gagarin and Alexei Leonov, along with other famous cosmonauts. Still, they wanted a type of fantasy Sci-Fi character. Thus, *Takoda: The Time Traveler,* came into existence.

Takoda, came from neither Russia's past or future. He was simply a time traveler that traveled in time on both Earth and Vanag. When the Americans and Russians eventually learned the history of Vanag, they would base their storylines on various time periods of this new planet they were now on. Once again, with

Takoda, the goal was to teach the Russian language and glorify Soviet, now Zotovan, communism.

"Good Goliath," Michaela stated at the end of this viewing, "these Earth people, that is the Americans and Russians, cunningly developed a way to teach their languages in the regions of Vanag where they now dwell."

"True," Lin added. "And as for the Russians, they also have a time traveler. But they have no idea that, we, that is the Time Maidens, are monitoring every move they make as they slowly gain control of their region on this other planet."

"Ha!" Rowena said with a laugh. "I see that they published a comicbook about Laika. Dogs may as well be a mythical creature on Vanag as they don't exist there." Rowena then gently patted Laika on her head. The little dog followed Rowena all over the kingdom. "Let them make their cigarettes in the future on this world in honor of my Laika, and even a large memorial statue of her like the one in Moscow, or stuffed toys. Meanwhile, Laika is still alive and well here with me." (Rowena had rescued Laika from certain death on Sputnik 2 when first becoming a Time Maiden.)

"Something else regarding these Earth people," Michaela also said, "They kind of remind me of the early people of Earth mentioned in the holy writings of the Book of Genesis when they were building the Tower of Babel. 'Yahweh came down to see the town that the sons of men had built. So they were a single people with a single language!' said Yahweh. 'This is but a start of their undertakings! There will be nothing too hard for them to do.' "I wonder what else these Earth people on Vanag will come up with?"

As the Time Maidens continued to view the history of the Americans and Russians on this other planet, much more was in store for this world that was over one hundred years behind Earth. And the holy writings, of the Bible that Michaela quoted would also play a part in teaching English to the Ucellans. How?

"In the beginning God created the heavens and the Earth." Could the planet Vanag also be a part of this creation? Some of the Americans on the USS Tampa believed so. And especially one seaman. At least for awhile. As noted earlier by the Time Maidens research, the two main religions for at least Trozny, Zotova and the Ucellan islands, are the Aelianans and the Mozdoks. Enaim, in the southern hemisphere, was made up of many fragmented, less significant beliefs. Was there room for the Judeo-Christianity faiths on Vanag?

Troy Cunningham is a twenty-one-year-old from Mineral Springs, Arkansas. This was a small town with around twelve hundred people. Troy was the son of a minister in the local United Methodist Church. While growing up, Troy was being groomed by his father to also become a preacher and one day become the pastor of the church. Troy did teach Sunday School and seemed to have a way with the children and young people in the church. He had a great knowledge of the Holy Bible, and knew everything about the people, places and events in the scriptures.

While Troy had a great connection with the young, he would rub many people older than him the wrong way. Including his father. Why? Troy was a haughty young man. He thought that he was better than everyone else because of his Bible knowledge. His father would tell him that his condescending attitude had no place in God's house.

Right after graduating from high school, and on the eve of going off to Bible college, Troy and his father had a big argument over his lack of humility. The result: Troy left and joined the U.S. Navy. He proved to be a smart boy and qualified to be a part of a crew on a nuclear submarine. This was how Troy was accepted to be a part of the crew on the recently new, and latest Los Angeles class submarine, the USS Tampa. And now, here the boy from Arkansas was on another planet. What next?

The Time Maidens followed this latest character from Earth, now on Vanag, and how he would have an impact on this alien planet. The five former Earth girls themselves were amazed, perplexed, and yet shocked at how Troy Cunnimgham would eventually have an impact on Vanag.

How, though, would this preacher's son along with the Holy Bible come into the picture? Just as the three young seamen taking the lead on the comicbook program, Troy Cunningham reasoned that he could do the same using the Bible. "*Let There Be Light*," was another early Bible scripture found in the Book of Genesis. Troy planned on bringing "light," as it were, to the Toramans and other Ucellans. Troy, too, could have Bible comics drawn and then copied or printed to teach English to the young. Many back in his church stated that Troy was a lively, animated Sunday School teacher, and he could do the same thing with his form of comicbook.

Nevertheless, even though Troy had the ideas, he would need help. There were other seamen on the Tampa that could draw fairly well. But the main person that stepped up to assist him was Leah Jordon. She was the young African-American from Mobile, Alabama. Leah was part of the experiment of the six young women that the navy wanted to evaluate with a mostly male crew on a submarine.

Leah sang in the choir at one of the Baptist churches she attended in her hometown. But the young eighteen-year-old also had a good knowledge of the Holy Bible. She agreed that Troy Cunningham's idea of a series of Bible comicbooks was a good idea. When Seaman Cunningham presented this idea to Captain Albritton, the *XO* replied, "Why not. The more the merrier." That is, ways to teach English to the Toraman-Ucellans.

Troy, Leah and their artists collaborators got busy. They started out with God creating the heavens and the Earth. Also including Vanag. Next came Adam and Eve, Noah and his ark, and the Tower of Babel. Then Abraham and his family. Of course Moses and the Red Sea, along with Joshua would follow. The Bible comics also proved to be a success with the young Ucellans.

As a result of this modest, but steady popularity, other comics were forthcoming. Samson, along with Kings David and Solomon, would follow. And many famous women in the Bible. It was claimed by both comicbook groups that the Americans had set up that there was no competition between the two. But in actuality there was. Both tried to outdo the other in graphics, later in color, and in teaching English.

Two young Toraman girls, both fifteen years old, also joined the team of Bible comicbook creators, as they could both draw. One of these North Ucellan girls was named Donya, a cute young blonde. The other was Lipari, a dark-haired girl, also attractive. The girls were both fast learners and quickly picked up on the English language by being around the Americans while working on the comics. In turn, Donya and Lipari taught English to their families and classmates. There were schools in the major Ucellan cities. Donya and Lipari appeared to be close-knit with Troy Cunningham. At first, they viewed him as an older brother. But this relationship would eventually change.

Another idea that Troy and Leah Jordon came up with was watching Bible-themed movies. The Tampa had over a dozen *VHS* players onboard and a videotape library of nearly one thousand movies. On the Tampa was one Steve Litten. This twenty-two year old seaman was an electronics expert. Using extension cords from the submarine, he was able to set up a movie theater on the dock. The Americans had the Toramans construct a large flat board. It was then painted white. This was the movie screen.

A canopy was next constructed for this outdoor movie theater. Seaman Litten then borrowed several speakers that he obtained from other sailors. There were quite a few stereo systems on the Tampa, as the crew could use headphones to listen to their music in the sleeping quarters. This outdoor theater on the dock could seat two hundred people. The Toramans would sit on blankets to watch movies. A modern marvel for them. This was like being at a Drive-In movie theater back on Earth. Minus the cars, of course.

The first movies featured by the Bible comicbook group were *The Bible, The Ten Commandments* and *Ben Hur.* All Bible-based movies. But not to out done, the other comicbook team also wanted to show movies. Many more videotapes on the submarine's library included *Disney, Superman* and other action movies. From noon to late at night the movies from Earth were featured. The Toraman-Ucellans loved them and continued to learn English.

Captain Albritton asked Seaman Cunningham to report back to him on the progress of his comicbook and movie program. In the captain's cabin, the young, handsome, curly-haired blonde saluted and then proceeded to explain the work and progress of his team. He spoke highly of Leah Jordon. But then the seaman asked the captain a question: "Captain, are you familiar with some of the Apostle Paul's missionary journeys found in the Acts Of The Apostles in the New Testament?"

"Perhaps a little, Seaman." The captain was a Roman Catholic and recalled a few things from catechism while attending parochial school.

"May I share something with you, Captain?" Seaman Cunningham asked. When the captain nodded yes, Troy moved closer to his captain. He then opened up a King James version of the Bible. The passage that he showed and then read to the captain was from *Acts 14: 8-13.* It read as follows. '*And there sat a certain man at Lystra impotent in his feet, being a cripple from his mother's womb. The same heard Paul speak who steadfastly beholding him, and perceiving that he had faith to be healed. Said with a loud voice, Stand upright on thy feet. And he leaped and walked. And when the people saw what Paul had done, they lifted up their voices, saying in the speech of Lycaonia, The gods come down to us in the likeness of men. And they called Barnabas, Jupiter: and Paul, Mercurius (Mercury), because he was the chief speaker. Then the priest of Jupiter which was before their city, brought oxen and garlands unto the gates, and would have done sacrifice with the people.'*

"Interesting, Seaman,' the captain replied. "But what are you getting at?"

"Don't you see, Captain," Troy answered. "Like the apostles that appeared to be gods to these ancient Greeks, we, too, with these people on this planet, appear superior." Then raising his arms heavenward, proclaimed, *"WE CAN BE LIKE GODS ON THIS WORLD."*

The captain wasn't sure what to think or say at the moment. He then replied, "That will be all for now, Seaman Cunningham." The seaman saluted and then departed.

Captain Albritton then began to think more about what Troy Cunningham had just siad. He tried to get to know a little something about each member of his crew. The captain knew that Troy was the son of a preacher, thus his knowledge of the Holy Bible. But this side of Troy that he had just witnessed, the captain didn't see coming. He actually found it to be disturbing. The last thing that the Americans from Earth needed to do was to elevate themselves as gods on this less-advanced alien planet. This was just the beginning of the dark side of Troy Cunningham.

"GREAT SAMHAIN," Rowena exclaimed. "This young man is disturbing."

"Yes," Michaela added, "and dangerous. 'We can be like Gods.' The Devil said the same thing in the first book of The Holy Scriptures." (The Jews referred to the Old Testament of the Holy Bible as The Holy Scriptures. Michaela was from ancient Israel.)

"Well, one thing is certain," Lin now said, "Troy Cunningham's father knew that he was haughty and lacked humility."

"True," Amaresh stated, "and we're seeing this dark side of him coming out on this other world. But perhaps, the black American girl, Leah, can balance him out."

"I don't know, Amaresh," Cuca concluded, "this young man looks like the type that could elevate himself over others." Cuca didn't know at this time just how right she was. Troy Cunningham would indeed prove to be dark and dangerous.

As time travelers, the Time Maidens had become quite the historians regarding their own world. They had to be when plotting time-jumps. But now, they were starting over with a brand-new world. An alien planet loctaed in another galaxy. And to top it off, this other world now had outside influences from Earth: Two nuclear submarines from the United States and Soviet Union, the two Cold War rivals of the 20th century accidently got sucked through a vortex and ended up on this planet called Vanag.

Earth and Vanag were similar in some ways, yet different in others. Both were inhabited by humanoids, but Vanag was over one hundred years behind Earth in social development. For the Time Maidens, as they studied Vanag via the planet-time scanner that the Aeduianns had also sent to this world, it was like starting over. They could now comprehend all of the languages spoken on Vanag, yet there were many new cultures to learn about. However, they could at least predict what these new and former Earth people may do. Namely, the Americans and Russians. They wasted no time in trying to transform the Vanagian people in their respective spheres of influence.

The Time Maidens, with help from their assistants, Justinian, Rebecca and Shako, searched through the time scanner to see what the Americans and Russians were up to now, and in the future. Vanag's future. At least the more prominent ones. They had already been following the life of the Troznyan girl, Kikimora, and her early connection with the Russians, now in control of Tannsisi, Zotova. But Justinian and Rebecca also began to focus on a young American woman that was part of the experimental crew on the USS Tampa. Why her? The two Time Maidens assistants in turn shared this information with Rowena.

Linda Flannery, would not only play an important role in the political development of first North Ucella, but also the other two large Ucellan Islands as well. Even though the young, white woman was only twenty years old when coming to Vanag, she would grow up fast and have a great responsibility.

This girl of Irish-American descent was from Bangor, Maine. She would prove to be quite an asset for the Americans and Ucellans. Linda, was a cute brunette with a gymnastic figure. She worked out before joining the navy, and continued to do so in the gym room on the Tampa. Linda was 5'6" and somewhat leggy. She had shoulder-length hair and wore bangs. There was a reason for this 1960's hair style.

As a little girl, Linda always wanted to become an *FBI* or some other type of government agent. Even a *CIA* operative. The Bangor girl was smart, but, as her parents were just factory workers for a paper company, she couldn't afford to attend college. Linda ended up as a cashier at a local supermarket after graduating high school. But after two years she grew restless and joined the navy.

However, Linda never gave up her interest in the *FBI* or *CIA*. She was obsessed with spy novels and television shows. Linda read all of the Ian Fleming, James Bond novels and saw every movie multiple times. During the long, cold Maine winters, she would stay in her room reading spy novels and books about real life spies checked out from the main library. Linda began to think like a spy.

The many spy television shows of the 1960's was something else Linda enjoyed watching and became an expert on. Even though most of these shows were originally aired around the time Linda was born, she was still a big fan of them. These included *The Man from U.N.C.L.E., I Spy and Mission Impossible* to name a few.

One spin-off from these 1960's spy shows was *The Girl from U.N.C.L.E.* The main charcter, April Dancer, was played by the actress Stefanie Powers. Even as a young girl, Linda copied this image. She saw these TV shows as reruns in the late 70's and early 80's. This was where the mid-1960's hair style came in. Now Linda was not April Dancer, but did resemble her.

During her last years of high school, Linda dressed in mini-dresses with matching Go-Go boots. Again, a throwback from the 60's. Linda had many dates, but any boy that asked her out had better be prepared to talk about the world of spies. She was given the nickname *Miss 007* and *Spy Girl.* However, Linda was serious about all of this and had a photographic memory.

Six months after coming through the vortex to this other planet, Linda, like all of the Americans on the Tampa, wasn't sure what the future would hold. She continued to perform her duties on the submarine, but wasn't sure how to interact with the North Ucellans. Linda wandered around the main areas of Torama, and was amazed at how many of the Toramans were learning English. But it was while she was browsing in an area by the main dock that something caught the Bangor girl's attention. A red flag, as it were, went up. On this day of the sixth month of *1 A.C.*, Linda's life would be transformed forever.

What did Linda observe at this vendor's stall? Two paintings. But not just any paintings. One was of a fairly attractive woman dressed in a blue jumpsuit. No women on Vanag wore a jumpsuit. At least not yet. But it was what was above the pockets on the jumpsuit that caught Linda's eye. A red star on one, and the cyrillic letters on the other: *CCCP,* meaning *USSR,* as in the Soviet Union. Was this a mistake, or a coincidence? Spy *Girl-AKA* Linda Flannery, didn't believe so.

"Oh, my," Michaela stated as she and the other Time Maidens viewed the time scanner back in their domain. "This is the painting of Valeria Rostova. The Russian political officer from the Vodyanoy."

"That's right," Rowena now said. "This is the painting by the young Troznyan boy when the Russians first came to port in that land."

"Yes," Cuca interjected. "This artwork has found its way from a port in Tellovaci, Trozny across the Kovda ocean, to a port in Torama, North Ucella."

"This shouldn't surprise us," Amaresh added. "That young Troznyan boy that painted this woman, sold his work to buyers that then sold it across the ocean. After all, to the Vanagians, this is an unusual painting. Hardly a comicbook character from the Americans or Russians."

"This planet, Vanag," Lin said, "may be over one hundred years behind Earth, but they have large ships, both sails and steam that can travel across oceans. There appears to be a lot of trading between Trozny, Zotova and the Ucellan Islands in the northern hemisphere. If I recall, this Troznyan boy also painted a portrait of the Vodyanoy. I wonder if it's here with this painting of the Russian political officer?"

"I think that we are about to find out," Rowena concluded.

With her mouth wide open, Linda Flannery continued to study the painting. The Spy Girl just had to have this portrait of a woman, obviously from the Soviet Union. *Are the Russians here?* Linda thought. *Were they here on this planet in the distant past? Time is all screwed up since we came through the vortex after the passing of Halley'a Comet back on Earth.* Linda concluded that she must have this portrait. If anything, to show it to the captain.

Captain Albritton never allowed any of the women to venture off the Tampa without a male escort. On this day, Ron Williams, an African-American from Jacksonville, Florida, was with Linda. When Linda saw this painting of a Russian woman, she exclaimed, *"I MUST HAVE THIS PICTURE.* Ron, find me an Ucellan that can speak English, so I can find out how to buy this painting." At present, all trade between the Americans and Toramans was on a barter basis. Trading items in exchange for something. Many of the Americans on the Tampa were handy at fixing things, and had the battery-powered tools to do the work.

Doctor Caldwell and Sylvia Rizzo were also providing medical care for quite a few in the city. So, the Toramans owed the Americans a lot. *"COME ON, RON,"* Linda now loudly said. "Find someone in this marketplace that can help us."

"All right, all right," Seaman Williams replied. "But you stay here. I'm not supposed to let you out of my sight."

"Don't worry," Linda said. "I'm not letting this painting out of my sight."

Crazy, excitable white chick, Ron said to himself. "Now where can I find someone that speaks English?" Ron now said outloud as he walked away from the vendor's stall.

Seaman Williams looked around as he walked through the crowd in this marketplace. All that he heard being spoken was Ucellan. But then, someone caught his attention somewhere nearby. He heard a faint, tiny voice yell out, *"I'M NOT PLAYING WITH BOYS ANYMORE. YOU'RE NOT COOL."* Ron stopped dead in his tracks and stood on his toes and looked around to see where this voice came from.

Someone is speaking English, he thought. The seaman continued to look around. *But where? I have to find this person.*

"JUST YOU WAIT," the little voice shouted again. *"I'M GOING TO TELL THE RHEA GIRLS ON YOU."* In a clearing of the crowd stood a little blonde girl about what would be considered five or six years old back on Earth. This little girl was obviously a comicbook fan, as she mentioned *The Rhea Girls,* and no doubt that was where she was learning English. And pretty good at that.

I must speak with this little Scandie girl, Ron Williams thought. "Scandie" was a nickname that the young American sailors had given to the blonde, North Ucellans, as they reminded them of the blonde people in Scandinavia, again back on Earth. It wasn't meant to be said in a derogatory way. "Hi," Ron said as approached the young girl, "I can see and hear that you speak some English."

"Yes," the girl replied. "I'm learning your language from the comicbooks and movies. I've read all of the comicbooks, and with my family, we have seen five movies. I like Pollyanna the best. (The Disney movie starring Hayley Mills.) The Toraman girl said "your language" as she knew the sailor before her was a stranger from the vessel. That is an American. Even though there was not a black, African race on Vanag, the Toraman people didn't appear to be alarmed by the presence of any African-Americans from the Tampa. If anything, they were fascinated by them.

Amazing, Ron pondered. *This little girl speaks almost perfect English, but with a North Ucellan accent.* (The Americans knew by now that there were two other large islands known as East Ucella and West Ucella. They had learned this from maps and what other Toramans had told them.) The seaman then stooped down and asked, "Sweetie, I need your help for a few minutes. My friend wants to buy something from a person in the marketplace. But we don't speak Ucellan. Can you help us? Please."

"I suppose so," the young girl replied. Ron then gently took the girl by the hand and made his way back to Linda at the vendor's booth.

"Linda," Seaman Williams said, "this is my new little friend. This scandie speaks remarkable English. But I didn't get her name."

"What is your name, sweetheart?" Linda Flannery asked.

"*PALAS,*" the little girl shouted and then jumped into the air as if she were about to fly. "I'm one of The Rhea Girls." Of course this wasn't her name. Obviously, this new American comicbook for the Ucellan children had made an impact on her.

"Yes, well," Linda remarked as she smirked at Ron Williams and then rolled her eyes back. *What have we done to these children?* Linda thought. "Can you help me make a purchase, Palas?"

"Sure," the girl answered. "But wait. What is a scandie?" This Toraman girl didn't miss anything.

"It's a name we 'visitors' from beyond have given many of the people in this land," Ron replied. "Especially to cute, little blondes like you."

"Ha! Ha!," the young girl said as she laughed. "In that case, you can call me Scandie."

Linda Flannery now shook her head and rolled her eyes back again at Ron Williams. But then proceeded to explain to the girl what she wanted to buy from the vendor, and how to go about getting it. The girl then switched to speaking in Ucellan as she pointed to the painting of this unsual-looking woman. At least unuual to her.

The woman vendor that appeared to be in her fifties explained to the young girl that she needed three large coins, as in Ucellan currency. There was no such thing as paper money on Vanag. Only silver-looking coins.

The largest one being the highest in value. Perhaps like dollars. Linda Flannery looked sad as she didn't have any Ucellan money. The older woman detected this, so made an offer to the young girl. That is, "Scandie." Did the Americans have something to exchange, or use for collateral until her potential customer obtained some currency? Scandie then told Linda and Ron what the vendor said.

The two Americans looked at each other with a perplexed look. "Wait," Seaman Williams then said, "You can use my wristwatch as collateral until you get some money. I'm sure you can find someone from the crew to loan you some." The watch appeared to be an expensive one.

"Are you sure, Ron?" Linda asked. "How do we know that this woman may not disappear with your watch?"

"I don't think that she will," Seaman Williams replied. "These Toramans don't want to get on the wrong side with us, as they know we are a powerful force. Let's do it. I know you want this painting."

Scandie then proceeded with the negotiating. She seemed to be quite good at it for her age. No doubt, the girl grew up in this marketplace. Seaman Williams took off his watch and handed it to the woman. The vendor then gave the painting to Linda. She began to study it throughly. This wasn't just a coincidence or a shot in the dark painting, as it were. Too much detail. The woman in the painting, (Valeria Rostova) was not a fantasy or comicbook character. She did indeed represent someone from the Soviet Union.

Linda reasoned that perhaps one of her fellow American sailors had painted this person. But she didn't think so. Linda inquired through Scandie where the vendor got this painting. The woman claimed a Troznyan merchant ship brought goods from the Port of Tellovaci. Tellovaci was the port city in Trozny located on the Acco Channel. Zotova was on the other side of the channel separating the two huge continents. As far as the Americans in Torama were concerned this was on the other side of the world. And it was.

Just as the two Americans were about to depart, the vendor said something to the young girl. "Wait." Scandie called out. The woman then presented another painting. Both Linda Flannery and Ron Williams eyes enlarged three times their normal size. They couldn't believe what they were seeing. This other painting was of a modern Soviet submarine. Linda and Ron weren't sure what class of submarine this was. The details in the painting were amazing. Whoever the artist was, had either seen a good picture, or a real submarine to have painted this. Once again, there were more questions than answers. At least for now.

Linda had to have this painting as well. She had Scandie barter for her again with the vendor. Still not having any North Ucellan currency, Linda would once more have to come up with something for collateral. It would be a bracelet she was wearing that belonged to her grandmother. Linda and Ron were sure that they could borrow some currency to get the watch and bracelet back.

As they headed back to the Tampa, Linda remarked several times, "Wait until Captain Albritton sees this."

"At this point in time," Ron said, "so much has happened, that nothing should surprise the captain." It had now been six months since the Americans had come through the vortex in the arctic.

"Oh, I think this will,' Linda concluded.

As the young Toraman girl, now called Scandie, had been a great help back at the marketplace, Seaman Williams told her to bring her entire family to the Tampa in three days, and he would give them a tour of the submarine. The senior staff was allowing this for a measure of goodwill with the North Ucellans. Many Toramans were waiting their turn to do this. This otherworldly vessel was something futuristic for them. And it actually was.

Once back on the submarine, Linda Flannery asked to see the captain. She had something very important to show him. Captain Albritton agreed to meet the young woman crew member in the excerise room. It was against regulations to be alone with a member of the opposite sex in his quarters.

When Seawoman Flannery showed the captain these two paintings, he at first thought that they were drawings for another comicbook. Perhaps a history related one. But then the young, female sailor explained to the captain where these paintings originally came from. *Is this a coincidence?* The captain also thought. But the Soviet woman, her uniform and this submarine were painted in authentic-looking detail.

Captain Albritton knew exactly what class of submarine this was. "Why, this is a Soviet Delta III Class submarine," the captain stated outloud as he held up the painting in its nice, well-built wooden frame. "We need to find out more information regarding this painting of the submarine, Seawoman Flannery. And the mysterious Soviet woman."

The captain further thought about the nuclear explosion that the Tampa detected from the other side of the world. Was there actually a Russian submarine on this alien planet? If so, how? And did the Russians use a nuclear weapon on this world? Good questions, but now for some answers.

Officially, Lt. Commander Vincent Cardova was the intelligence officer on the Tampa. The officers all had access to classified information. Yet, all of the crew could find out about some security matters via books on the submarine or diskette-floppy disks that could be used on the *IBM* computer. Captain Albritton knew a thing or two about Seawoman Linda Flannery. Namely her love of espionage.

As a result of this new development, the captain appointed Linda Flannery to be in charge of this investigation. The girl from Maine was elated. Now, she truly was a Spy Girl. And Linda would leave no stone unturned to find out the real source of these paintings.

The captain had access to some Ucellan funds to pay for items needed. There was actually a Toraman bank that extended credit to the captain. They could always settle up later with services performed by the crew. As the submariners came from a variety of backgrounds, they had many talents and could adapt to the present state of development on this planet and improvise. Captain Albritton made sure that Seawoman Flannery had pocket money, as it were, for this now-new spy agency. He believed in this young lady.

"I see that this young American woman is serious about her new role," Michaela commented.

"Yes," Lin added. "She is either dedicated to this new role, or patriotic to her country."

"Perhaps both," Cuca now said.

"Then again, she may be obsessed," Rowena stated. "This Linda Flannery seems to now have a cause on this world."

"I agree, Rowena,' Amaresh also had to add. "At first this young woman appeared to be lost after coming through the vortex, wondering if she would ever get back home. But now, she seems to be in a frenzy regarding this role as a spy. Let's find out more." The Time Maidens continued to follow Linda Flannery.

Spy Girl, that is, Linda, hit the payment, as it were, to find out more about the paintings now in American hands. All of the crew members on the Tampa, had civilian clothes that they could wear while on shore leave. As Linda was now in a different role than just a seawoman on the submarine, she was allowed to dress differently. At least while going ashore in Torama.

Seaman Williams was still assigned to accompany Linda whenever she left the submarine. They would also employ the services of Scandie for a while during the day after the young Ucellan girl got out of school. The Americans needed her to translate for them. Toraman children only attended school half a day. Most of them did some type of work to help support their families. Life was still hard at this time on Vanag.

Linda knew that as these paintings came from a land called Trozny, she needed to talk with sailors or merchant marines. Near the docks where the Tampa was located, were quite a few taverns that were frequented by sailors. One afternoon, the two Americans went inside one of these taverns. They even took Scandie with them. The reason for this was that they wanted to inquire if anyone had recently come back from the Port of Tellovaci, or would be going there in the near future.

With the two Americans, Scandie went from table to table, asking if any unusual-looking vessel was seen in the Troznyan port separating Trozny and Zotova. One old sailor said yes. "What did you see?" Scandie was told to ask.

"Why, a metal monster from the sea," the old sailor replied. He then proceeded to describe a big gray boat with a star on the middle of it, meaning on the outside of the conning tower. Linda and Ron both looked at each other in amazement.

This can't be another coincidence, Linda thought, then asked, "Scandie, can this man draw what he saw? Ask him." Scandie did as asked.

Someone in the tavern brought paper and what could have been similar to a pencil. The two Americans leaned over the man at the table and carefully watched as he started to draw something. The drawing was oblong and almost in the shape of a fish. But it wasn't a bad drawing, either. The old sailor even drew a star on the tower.

"*THAT'S IT!*" Linda exclaimed. "This man is drawing a Soviet submarine. Probably the same one in the painting."

"Now wait a minute, Linda," Seaman Williams said, "Don't go jumping to conclusions."

"Jumping to conclusions?" Linda replied. "That man drew a submarine. And as we know, no nation on this planet has a submarine." Spy Girl then asked Scandie to ask the old sailor what color the star was. The young girl asked, and the man replied, 'Red.'

There was no stopping Linda Flannery now, she just knew that a Soviet submarine, and from Earth at that, was somewhere in a land across what was called the Kovda Ocean. Spy Girl wanted to know if the vessel was still in the Port of Tellovaci? The answer was no. According to the old sailor, the submarine with the red star was not in this port for very long.

"Scandie," Linda said, "I need you to ask some more questions for me." The little Ucellan girl nodded that she would. Switching back and forth between Ucellan and English, Scandie asked the questions to the man that Linda wanted to know. Meanwhile, Spy Girl had a pen and small notebook and wrote down what Scandie told her via the old sailor.

According to the sailor, this "monster ship," left Trozny and sailed eastward towards Zotova. But to where in Zotova? There were many small ports in this large land. But the largest, most southern port would be in Tannsisi, Zotova.

"Good Goliath," Michaela stated as the Time Maidens observed this latest development on the time scanner. "Spy Girl is going to figure out that the Vodyanoy is in Tannsisi, Zotova."

"True," Lin said, "But with the current state of development on Vanag, it's not like she can find out in an instant whether there is a Russian submarine on the other side of this world."

"In addition," Amaresh added, "The Americans aren't about to leave their now home port in Torama to go out searching for the Vodyanoy."

"At least not yet," Cuca interjected. "There may be two modern submarines on this backward world compared to Earth, but the Americans and Russians are still somewhat limited in technology beyond their submarines."

"It doesn't matter," Rowena concluded, "this Spy Girl is crafty and determined. She will get to the bottom of this new mission for her."

Linda, Ron and Scandie left the tavern. The old sailor allowed Linda to keep the drawing of what was obviously a submarine. Linda would file this drawing with the paintings and now her notes. This was the beginning of her intelligence files. The seawoman reported back to Captain Albritton with her findings. He was impressed with what the young woman had found. However, Spy Girl was by no means through. She was determined to find out not if this submarine was real, but where it was located.

That very night, Linda, accompanied by Seaman Williams, returned to some of the other taverns. And with the permission of Scandie's parents, took the young girl with them to translate. The two Americans had grown very fond of Scandie, and rewarded her and the parents for her help. One might say that Scandie was somewhat on the payroll of the U.S. Navy.

This time, though, when Linda returned to the taverns by the docks, she was dressed and looked entirely different. She already had the captain's permission to do this. All of the crew on the Tampa had a few civilian clothes. Back on Earth, even on a submarine, there was shore leave if the vessel made a port of call. Spy Girl was wearing a blue and white polka dot mini dress, with matching white Go-Go boots. While on duty, Linda, like the other female sailors, wore their hair pinned back. But tonight her shoulder-length hair was down and she had bangs. Spy Girl really did resemble *The Girl from U.N.C.L.E.* Which is what she wanted.

However, Seaman Williams had to tell her, "Linda, you are going to attract a lot of attention to yourself. Heads will turn, especially in taverns when these Ucellan men see you. No woman on this planet dresses like this."

"Relax, Ron," Linda said. "I have you for protection. I want to draw attention for a good reason. We need to find a sailor that will be going to this land called Zotova. If we find one, then perhaps he can verify this Soviet submarine, if it's still there."

"That is if it even exists," Ron mumbled. Spy Girl smiled and confidently walked into a tavern with the seaman and Scandie. In this role, Linda Flannery had no fear. But one had to wonder. Did this Maine girl take this spy role seriously, or was she merely acting out a fantasy? Only Linda knew.

Like they had done earlier, the two Americans went from table to table and had Scandie ask a question. The sailors in these taverns were a rough bunch. However, they feared the "people from beyond," that is, Earth, because of the vessel that they all still lived in. The question Scandie asked in Ucellan was, "Is anyone going to the Port of Tannsisi soon?" At the first two taverns they did not have any success as all of the sailors either shook their heads or replied no. There were many small shipping companies in North Ucella. Not all sailed to Trozny or Zotova. But by the third tavern, Spy Girl found what she was looking for.

At one table, a younger sailor, most likely around the same age as Linda and Ron, told Scandie that the steamer he worked on was indeed going to this port in Zotova. And in two days. *Jackpot,* Spy Girl thought. The Americans asked if they could sit down and join this sailor. Another sailor that looked a few years older was also present.

Ron saw to it that, whatever they were drinking, they were bought another round. The drink did resemble some kind of beer. Who knows what it was made out of on this planet? Linda asked Scandie once again to ask and find out what she wanted to know.

First of all, the sailor went by the name Redan. He was a native of Torama. Redan had some schooling but made more money as a merchant sailor. He still lived at home with his parents and a sister who was a couple of years younger than him. By now, it was an established fact that this part of the world was like industrial America and Europe over a hundred years ago. Life was still hard. Linda thought, though, that Redan wasn't a bad-looking fellow. He was also blonde, a scandie as it were, with broad shoulders and strong arms. No doubt he got a good workout from shipping.

Redan explained that over the past three years, he had traveled the world. In at least two of the main Ucellan Islands. Along with Trozny and Zotova. *Ah,* Spy Girl thought. *This guy has been to Zotova before.* The Americans knew from their research and maps that they had obtained in Torama, that there were three main, fairly large Ucellan Islands. Redan stated that he had been to one of the other islands, that is East Ucella, but not to the other one. This would be West Ucella.

Curious, Linda asked Scandie, "Find out from Redan why he hasn't been to West Ucella. After all, it's not that far away." Scandie found out and translated.

Redan told the Americans that because of the war and now plague, everyone stayed away from West Ucella. *War and plague,* Linda thought. Everyone on the Tampa had heard that there had been some type of civil war between the two Ucellas. That is East and West Uclella. But now a plague? Everything was still somewhat sketchy as the reports coming out of West Ucella were confusing. Spy Girl reasoned that they could look into that later. For now the mission was to solve the mystery of the Soviet submarine.

Linda asked Redan if he would help in solving this mystery. He would have to be discreet, of course. Speaking through Scandie he replied that he would. The young merchant sailor asked if Linda and Ron would come to the home of his parents for dinner the following night and they could talk about this further. If this is what it would take to get Redan to help them, Linda and Ron agreed that they would accept the invitation.

As the Toramans were in awe of the Americans and their futuristic vessel, that is, futuristic for them, the North Ucellans looked up to them. To have any of the crew from the submarine come to a Toraman's home was a great honor. It was like having royalty. Captain Albritton had informed the crew that as long as it appeared safe, the crew should interreact at the homes of the people. This was good for both the Americans and Ucellans. And not to lord it over the Toramans. Thus far, the cusine was safe and delicious. The people of Earth in this land were still learing about the food of this world.

Ron Williams brought along a bottle of wine from Napa Valley, California, for this occasion. There was still a good supply of liquor on the Tampa as it was used sparingly and only for special occasions. Besides, the crew was experimenting and enjoying the many varities of Ucellan liquor in Torama. Ron and Linda were dressed in their formal U.S. Navy uniforms. Redan's parents marveled at the handsome black man from beyond, and the pretty young white woman. Once again, Scandie accompanied them as their translator.

However, there was someone else in the household that added to the joy of this occasion. Redan had a younger sister. Her name was Tixae. This Toraman girl would be about eighteen years old. Tixae had jet-black hair, along with beautiful green eyes. But nothing like green-eyed people from Earth. The Ucellans were a mixture of Troznyan and Zotovan blood. But then, as a result of this continued mixed blood, a new type of race came out of this union. Tixae was attractive.

The majority of Toramans, like other Ucellans in the major cities, lived in a type of tenant house where many were joined together. Rather small, but the families made do. Ron and Linda found out quickly that Tixae spoke a fair amount of English. Not anywhere as good as Scandie, but not that far behind. This would also prove to be a good thing. Tixae was a big fan of *The Astro Girls* as well, and had been exposed to Troy Cunningham's Bible comics and movies.

Formalities aside though, time was running out. The next day Redan's ship would be leaving port for first Trozny, then Zotova. Linda needed to give something for Redan to take on his journey. A poloroid camera. Quite a few of the crew on the Tampa had this then popular instant camera. It shouldn't be too difficult for Redan to learn how to use the camera.

The difficult part would be how to take a picture discreetly, in a world where cameras didn't yet exist. After a lovely dinner, as it was still light outside, Linda had Redan step outside onto a small backyard terrace. Speaking through Scandie, she wanted to instruct Redan how to use the camera. Ron joined them as well.

As Linda explained how to use what to her and people from Earth was a simple device, she really did feel like a spy. Spy Girl was instructing her first "operative" in an act of espionage. Even if it was just a simple picture. Linda got up close to Redan and showed him how to look through the viewing hole and hit the click button. Linda had on makeup and Chanel perfume. This was a bit overwhelming for Redan. If he remained still, the camera would do the rest. Linda, stood back a few feet so Redan could focus in on a mostly head shot of her. The American-Earth girl smiled. Redan focused and then gently tapped the click button.

Within a few seconds the poloroid picture came out and began to develop. Redan handed the camera back to Linda, and then she did the rest. When the picture became clearer, Linda thought, *Not bad for a close-up.*

When Redan saw the picture he had just taken of the pretty Earth girl, he asked Scandie to ask if he could keep this picture of Linda. When Ron Williams heard what Redan had asked, he thought, *This Ucellan guy has the hots for Linda. He would swim across the ocean to this other country to take a picture if it meant getting on Linda's good side.*

Spy Girl hestitated about this requests for a moment, but then agreed that Redan could keep the picture of her. However, he was not to show it to anyone. Keep it concealed. And the camera, too, until the time was right to take a picture of the submarine. If it could be found. Linda instructed Redan what to look for if the submarine was there, he couldn't miss it. Everyone then called it a night, as Redan would be departing early in the morning. His family no doubt wanted to spend some time with him, as he would be gone nearly six weeks.

Right before sunrise the following morning Redan's ship would be leaving for its destinations. The steamer was loaded with a variety of goods to be sold and delivered at various ports. Redan's sister, Tixae, was present to see her brother off. Spy Girl thought that it was a good idea to also see her new "operative-friend" off. Tixae gave her brother a big hug. Spy Girl also gave the Toraman sailor a hug. He was determined to find out about this other submarine, and said so in Ucellan to Linda. She knew what he was trying to tell her. With that, Redan went aboard his ship.

From this point on, Linda and Tixae began to draw close. With Tixae's English improving each day, Spy Girl could use her services, too. And Tixae was growing fond of the American and wanted to be close to her. Linda returned to the Tampa to give Captain Albritton an update. All that the Americans could do for now is wait. Hopefully, Redan would turn up with something and solve this Soviet submarine mystery once and for all.

Linda also informed the captain about what Redan told her regarding a civil war between East and West Ucella, followed by some type of plague on the western island. Captain Albritton had heard bits and pieces of this as well. For now, the Americans were still trying to improve relations with North Ucella. Nevertheless, they needed to find out more about the other two Ucellan islands. Evidently, all three large island nations were closely related and had a connection with one another. That is until a deadly plague struck West Ucella.

Now that Spy Girl considered herself in intelligence work, she volunteered to find out more about East and West Ucella. The captain thought that this was a great idea. Captain Albritton promoted Linda Flannery to an ensign. He had the authority to do this. Especially now that the Tampa was no longer on Earth. Ensign is considered a commissioned officer of the lowest rank.

But this was quite a step up for a former seawoman. Once again, Spy Girl was elated with another mission and new zeal. Linda had almost forgotten that she was no longer on Earth. Linda set out to do more intelligence gathering work.

The Time Maidens moved up the time scanner a few more years. Spy Girl would eventually become the director of a large intelligence ageny similar to the *U.S.-CIA* back on Earth. This American-inspired agency on Vanag would be known as the *UIA*. What did this stand for? More about that later.

Meanwhile, on the other side of the world in Soviet-Zotova, another young woman with zeal and determination was also busy at work in the intelligence field. Kikimora. Tannsisi was pretty much already transformed into a Soviet style city. But there was a whole country yet to become a second Soviet Union. This would require a lot of work. Valeria Rostova was teaching Kikimora everything she knew. Kikimora was a fast learner and had her own plans in making Zotova a "socialist paradise." Just what was this other "spy girl" up to?

For this next exploit involving the Russians on Vanag in what they called *1 A.E.* (After Earth), it had been four months since these people from Earth arrived on this planet. Lin and Michaela were now viewing the latest developments regarding the Russians. The other three Time Maidens and assistants were also viewing other events on the time scanner. These events were taking place so rapidly, it was hard to keep up with them. They would all compare notes later.

"It looks like the Russians are serious about making Zotova into another Soviet Union," Lin remarked. "I suppose that they imagine that as long as they are stranded on this other planet, they may as well make the best of it. They have the power now to make changes. The Russians need something to keep them occupied and in control until they get home."

"If they get home," Michaela added. "They are a long way from Earth. The only way these two groups of Earth people can get back home is if the Aeduians helped them. Something tells me that this is not going to happen."

On Earth during the 1920's, the Soviet Union started what was called Five Year Plans. These plans were a series of nationwide economic plans. Many did not reach the goals set by the government or ended in disaster.

However, there was now a small nucleus of Soviet-Russians on another planet. Zotova, was in chaos even before the Russians came through a vortex and ended up on Vanag. The Russians may have been in control of Tannsisi, but the other cities and towns were still in dismay. And, after the nuclear strike against Zelessio, there was even more disorder. As the majority of crime bosses and warlords perished in the nuclear attack of that city, there was a vacuum so to speak with power or authority. Zotova was also in economic shambles.

Still, the Russians, as the new masters of the land, intended to change this current state of development. Especially the political officer Valeria Rostova with the opportunist Kikomora at her side. Having this Russian and Troznyan woman as your enemy could prove to be dangerous. But if you were their friend, or cooperated with them, you would be rewarded. Valeria Rostova as well as the rest of the Russians from the Vodyanoy knew that they must be in control of this vast land in order to survive on this alien planet. And they needed to be in full control soon.

Under the direction of Valeria Rostova, a new Red Army was formed in Tannsisi. She appointed the six Soviet marines, or special forces, to be in charge of training. They had already seen combat when they took out the previous crime boss in Tannsisi. The new Zotovan in charge of the city, Commissar Tefano, as he was now called, signed over his private army of around one thousand men. They were mostly cuthroats and thugs. But the Soviet marines quickly whipped them into shape.

The new recruits were trained in small groups of ten at first for basic training. Many were learning Russian, and Valeria and Kikimora had found young Zotovans that had pretty much mastered this new Earth language now being spoken in Tannsisi. They were on hand to translate for the Russian instructors. The Russians were determined to make these Zotovans into a professional army. They were mostly being trained in counterinsurgency. The same type of warfare the Russians were engaged in on planet Earth in Afganistan. The days of lining up and firing at one another, like soldiers back on Earth during the days of the Napoleonic era were gone. First on Earth , and now on Vanag.

As there were so few AK-47's in the arsenal on the Vodyanoy along with ammo, this new Soviet-Zotovan army would have to make due with muskets. Quite a few from the crew grew up on collective farms in the Soviet Far East. Because of this background, they were experienced with rifles. Some even left over from World War II. But these Zotovan muskets were even more primitive than the old Russian rifles. There were three crewmen on the Vodyanoy, actually all with the first name Ivan, that were assigned to see if they could improve or modify these Zotovan weapons. With the current state of development on Vanag this would not be an easy task.

Nevertheless, the three I's (Short for Ivan) put their heads together and set out to see what they could do. The first thing they did was visit the factory in Tannsisi that manufactured the muskets. The factory was still way behind compared to the gun factories back in the Soviet Union or anywhere else on earth, but some adjustments could be made.

These young Russian men helped the manufacturers develop a more accurate musket ball. Quicker to load, even though, for the time being, only one musket ball at a time could be loaded. Next, the Russians showed the Zotovan soldiers how to take better care of their guns. Including keeping the rifles clean so they wouldn't jam up and explode back in their faces. This had been quite common.

When the Russians took over control of Tannsisi, they had all weapons confiscated and locked away in several guarded warehouses. Only those that would be serving in the Soviet-Zotovan Red Army, or a few trusted others, would be issued a gun. When other cities and towns came under direct Soviet rule, this same policy was enforced.

There was a railroad network linked up to major Zotovan cities. This network was much like the early railroads on Earth. But the Zotovans were still working out the kinks. As many of the sailors on the Vodyanoy were mechanically inclined and modifying tools available, the Russians were able to update and improve somewhat with the engines and trains. Similar also to trains in the early period of Earth, the Zotovan trains were fueled by a type of coal. As long as this Vanagian coal was available, the

Russians could hopefully reach their goals of improving life in this new country.

Each city and town would need to be evaluated in order to move and ship goods throughout Zotova. Again though, an army was needed. The Russians had no idea what the next city or frontier town would hold for them. During the Great Patriotic War, in the Soviet Union, sewing brigades made up of women were formed to keep the Red Army in uniform. Even if most of the brigade had to sew by hand. Valeria Rostova saw to it that many women in Tannsisi made up this first brigade. Right now the economy was pretty much on a trade barter basis.

With all of the crime bosses gone in Tannsisi and no longer controlling the food, the new centralized government set up by the Russians took over with food distribution. The soldiers in the new Red Army, along with the women in the sewing brigades were paid in food or other goods.

Famine had been rampant in Tannsisi until the Russians came on the scene, and still was in other Zotovan cities. This would be a thing of the past, starting in Tannsisi. There was plenty of food now and equally distributed. Soup kitchens and food pantries were also set up. Everybody in Tannsisi received three meals a day. The Zotovans knew nothing about communism, but would soon learn. The fact that famine disappeared in Tannsisi made these Vanagian-Zotovans view the Russians and communism as saviors.

Kikimora, also had a plan and agenda. First and foremost, any Troznyan girls and young women that had been kidnapped and sold as workers and or sex slaves held in Zotova would be freed immediately. Starting in Tannsisi, Kikimora was able to rescue or repatriate many of these young women in the city. Some wanted to return home to Trozny, others didn't. Kikimora recruited the Troznyan girls that wished to stay. But for what purpose? Why, as spies or intelligence personnel for a new spy agency. The Zotovan *KGB.* Valeria Rostova applauded this move by her new assistant. These Troznyan girls would prove to be quite the asset.

Even the Troznyan girls that returned to their towns and villages kept in touch with the new Zotovan *KGB* by letter. Kikimora wanted these young women to be her eyes and ears back in her homeland. A building was taken over in Tannsisi and set up as an intelligence center. A huge red Soviet flag was made and flew over the top of this building. The original flag of the Soviet Union displayed a yellow hammer and sickle along with a lone star. But with this new flag were two yellow stars. One represented the Soviet Union back on Earth, and the other, Soviet-Zotova. The other Soviet Union now on Vagag.

In a short time there were nearly one hundred young women working for the Zotovan *KGB* in this building. And a few men here and there. But as the new *KGB* was founded by Valeria Rostova and Kikimora, they had come to trust women more.

The *KGB* women at first worked in the office. They compiled books, newspapers and whatever else that pertained to Zotova and beyond. As there were no computers except on the Vodyanoy, all of this research was filed away by category or written down by hand. The Troznyan girls, along with a few Zotovans, were required to learn Russian.

The sewing brigade was rapidly turning out uniforms for the Zotovan Red Army. The Russians on Vanag believed from the start that their Soviet-Zotovan army should have the best. As they had a few army uniforms on the Vodyanoy, they could see about manufacturing clothes patterns. These were the one-piece hooded, leaf-pattern camourflage uniforms worn by the Spetsnez forces in Afghanistan.

Eventually, a lightweight helmet was also added. During the cold weather in the northern areas of Zotova, the soldiers had fur ushankas (Hats) made from Vanagian animal skins. The hat even had ear flaps. The Soviet-Zotovan Red Army looked impressive. Even if they were only equipped with a musket and dagger.

Valeria Rostova and Kikimora wanted their *KGB* spy girls to look professional as well. Once again the sewing brigades were the answer. At the main *KGB* headquarters on Earth in Moscow, Soviet women had a standard uniform. This consisted of a black skirt, black high heels, with a white blouse. Valeria, as a political officer, was about as hard-nosed as they come when it came to her job as a serious Marxist-Leninist. But she was also a woman and believed that Soviet women could flaunt their beauty. She had the *KGB* uniforms for the women on this planet a bit more revealing.

This uniform was tighter, shorter and a bit less modest. No women in Zotova, or, for that matter, anywhere on the planet dressed like this. At least not yet. But that would soon change with influence from Earth. Many Zotovan men couldn't help but stare as they observed these "new government" women strolling down the streets of Tannsisi in groups on their way to work. Also, on the right collar of their white blouse, the *KGB* girls wore a small pin. It was the emblem of the *KGB*. A blue-gray shield with a sword. In the middle of the emblem was a red star with a yellow hammer and sickle inside the star.

Valeria Rostova once again called on the services of Tatiana Semerova, Svetlana Lebedeva and Anastasia Macogonova. These three young, civilian women on the Vodyanoy were nicknamed by the crew the "Soviet Princesses." This latest assignment for the Soviet Princesses was twofold. One, to teach Russian in small groups to the new *KGB* girls. Two, to doll them up, as it were.

Very few women on Vanag wore makeup. Only the wealthy. And they were few and far between. But these three Soviet Princesses figured out a way to manfacture makeup. Most of the product consisted of water, oil and wax. This could all be found in Tannsisi.

The Russian Earth girls then taught the Vanagian girls how to apply their makeup and variuos hairstyles. It was Kikimore that came up with the phrase, "Beauty and power." These *KGB* girls may have looked beautiful and had pretty smiles, but they had the power to make life miserable for anyone that opposed the new order. Some could even order a person to be put to death.

By day, the intelligence girls worked at *KGB* headquarters, but at night, or on their days off, they mingled with the population. Some even posed as prostitutes, like spy girls did on Earth. This was a new role for the women of Zotova. Up until now, with the new Soviet rule, women had few rights. Overnight, they now had authority. The spy girls that posed as prostitutes would frequent taverns or parks. Even though the Russians were pretty much in control of Tannsisi, there were still opposers. Basically, this had been a crime-ridden city. And it was most likely still that way in other Zotovan cities.

Once it was revealed through the spy girls who was not for the new Soviet-Zotova government, they were rounded up and put in a labor camp. This was right out of the *KGB* manual from the Soviet Union on Earth. Free labor so to speak, as the new Soviet Union expanded with their work programs.

As for Kikimora, how did she dress as second in command to the Zotovan *KGB*? Kikimora was an attractive young woman herself. She had special dresses made for her. The dresses came to her mid calves, but were also very formfitting. The dress could be black, but with a white cape. Or a purple dress with a red cape. This top spy girl had many different color dresses and capes made for her attire. Kikimora, too, had matching high-heels made for her dresses and quickly learned how to walk in these Earth-style shoes. This was a far cry from the animal skin clothes she used to wear when the Russians first met Kikimora and Baba out in the middle of the Targu Ocean.

To many, Kikimora may have looked attractive, yet there was a sinister air about her. Under the reign of Josef Stalin and his security chief Lavrentity Beria, millions pf people in the Soviet Union died or were exiled to labor camps. When Nikita Khrushchev came to power, Stalin and Beria were exposed for their vile deeds. Stalin had already died, and Beria was executed by the new ruling leaders. This was considered a dark period for the Soviet Union.

Books were written about Stalin and Beria. Some of these books were in the Vodyanoy's library. The purpose of these books was to reveal how Stalin and Beria perverted communism. As Kikomora had learned the Russian language so fast, she read these books and learned about these sinister deeds. *If done in secret, can these same ploys by Stalin and Beria be used on my world? In Zotova with the new KGB?* Kikomora thought. Time would tell. The Russians also gave Kikimora a Makanov pistol to carry. No doubt, if needed, she would use it.

So, in reality, it didn't take long for Soviet-Zotova to have an ever-growing army and spy network. In addition, the railroads were improving every day. This would be a link to the rest of Zotova, which in turn would improve the economy and living conditions for the Zotovans. The Russians began to proclaim to the Zotovans about a "workers paradise." Perhaps even better than the one the Russians were still attempting to achieve on Earth.

On Earth, the Soviet Union was known for its large, colorful poster boards and statues glorifying communism. The Russians were doing the same thing here in Zotova. The faces of Marx, Engles and Lenin were on these posters. Also famous Russian cosmonauts, along with space rockets and other scientific achievements. Even larger-than-life statues were being erected. The Russians employed a large group of Zotovan artists and sculptors. The population of this Vanagian nation were learning fast about the people and heritage of the new government of their land.

There was also another young and brillant Russian from the Vodyanoy that was about to come out of the shadows and make a lasting contribution on Vanag. His name was Mikhail Popovich, but had the nickname *MIG Boy.* He was from Volgograd. Mig Boy was obsessed with airplanes and the Soviet Air Force., and wanted to become a *MIG* pilot, but because he didn't have the technical background, this goal was beyond his reach. Mikhail was conscripted into the navy. Yet, *MIG* Boy never gave up his love of aviation.

While growing up, *MIG* Boy read every book or manual he could get his hands on about aviation and the Soviet Air Force. When a nearby air force base had their annual day for the public to visit, *MIG* Boy was present.

When some of the older Soviet planes and jets were no longer classified, Mikhail learned everything he could about the aircraft. *MIG* Boy knew where every nut and bolt was in these planes and also like Linda Flannery, had a photographic memory. If he had the tools and supplies to do so, Mikhail could probably construct a simple airplane. However, the technology wasn't present on Vanag just yet.

MIG Boy, though, had another idea. Hot air, or Zeppelin balloons. There balloons on Earth were manufactured with nylon. Nylon is made from petroleum. Petroleum existed in places on Vanag. The Americans and Russians knew this. However, the Earth people didn't have the drills and oil wells yet to extract this petroleum. Like other things this technology would come later.

These Zeppelins would have to be manufactured from canvas. Hot air ballons need helium to power these airships. Helium could also be found on Vanag, and in Zotova. With help, *MIG* Boy could extract this helium. Before long, *MIG* Boy had manufactured two prototype Zeppelins from a warehouse in Tannsisi. The canvas on the blimp was dyed gray. Painted on the gray airship was a large, red hammer and sickle. One of the symbols of Soviet-Zotova communism. This would be clearly visible from the air.

The passenger compartment under the airship could carry twenty-four people. In this case twenty-four Soviet-Zotovan soldiers. The Zeppelins could sit on top of a flat train car until it got near its destination. Then the blimps could become airborne. *MIG* Boy would pilot one blimp, while a Zotovan was trained to pilot the other. Obviously, under the best of circumstances, blimps could be volatile and dangerous. Recall the German Hindenburg disaster in 1937 on Earth. *MIG* boy crossed his fingers, while the young Zotovan pilot didn't know any better.

When Soviet-Zotovan troops were about to enter a new city, the airships would take to the skies. Even if any opposing army attempted to shoot at the airships, it would be futile. They were too high up for any musket ball to do any damage. Zotovans in these cities would be in fear and awe when they observed these "otherworldy" objects over their city.

The airships would set down on the outskirts of the city. The special forces would then jump out and enter the city from the opposite side where the train carrying the main forces would stop. In this way, the "airborne" forces would launch a surprise counterattack and act as reinforcements for the main frontal army disembarking from the train. This was how each Zotovan city would eventually come under the control of the Russians. Once a city was secured, other Soviet-Zotovans that had been trained in various skills would enter the city and begin to modernize this backward culture. The *KGB* girls would then come in various guises to follow up in the intelligence work.

The Russian senior staff on the Vodyanoy, Valeria Rostova, and now Kikimora, didn't see why this plan wouldn't work with miminal opposition. When Captain Starinov saw the drawings, and then the two actual airships in the warehouse, he was amazed. "Imagine that," the captain said, "we actually now have air power on this world."

"Whew," Lin said as they were about to conclude this latest saga of the Russians on Vanag. "Who would think that a new Soviet Union was possible on another planet."

"Yes indeed," Michaela added. "This Troznyan girl, now working with the Russians is also a shady, dangerous character. I bet that our Celtic Time Maiden sister, Rowena, would love to meet Kikimora in a dark alley, as they say, and take her out."

"Let's not give her any ideas," Lin concluded. "Like the Aeduians, we really can't change the developments on this other world. At least not much. Even if the Americans and Russians have. We can only monitor and observe how this history unfolds on Vanag."

The assistants of the Time Maidens continued to pull up more information regarding the planet Vanag. Especially the history of events after the arrival of the people from Earth. Justinian and Rebecca had some more details and facts to share.

Cuca had joined Rowena to watch and study these latest developments. The Time Maidens sometimes worked together as a group. Other times perhaps just two or three of them took part in viewing developments on the time scanner. The reason being was that so many things were unfolding regarding the Americans and Russians so rapidly, that it was hard to keep up with it all.

"I'm so glad that you could join me, Cuca," Rowena stated, "as we watch the time scanner with this information that Justinian and Rebecca complied for us regarding the Americans."

"I wouldn't miss this," Cuca replied. "We know that the Russians are gradually transforming Zotova into another Soviet Union. Let's find out more what is happening with the Americans in North Ucella.

While Linda Flannery, or Spy Girl, patiently waited for Redan to return from Trozny and Zotova, to confirm whether or not a Soviet submarine was also present on this world, she kept busy with other intelligence gathering work. Spy Girl would not slt stlll.

Linda wanted to find out everything about the recent Ucellan Civil War. The Time Maidens had already learned that the three large Ucellan Islands were populated by people originally from Trozny. Similar to the Norsemen, or Vikings, Troznyan seafarers set up colonies on these islands. This took place nearly four hundred years ago.

As Captain Albritton realized, intelligence gathering was vital if the Americans were going to make an impact on this world. For this reason, now that Linda Flannery had been promoted to an ensign, or commissioned officer, she was relieved of her main duties on the Tampa. The captain told her, "Keep digging on anything of importance regarding this world and how it may affect us."

"Aye, Aye, Captain," Spy Girl replied. "It will be an honor.'

The captain saw to it that Ensign Flannery was set up in a small house in Torama, not very far from where the Tampa was docked. This would be her office. The Toramans that worked close with the Americans provided Linda with some furnishings such as a desk and wooden cabinets to store files. Spy Girl could have access to the technology on the submarine such as the copy machines. She immediately began to build up her files from newspaper articles from Torama's main newspaper. The paper was a simple journel, yet informative and to the point.

Ron Williams would continue to assist Linda in her intelligence work, but he still had duties on the Tampa. Spy Girl, though, had two additional recruits for her tiny intelligence network. Young Scandie, of course, who would continue to be her translator, and her new friend Tixae, Redan's sister. Both of these young Toraman girls would prove to be invaluable for Spy Girl and the Americans.

Spy Girl was always one step ahead. She had a plan involving Scandie. The little Ucellan girl could pretty much read, speak and comprehend the English language, but Linda had another assignment for Scandie: Learn Russian. What! This Ucellan girl was going to learn a third language. Why not? She had the young mind and determination to accomplish this. But again why Russian?

Spy Girl was convinced that a Soviet submarine was on this planet. The paintings of the woman, that is, Valeria Rostova, and the submarine, were real. It wasn't a fantasy or something out of a comicbook. For this reason, if the Russians were on this planet Vanag, then someone had better learn Russian. As far as Spy Girl was concerned, that someone was Scandie.

There were actually two other crew members on the Tampa that also spoke Russian. On every U.S. Navy ship or boat, at least one person of the crew had to speak and understand Russian. This was all a part of the Cold War. One crewman learned the language in college, while the other had grandparents that were Russian.

Spy Girl began to compile newspaper articles pertaining to this recent civil war between East and West Ucella. In a short time Tixae, too, rapidly could understand English. With Scandie's help, she learned how to read and write English. Tixae then translated for Linda, the newspaper articles. Tixae, even wrote out the articles by hand in English on paper for her new friend and boss, Spy Girl. Additionally, Linda, with Scandie and Tixae's help interviewed a number of sailors from Torama that, although the North Ucellans were not directly involved in the war, still had knowledge of the conflict.

No civil war can easily be defined, including the ones fought on Earth, and there were many down through the ages. The same applied to the Ucellan Civil War. The three main Ucellan Islands, although closely related, were still considered independent island nations. Yet, there was a common bond. Fifty years before the Earth people arrived on Vanag, East Ucella, which was much more powerful than their western island cousins, began to impose their will on the West Ucellans.

Perhaps East Ucella wanted more land for farming and to control West Ucellan cities, as the planet was slowly becoming industralized. Then, too, there were the fishing rights. Fishing was an important industry for the three Ucellan islands. The fishing industry took place in the great sea that the Ucellan islands were all a part of. This sea had a strange-sounding name that the Americans would eventually change.

As East Ucella gained more control over their western cousins, the people of the land became like indentured servants.

This was one step above a slave. The West Ucellans no longer controlled their farms or cities. The people of West Ucella eventually lived in poverty.

A few uprisings were attempted, but were brutally crushed. Finally, one West Ucellan by the name of Kalodi rose up and started a following of West Ucellans that were determined to take back their land. This rebel leader had great charisma. His rebellion against the occupying East Ucellans started out in the rurals, but then quickly spread to the cities and towns. The rebel base camps were hidden in the mountains. This made it almost impossible for the invading East Ucellans to flush the rebels out.

By day the battles were fought in the mountains and forests. At night the rebels attacked the cities. A bloody urban warfare resulted with the death toll mounting on both sides. East Ucella continued to send more forces in what was rapidly becoming a costly war. This Ucellan civil war started about ten years before the arrival of the Americans. It dragged on for seven years.

West Ucella had a somewhat powerful navy. They had several fleets of warships or Man-Of-Wars. This navy was for the purpose of protecting the island nation's fishing rights, along with escorting merchant vessels to Trozny, Zotova and Enaim. At the outset of East Ucella's occupation, the West Ucellan navy worked alongside their eastern cousins. But as the occupation became more brutal, the West Ucellan navy also rebelled against the invaders.

What stand did North Ucella take during this civil war? Officially, they claimed to be neutral. Still, there was financial gain to be made from both sides of this conflict. Both of the navies of East and West Ucella had unofficial ports in North Ucella. East Ucella would go to Torama for ship repairs and supplies. As for the West Ucellans, they had a port in a city called Cakovica in North Ucella.

The capital of West Ucella was a city called Ruteni. The city was completely under the control of East Ucella. The capital city of East Ucella was Gosalia. As these were island nations, both capitals were port cities. East Ucella may have been winning the land war in West Ucella, but they were having difficulty controlling the sea separating the three major islands. There were fierce navel battles at sea between the two opposing Ucellas.

Even the capital city of Gosalia was not safe from offshore bombardment from West Ucellan warships. Smaller towns along the coast of East Ucella were also raided and plundered. The West Ucellan naval forces used these spoils of war to help pay for their war effort.

This bloody war continued on at great cost for both sides. Gradually, the West Ucellan forces retook their cities and defeated the occupying East Ucellans. However, West Ucella was in chaos. The rebel leader Kalodi, proclaimed himself the new ruler of his land. Suddenly though, events took a dastardly turn. This was three years before the Americans arrival on Vanag.

"Goodness," Cuca remarked at this point of the viewing. "Just when you think that things couldn't get any worse."

"Oh, but they can," Rowena added, "they can and will."

Linda Flannery also discovered all about this war in her research and interviews. But what was this dastardly event?

For this next phase of what was unfolding for the Americans on Vanag, Rowena and Cuca invited the other three Time Maidens to join them. Rowena and Cuca took turns bringing the other Time Maidens up to date regarding the Ucellan Civil War. And there was more to explain about Linda Flannery, or Spy Girl.

The dastardly event that next struck West Ucella was a pandemic, or plague. As this pandemic originated in Ruteni, the capital of West Ucella, it became known as the Ruteni Influenza. By now the Ucellan Civil War had come to a halt. East Ucellan soldiers retreated from West Ucella and returned home before the pandemic enveloped the whole island. Three quaretrs of Ruteni had been destroyed in the war. Famine also gripped the land. Over a million West Ucellans would perish as a result of the famine.

Undoubtedly, because of the seven-year civil war, and now famine, the population of West Ucella was weary and malnourished. For that reason, the immune systems of the people of that nation were comprosimed. A killer virus set in and spread rapidly. Before the civil war, the population of West Ucella was around four million. The Ruteni Influenza would kill nearly a million. Along with the famine, half of the population of West Ucella vanished almost overnight. Huge funeral pyres lit up the night sky to burn the dead. Offshore ships could witness these mass burnings.

Even the rebel leader Kalodi died from the killer flu. Now, too, West Ucella suffered from a power vacuum. Both Linda Flannery in her research-investigation, and the Time Maidens viewing this event on the time scanner, thought that this pandemic was reminiscent of the Black Death on Earth during the Dark Middle Ages. It was Michaela that stated, "This reminds me of mission nine."

A naval blockade, or quarantine, was set up around West Ucella. Even the ships that made up the navy of West Ucella participated in this quarantine. Although this was their countrymen dying back on the homeland, the West Ucellan navy realized that the Ruteni Influenza could not be permitted to leave the island. Nevertheless, West Ucellan ships sent food on rafts to their sick and starving countrymen.

How, though, did North and East Ucella react to the pandemic? North Ucella felt the need to send humanitarian aid, but these northern cousins realized that they couldn't send any of their citizens to the actual island nation. They followed the example of the West Ucellan navy. North Ucella sent food and supplies also on unmanned rafts from larger cargo ships. As for East Ucella, they were morally and financially bankrupt as a result of this civil war.

East Ucella did feel responsible for the tragedies inflicting West Ucella. First and foremost, East Ucella had occupied the land of their western cousins for fifty years, which resulted in a civil war, famine, and now a pandemic. A new leadership had come to power in East Ucella that replaced the military dictatorship that caused all of these troubles upon West Ucella. But East Ucella was stil recovering from its own losses due to the war. There was very little they could do to help West Ucella. For now, a quarantine around the island nation was needed to keep the Ruteni Influenza from spreading to other lands. By and large, the West Ucellas were on their own.

Like with many pandemics and plagues, younger people and children appeared to have a stronger resistance or immunity. Even now, this was proving to be a nightmare world for the young in West Ucella. With more than half of the adult population gone, bands of children roamed the countryside and cities fending for themselves.

The Time Maidens were aghast at what was transpiring in West Ucella. "This is so awful what these poor people are going through," Amaresh commented.

"I agree," Michaela affirmed. "With so many children being orphaned, I think that we should consider making multiple, massive time-jumps to rescue these Vanagain-Ucellan children. The Aeduians would welcome them all."

"They would add to the growing number of children from Earth, that would become Aeduians," Cuca added. "This world of Vanag is ripe for the rescue of children."

"Something tells me the Aeduians would not permit this interference on such a massive scale," Rowena stated. "Who knows how something like this would affect this planet in the grand sceme of things."

"I agree, Rowena," Lin concluded. "But I think we should realize by now who can and will interfere. The Earth people. In this case, the Americans. They have the technology and the means to find a cure for this pandemic. Linda Flannery will take all of this information she has gathered to her superiors, and that we have viewed on the time scanner. For whatever reason, the Aeduians have not prevented these people of Earth from interfering on this planet. I believe our job for now is to also gather information regarding the planet Vanag."

True to what Lin said, Spy Girl gathered up her findings concerning the Ruteni Influenza, and reported back to her superiors on the USS Tampa.

As a team, the Time Maidens once again scanned several years forward using the time scanner. The former Earth girls were following up on the Soviet-Zotova Five Year Plan. The next phase of the Russians was knows as *Mother Zotova.* What was this all about?

The Soviet Union often referred to itself as Mother Russia. Motherland was used as a symbol of Russia during a time of crisis. This was especially true when Nazi Germany invaded the Soviet Union during World War Two. Even the atheist leader, Josef Stalin proclaimed, *"DEFEND MOTHER RUSSIA,"* during this invasion.

One of the fiercest battles of World War Two was the Battle of Stalingrad in 1942: By the end of this seven-month battle, there were over two million military and civilian casualties. Although this was a victory for the Russians in the war, Stalingrad left a deep emotional wound in the hearts and minds of the Russian people.

From the years 1959 to 1967, a two hundred and seventy-nine-foot statue was erected in the rebuilt city renamed Volgograd. *This Motherland Monument* became a symbol of Soviet Russia. Now, another statue, identical to the one on Earth, would become a symbol of Zotova on Vanag.

During this same time period, Tannsisi was renamed *New Moscow.* This statue and the capital city of Zotova underwent a massive refurbishment. The Zotovans in this city were happy to be a part of this work program. This is how they would be fed and have proper medical care. With the assistance of Doctor Yelena Inanova and her assistants, the medical care in New Moscow had an enormous overhaul. The Russians updated the Zotovan doctors, healers and nurses in the city.

Manpower also came from people that were sent to labor camps from those that resisted the Russians and the ever growing Zotovan communists. This immensly cut down on any rebellion against the new regime. Once the sentence of the rebels was up, they could either conform or end up as slave laborers again. As a result of this manpower, and Russian technology, New Moscow was transformed into a new, modern city. Huge apartment buildings were built, similar to the ones in Moscow on Earth. They were built even better, as there was not a rush or housing shortage. New Moscow only had a population of around three hundred thousand.

What of the new Motherland Monument statue? The Russians had the blueprints and dimensions from a book in the library on the Vodyanoy. Although Vanag was over one hundred years behind Earth of the 1980's, there were skilled craftsmen and sculptors. The very best from Zotova were sent to Tannsisi-New Moscow. Many of these sculptors had been creating statues and monuments of the goddess Aeliana, throughout the land. One fifty feet tall was destroyed in the now nuclear wasteland of Zelessio.

With the backing and determiniation of the Russians, along with thousands of Zotovan workers, the new Motherland Monument was constructed and completed in a little over two years. The colossal statue was a crowning achievement that stood over the harbor in New Moscow. The female statue was an exact replica of the one in Volograd. Even with the huge sword in her hand. The monument projected a powerful message against any enemies of Soviet Zotova.

Even so, there was another underlying factor for this statue that the Russians had in mind. They knew of the Aelianan religion. The Aelianans were followers of the mother goddess Aeliana. Soviet communism and religion were rarely compatable on Earth. Most hard-line communists agreed with what Karl Marx had stated: "Religion is the opium of the people." But the Russians had to walk softly regarding religion on this other world.

Aeliana, the mother goddess on Vanag, had many devout followers. They had been worshipping this goddess for thousands of years. Could Aeliana be replaced by another type of mother-goddess? The Russians now on Vanag believed so. Thus, in a short time, Mother Zotova did indeed push Aeliana into the background. The majority of the Zotovans did begin worshipping this symbol of communism now in control of their land. The image on the first postage stamps used by the mail service created by the Russians was none other than the image of Mother Zotova.

"*THIS IS AMAZING*," Amaresh exclaimed. "But what a sly move these Russians pulled off."

"Sly indeed," Michaela added. "Almost overnight the Russians did succeed in making the goddess Aeliana disappear and replacing her with a Vanagian Mother Russia."

As the Time Maidens had concluded, the Americans did indeed take an interest in the Ruteni Influenza and the people of West Ucella. When Spy Girl presented her findings to her superiors, they, too, wanted to find out more about this deadly virus. Especially Doctor Caldwell and Sylvia Rizzo.

Captain Albritton and Doctor Caldwell, along with Linda Flannery, sought out Benatta, the current leader of North Ucella. Benatta's wife, Kureyri, was actually making good progress in learning English. The captain, doctor and Spy Girl wanted to find out more about this Ruteni Influenza. Scandie had accompanied the three Americans to act as their interpreter. This little Toraman girl was quite remarkable. As Scandie now almost lived on the Tampa, there was a joke among the crew that she was the youngest person to ever be employed by the U.S. Navy.

Benatta related what he knew had transpired in the declining days of the Ucellan Civil War. There were underwater telegraph cables that connected with all three of the Ucellan Islands. There had been some news and communication, but as soon as the East Ucellan army evacuated from West Ucella at the war's end, events took a dark turn. This was the beginning of the Ruteni Influenza. Communication became sporadic, then ceased.

Once it became apparent that a deadly plague had afflicated the West Ucellans, the naval blockade involving North Ucella, East Ucella and the West Ucellan navy was imposed on the stricken island nation. A quarantine had to take place in order to contain the Ruteni Influenza. This was the only measure that the Vanagians in this part of the world could do.

The Americans realized that they would have to sail to West Ucella to investigate this pandemic further. Captain Albritton and Doctor Caldewll informed Benatta of their intentions and asked for his cooperation. The North Ucellan leader said that he would do all that his country could do to assist.

While the Americans made preparations to pull up anchor, as it were, to set sail for West Ucella, Benatta was asked to help prepare the way. The Earth people wanted some type of approval from the Ucellans before heading to West Ucella. As North Ucella was now the most powerful of the three island nations, they were in the best position to do this.

Benatta would send his main flagship of the North Ucellan navy. The ships making up the quarantine would be informed of the arrival of the Americans. Even in this age of almost no modern technology, word had already spread of "the people from beyond" in a huge metal vessel. Word of mouth, letters and the telegraph could spread news in a short time once it began to circulate.

Before departing, the captain saw to it that Lt. Cordova remained in Torama with twenty sailors from the crew. It was important to maintain an American presence in the city. By this time, though, the Americans were pretty much viewed as saviors by the North Ucellans. Most of the Americans tried to remain humble regarding their presence on this world. Except for Troy Cunningham. He was already starting to view himself as some type of prophet to the people of Vanag.

Lt. Cardova and his men were put up in the best hotel in the city. This hotel was an old establishment in more ways than one. The building was over seventy years old and lacked any modern conveniences compared to what the crew was used to back home and on the Tampa. Yet, the Americans found this to be an interesting experience. It was the best the Toramans could offer, and the hotel staff was very devoted and waited on the visitors as if they were royalty. The crew would later reflect that being in this hotel was like going back in time to the era of their great-grandparents.

Without further delay, the USS Tampa left the Port of Torama and set a course for Ruteni, West Ucella. The flagship of the North Ucellan navy was already a day ahead of the Tampa. Instead of crusing underwater, the submarine would be sailing on the surface of this sea in the middle of the three large Ucellan Islands. The Americans wanted the naval blockade to observe the submarine coming their way.

As the USS Tampa approached the blockade, the Ucellan naval ships did indeed allow the strange, powerful-looking vessel to sail through the blockade. The North Ucellan flagship had seen to that. And, although there was no tension, if there had been a confrontation, none of these Ucellan warships were any match for a Los Angeles class submarine.

Also onboard the Tampa were Kureyri, Tixae and, of course Scandie. They would be needed as interpreters, although they would not be going ashore. The Americans had a plan to ensure that no one would be exposed to the virus.

"All right," Captain Albritton said to all of those involved from a briefing room, "we're here off the coast of Ruteni. We all know what to do."

"Aye, Aye, Captain," Linda Flannery confirmed, "I have my agents, or girls, on standby with a radio to translate when we make contact." As this mission called for intelligence gathering, Spy Girl was involved.

"We will do our best to give you a firsthand report, Captain," Sylvia Rizzo added. "The other sailors and I are ready to gear up."

It was decided that Doctor Caldwell should remain on the Tampa as he was the submarine's medical officer. By now, Sylvia Rizzo, although still technically an intern, was really now a doctor herself. She had been exposed and learned a lot since coming to this world. Two other sailors that had some medical experience would accompany Sylvia. As for protection, the three Americans would be wearing radiation suits with a self-contained breathing apparatus. All U.S. navy nuclear submarines had a limited supply of these protective suits.

The Tampa was anchored off in still, deep water. The plan was for Sylvia Rizzo and the two sailors to use a small boat provided by a ship from the North Ucellan navy. They could then paddle ashore to a beach. As it was early morning there was a crowd of people aleady watching from the shore. No doubt they were anticipating some food. A ship from the West Ucellan navy had already sent a large raft ashore with food. They were preparing to launch two more.

As the Americans paddled ashore, a group of about fifty children and three adults watched the strange looking visitors stop the boat on the beach, and then pull it out of the water. To these West Ucellans observing these three figures dressed in their protective suits, that may as well have been aliens. They in fact were. Sylvia had a small radio attached outside her suit on her upper chest. The Americans also had communication devices inside the protective hoods over their heads. This was so they could communicate with the Tampa.

These children remind me of something out of a Charles Dickens novel, Sylvia thought as she surveyed the crowd. "Captain, we're ready." Sylvia said through the radio in her head gear. "Kureyri, inform everyone present that we mean them no harm.' Kureyri did as asked. No one seemed to be alarmed that another voice speaking in Ucellan came from a device from this woman dressed in a strange suit. Perhaps the West Ucellans were in a daze as a result of the Ruteni Influenza.

Kureyri and Tixae took turns speaking through the radio from the Tampa, saying, "Please. No harm will come to you. The people before you need a few volunteers to draw some blood. It won't hurt very much." The two North Ucellan women stated this several times. But it wasn't until some of the children in the group heard a young girl's voice ask the same thing that they took heed. This was none other than Scandie now speaking.

Several children approached Sylvia and the two other sailors. All Sylvia and the other two Americans needed to do was prick a finger of each volunteer and then let a drop or two of blood drip into a small glass vial. After each American did this procedure with three children per person, they knew that they had enough volunteers. The vials were then placed in a medical kit that Sylvia was carrying.

But now the hands-on doctor, wished to get some blood samples from an adult or two present. As they weren't dead, perhaps they had an immunity as well. Tixae translated through the radio to the adults what they needed. Two stepped forward and complied. To Sylvia, the adults looked thin and fatigued, but otherwise fairly healthy. Once they had enogh blood samples, the three Americans needed to get back to the Tampa. Tixae then thanked the children and adults and informed them that a large raft was on its way with food. The West Ucellan navy had just launched another one for its people.

Sylvia Rizzo and the other two crewmen from the Tampa returned to the submarine. In the sickbay-medical lab on the boat, Doctor Caldwell and Sylvia could run tests on the blood samples and begin to look for a vaccine for the Ruteni Influenza. In the meantime, the USS Tampa set a course for another port of call. Where was this next port of call?

"It appears that the Americans and the USS Tampa are making the rounds in this region of Vanag," Rowena stated. The Time Maidens were in the conference-planning room viewing the time scanner. "I would say that this is phase three of their mission involving the Ucellan Islands."

"I wonder what's next?" Michaela asked.

"The planet-time scanner will show us," Lin replied.

The USS Tampa was sailing, once again above the surface of the sea. Its destination was *Gosalia*, the capital of East Ucella. Preparations had been made by the North Ucellans for the arrival of the American submarine. North and East Ucella maintained good relations, with North Ucella usually taking the lead.

As a result of Earth-American technology, it didn't take long for Doctor Caldwell and Sylvia Rizzo to develop a cure or vaccine for the Ruteni Influenza. But how could the vaccine be administered? There simply wasn't enough hypodermic needles on board the Tampa. But once again, good old American know-how would find a way.

What was equivalent to sugar could be found in abundance in East Ucella. How could this help? On planet Earth during the early 20th century the polio epidemic swept the globe. Including the United States. Once a vaccine was developed for polio during the 1950's and early 1960's, a sugar-cube was used to administer the vaccine. Doctor Caldwell and Sylvia Rizzo believed that this same method could be used for the vaccine against the Ruteni Influenza. The Americans would need the help from East Ucella to develop millions of these sugar-cubes, but it could be accomplished.

Many of the crew on the Tampa had met sailors and other merchants from East Ucella. After all, Torama was a port city. Word had spread to this other island nation of a strange-looking vessel and its unique and marvelous crew. Benatta, had telegraphed the leaders in Gosalia, regarding the Americans sailing their way. He advised the East Ucellans to cooperate with these "people from beyond" that could perform great works. And to show North Ucella's support of its new friends, Benatta's wife Kureyri, was traveling with the Americans.

Also onboard the Tampa was Tiffany Ash. Aka Miss Tampa. The beauty queen was more than just a pretty blonde with a great body. Tiffany was a smart young lady that did well in high school and was set to attend the University of South Florida. To everyone's surprise, Tiffany could actually speak the Ucellan language fairly well. How was this possible? Like others from the Tampa, Tiffany had made friends with a small circle of Toraman girls around her own age. Miss Tampa was teaching her new friends English. They in turn were teaching her Ucellan.

Tiffany was becoming quite the business entrepreneur. With her new Toraman friends, she was setting up a small women's clothing factory. As these Toraman girls could all sew, they were designing and making dresses, blouses, slacks and pantsuits. In turn, little dress shops were being opened in several locations in Torama. The young girls and Toraman women were gradually buying these 20th century Earth fashions. It was quite the sight to observe Ucellan women dressed in clothes that resembled the Victorian era one day, and the next day strolling around in 1960's-1980's western style clothes with influence from another world: Earth. This was just the beginning of Tiffany Ash's clothing empire.

Yet, the beauty queen from Tampa also had a caring heart. Tiffany's parents had been involved in many charitable causes in their native city. Tiffany grew up taking part in these charitable events. From history lessons, Tiffany recalled the Cooperative for American Remittances to Europe. (The *CARE* Package Program.) Food and other items were sent overseas in the aftermath of Worl War Two. Tiffany had a plan for something similar in West Ucella.

Upon arriving in the Port of Gosalia, the senior staff of the Tampa had a brief meeting with the new coalition of leaders now representing the government of East Ucella. This six member coalition was much more moderate than the previous military dictatorship that had caused the Ucellan Civil War. The goal of the new regime was to rebuild the economy that had been bankrupted as a result of the war. Along with this, though, the East Ucellans wanted to do all that they could in helping West Ucella. There was a new general national shame throughout East Ucella for causing the civil war and the Ruteni Influenza.

Captain Albritton, along with Doctor Caldwell taking the lead, was taken to a sugar mill. The mill was very 1880's-looking, but sugar-cubes containing the vaccine could easily be produced here. The Americans had calculated that over four million cubes had to be made in order to cure the people of West Ucella. Other sugar mills were also recruited for this operation.

The USS Tampa then departed for Torama, North Ucella. The port was now the submarine's home away from home port. However, over a dozen Americans remained in Gosalia to oversee this vaccine for the Ruteni Influenza. Sylvia Rizzo took the lead.

Miss Tampa and Tim Spivey were part of this group. The beauty queen was organizing groups of East Ucellans to put together *CARE* packages. These consisted of non-perishable foods and hygiene products. As for Sci-Fi Guy, Tim Spivey, he was setting his sights on having his comicbooks available in East Ucella. There were millions of young people in this land that also needed to learn English. Actually, Tim Spivey and Tiffany Ash were starting to take a liking to each other.

As the vaccine sugar-cubes became available, the first ones to take them were Sylvia Rizzo, Tiffany Ash, Tim Spivey and the other Americans with them. They were going to actually go back to West Ucella to help administer the vaccine. Starting in

Ruteni. Some East Ucellan nurses and other volunteers were also vaccinated so as to accompany the Americans. No soldiers, though, from East Ucella would be permitted to go to West Ucella. Too many bad memories from the civil war may still be lingering.

It would take fourteen days for the vaccine to take effect. On day twelve, the Americans and East Ucellans prepared to sail to the western island nation. It would be a two-day journey across the sea by a steamer. On the ship were ten thousand sugar-cubes of the vaccine. Along with the medicine were thousands of *CARE* packages that Miss Tampa had organized for the relief of the West Ucellans. Meanwhile, the sugar-cube vaccine would continue to be produced in East Ucella.

When the Americans and other health care workers landed on the shore outside Ruteni, there was a crowd of West Ucellans. Mostly children. Sylvia Rizzo immediately asked for the East Ucellans that had accompanied her to start dispensing the sugar-cube vaccine. As the cubes resembled some type of food, the children readily took it and swallowed the cubes down. A couple of American sailors had brought containers of fresh water to drink after the cubes had been taken orally. Many of the children drank out of the same cups. But after what the West Ucellans had been through, this was the least of their worries.

Sylvia, along with the American sailors and East Ucellan health care workers, made their way to the actual city. Ruteni was about a half-mile walk. The people on the beach and others began to follow them. The dozen American sailors involved in this operation did have their side arms. So far, there didn't appear to be any danger. The inhabitants of Ruteni were very weak and malnourished. The war and influenza had reduced the West Ucellans to this state.

Once at what used to be a marketplace, Sylvia instructed the health care workers to set up shop. That is the place to dispense more of the vaccine. The Americans sailors assisted in directing the people in an orderly manner as they got in line to take the vaccine. The West Ucellans were told that this medicine would put a stop to this deadly sickness in their land. Before they knew it, this group of people had taken the sugar-cubes containing the vaccine. But others were coming as word had spread about a cure for the pandemic. Sylvia spent the rest of the morning in this Ruteni marketplace.

By now, the East Ucellan health care workers and nurses knew what to do. More sugar-cube vaccines were available and coming from the East Ucellan ship. Moreover, other ships were on the way. The sugar mills back in East Ucella were working nonstop to produce millions of sugar-cubes needed to stop this pandemic once and for all in West Ucella.

Along with the vaccine on this first ship from East Ucella, was Tiffany Ash, Tim Spivey and their East Ucellan volunteers that helped put together the *CARE* packages. The next phase of this operation was to start taking the over two thousand of these *CARE* packages ashore. Like the vaccines, more of these packages would be forthcoming.

Miss Tampa directed this first distribution of the much-needed packages. The packages were being given out one per person for now in a former school not far from the marketplace. Because of her dynamic personality, and the fact that Tiffany was mastering the Ucellan language, the volunteers of this charitable work were eager and willing to keep the *CARE* packages coming.

The Americans had provided a cure for the pandemic and took the lead in organizing the first phase of distributing the vaccine. It was now time for the East Ucellans to take over. The sailors on the ships of the West Ucellan navy would also be available. The vaccine would be given out in all of the major cities and towns of West Ucella. From there, the health care workers could fan out into the rurals and countryside. As remarkable as it seems, in eight months there was no longer any evidence of the Ruteni Influenza.

The time had come though, for Sylvia and the rest of the Americans with her to join their copatriots from the Tampa in Torama, North Ucella. The steamer that had brought them to Ruteni, West Ucella, would take them to this other island nation. While sailing in this Vanagian sea, Sylvia, from the open deck, remarked to her fellow counrtymen, "This sea has a long, strange-sounding name. I'm going to start calling this body of water the *American Sea.*" In a short time this sea would come to be called just that.

"Once again, the Americans saved the day," Cuca remarked at the conclusion of this viewing. "It appears that these people from Earth may be viewed as saviors. At least to the Ucellans."

Especially the West Ucellans," Amaresh confirmed. "Without the vaccine that the American doctors created, West Ucella would have remained under quarantine and in the dark ages."

"What's interesting, and possibly alarming," Rowena added, "is how they changed the name of this Vanagian sea. What else will they and the Russians continue to change?"

Lin concluded by saying, "Well they are now the masters on this new planet for them."

It was the early part of 2 *A.E.* (After Earth.) The Russians had indeed been active on this other planet since coming through the vortex in Antarctica. By now, these Earth people had to conclude that the passing of Halley's Comet had something to do with this vortex. It was still mind boggling for the mostly scientific-minded Russians, or Soviets as they were also called.

Observing the time scanner back in their domain, the Time Maidens continued to do their research regarding the Earth people now on Vanag. "We're now in the second year of this new calendar according to the Russians," Cuca commented. "After Earth, as they call it."

"Yes," Rowena added, "and they are staying busy with their new projects and modernizing this backward land of Zotova."

"This was the beginning of the Russians' first Five Year Plan," Lin stated. "And to their credit they are having more success than the plans in the Soviet Union on Earth."

After gaining control in Tannsisi, and with the destruction of Zelessio by a nuclear cruise missile, opposition from small, renegade gangster armies gradually ceased. Even in the rurals and countryside. The rebel Zotovans were no match for the Russians' well-trained fighting tactics and the ever growing Zotovan army that they had recruited and trained. Not to mention the effectiveness of the huge Zeppelin airships visible from the sky when conquering a major city or town. The mere sight of these gray airships with the large red hammer and sickle was enough to cause the Zotovans on the ground to freeze in either awe or terror. Before too long, city after city surrendered to this new powerful government and army.

Once in control of a city and rural frams, the new Zotovan communists seized all food and took over any industries. Food was then evenly distributed among the population. There had been food shortages throughout Zotova for many years as a result of the gangster warlords that had controlled the land. Still, the Russians and Zotovan communists now in control expected all able-bodied Zotovans to also work and contribute to the new government. The constitution of the USSR stated, Work is the duty of every able-bodied citizen according to the principle: "He who does not work, neither shall he eat."

"*HOLY MOSES,*" Rebecca Canus exclaimed. Justinian and Rebecca were present at this viewing as well. "They took that right out of the Holy Bible. It's from *2 Thessalonians 3:10.* I remember this from Sunday School. This is why we worked so hard on the farms and plantations."

"Interesting," Amaresh added. "A communist, atheist government borrowed from a holy book."

If the people worked, they would have plenty to eat, medical care, education for their children, and eventually decent housing. At present many of the cities across Vanag resembled pre-industrial squalor during the same time period on Earth.

The central government controlled by the Russians in Tannsisi now made all of the decisions for the entire country of Zotova. And Tannsisi's name would change. Henceforth, the city was now *New Moscow.* All industry was to be updated as best as the Russians could accomplish at this time. They had the knowledge of technology from Earth of the 1980's. The Zotovans had the manpower, along with the raw materials. Many still untapped. They just needed a little push and guidance to get up to speed with late 20th century technology. But it could be accomplished.

As for the farms in the countryside, this new Russian-backed communist government of Zotova, followed the Soviet-style collective farms. Once again, everything was controlled by the state or central government. It was a rough start at first. But eventually there were great yields and bumper crops. In a short time, there was plenty of food for Soviet-Zotova.

Issac and Chaya Nimrosensky, as biologists, had brought many seeds of various plants on the Vodyanoy. These seeds of course were to be part of the program to grow food in the future, in secret Soviet bases in Antarctica. Underground chambers with artificial lighting, or greenhouses were to be constructed to grow a variety of food. Hydroponics could also be employed.

The two scientists were now going to institute these same projects on Vanag. They had a limitless supply of Zotovan argricultural workers for the labor involved. At first, the Nimrosenskys had greenhouses constructed outside of New Moscow. In this controlled environment, plants could be safely grown and protected until they could take root in Vanagian soil.

Vanag had its fruits and vegetables. Some similar, others different. After all, this planet was a different world, unique in its own way. The Nimrosenskys had brought over fifteen hundred packets of seeds from many fruits and vegetables and other important plants. Including tobacco.

Protected in greenhouses, all of the plants did well, and would, in turn, produce more plants. With the tobacco plants, it wasn't long, for better or for worse, that the Russians were manufacturing packs of cigarettes in great quanity. There were name brands such as *Orbit, Cosmos, Sputnik* and even *Laika,* after the first dog in space. Laika was already a popular cigarette in the Soviet Union on Earth.

"Oh, my. My little darling, Laika," Rowena stated when seeing this on the time viewer as she patted the little dog on the head. (Laika accompanied the Celtic Time Maiden everywhere she went in the kingdom.) "Now you are popular not only on Earth, but on this other planet as well, thanks to the Russians. But why name this dangerous product after you?" Rowena continued to gently pat Laika's head.

With industry and agriculture being updated, the Russians turned their attention to housing. There had always been a housing shortage in the Soviet Union. The Russians now on Vanag intended to see to it that every Zotovan had a decent place to live. It may be modest, but the Soviet-Zotovans would have a place to call their own.

There were plenty of quarries outside most cities and towns in Zotova. Stones and other materials could be extracted to build homes and other new buildings. This great building project would take place starting in New Moscow and other major cities.

Taking one block at a time, the shantytown dwellings would be demolished. Then well-built apartment buildings would be constructed. Again, with Russian know-how, Zotovan manpower and plenty of resources, these new complexes could be built. The organic materials were also available throughout Zotova to make cement. And throughout most of the interior of this land were plenty of forests with trees to obtain lumber. Then, too, there weren't as many people living in Zotova as there had been in the Soviet Union on Earth. As a consequence of this factor, it would't put a great strain on the resources of Zotova.

Even in the desert area of Zotova, not too far from the wasteland of the former city of Zelessio, there was a plan for more housing. In this region similar to Outer Mongolia, were many caves and underground caverns. Comfortable dwellings could also be carved out to live in as well. These dwellings had a naturally-controlled temperature and environment. These dwellings proved to be very comfortable and luxurious. Mining commuities were established in this region, as there was iron ore, copper and tin deposits to be extracted for industry.

There was no indoor lighting and plumbing as yet, but the Russians were working on that, too. Each city and town would have a Soviet-Zotovan commissar in charge. These officials were all loyal and under the direction of the Russians and New

Moscow. Tefano, the former gangster and crime boss, would in the near future become the first premier or General Secretary of Soviet-Zotova. But he was nothing more than a figurehead while the Russians set up their new, offworld country.

In the meantime, millions of Zotovans had jobs with other benefits. Such as access to food, health care and housing. And many Zotovans were learning to speak Russian while converting over to Mother Zotova and communism. Red banners were visible everywhere promoting these great, scientific-socialist achievements. Even the fantasy character *Red Queen's,* image was highly visible for the benefit of the young people.

Speaking of the real Red Queen, that is Tatiana Semerova, what was her role in all of this? The girl from Archangel traveled by train to various cities where these grand Soviet projects were taking place. By day, Tatiana reported for the new Zotovan news agency Tass based in New Moscow. But at night, she would become Red Queen. Her comicbook creators accompanied her to help promote this character and the many comicbooks being printed. The young Zotovan population that were rapidly learning Russian loved the comics and stories based on Red Queen. And the other comicbooks such as *The Snipers, The Night Witches, Takoda, The Time Traveler,* and other real-life comicbook heroes from the Soviet Union. During the day no one recognized Tatiana as the Tass reporter, as she dressed down. But at night, promoting special events, everyone was in awe of this new mythical beauty. Even Miss Tampa would be impressed.

Two other young, lovely beauties that went on tours and to set up classes for Zotovans to learn Russian, were Svetlana Lebedev and Anastasia Macagonova. Or the Soviet princesess, as the male crew of the Vodyanoy had nicknamed them. If Svetlana ever got back to Earth, her great uncle, a member of the politburo would be proud of her. As these two young ladies were to become schoolteachers, this was a good job for them. And there were plenty of young Russian sailors from the Vodyanoy, along with young Zotovan men that had their eye on both Svetlana and Anastasia.

On the other side of the vast land of Zotova, to the west of new Moscow, was the second largest city. This was *Klarus.* This city also became a beehive of activity for the new country. Klarus was remamed *New Leningrad.* In one of the updated factories, doll-like or a type of action figure began to be manufactured. The figures were five inches tall. These, of course, were the comicbook characters. Red Queen was the most popular.

The Vanagians were just beginning to understand how to make plastic. These early action figures were made mostly of wood, but with a very detailed porcelain face of the character. Hundreds of women were employed to make these action figures and hand-crafted clothes. The factory could barely keep up with the demand of this new novelty for Zotovan children.

Also in New Moscow and New Leningrad, the Russians set up what was known as the *Young Pioneers.* This was the organization in the Soviet Union to indoctrinate the young people to communism. Most of the crew on the Vodyanoy had been Young Pioneers. Overnight, hundreds of thousands of Zotovan youths appeared in black and white uniforms, along with red handkerchiefs and a pin with the face of Vladimir Lenin. Even more factories were busy making all of these uniforms and accessories.

As to be expected in every city and town, Valeria Rostova and Kikimora sent in their white-bloused and black-skirted girls. A Zotovan *KGB* office was set up. Once again, these young women would be the eyes and ears for this new version of the *KGB.* There were even a few young men in the spy agency, but the women made up the majority of agents. Valeria and Kikimora trusted the women more than the men. These young women proved to be very effective. Under communism, men and women were equals. This hadn't been the case in Zotova before the Russians came to this land and world.

"We know that the hammer is a symbol of the Soviet Union, and stands for the industrial worker," Michaela remarked. "And the Russians are gradually controlling everything related to industry."

"And as for the sickle," Amaresh spoke up, saying, "It represents the peasants or agricultural working class. All of the farms in Zotova will be under the control of New Moscow, or should we say the Russians."

"And how about these huge posters and banners everywhere," Rowena added. "Not to mention the Zotovan youth as Young Pioneers."

"One thing is different though with this new Soviet Union on Vanag," Lin observed. "On Earth, the Soviet Union had a hard time getting established. After the 1917 Bolshevik Revolution, Russia was plagued by civil war, famine, and World War Two, followed by the Cold War. The expensive arms race with their rival, the United States, bankrupted the Soviets. However, socialism in this new country of Zotova appears to be working, as there have been very few obstacles."

"The people of Zotova really do believe that with this new government, they are living in a socialist paradise." Amaresh went on to add.

"So here we are again," Cuca said. "Americans and Russians from Earth, now on another planet in another galaxy. What a paradox."

"Let's not forget this comicbook character, Red Queen, or should we say Tatiana Semerova." Michaela stated while shaking her head. "Vanag's first action figure."

"Oh, I don't know, Israelite Girl," Rowena acknowledged, "I find this concept very interesting. In fact, I think that there should be dolls and action figures of all of us Time Maidens. On both Earth and Vanag." Rowena had a twinkle in her eyes as she looked at Michaela.

"GOOD GOLIATH, Rowena," Michaela replied. "That's the last thing we need." The other three Time Maidens chuckled. Rowena was once again poking fun at Michaela.

For this next viewing, the Time Maidens and assistants went to Lin's palace. After a meal, they all went to a lounging room where a large video screen was available to view what the planet-time scanner satellite orbiting Vanag could project back to the kingdom. The domain of the Time Maidens.

"Let's see what the Americans are up to again," Lin stated. "No doubt they will continue to make an impact on the Ucellans." The Time Maidens programmed the time scanner for the year 2 A.E. It was already the third month into this year.

"I have to admit that all of this research is getting very exciting," Rowena said. "But also quite alarming."

Redan was back from his voyage to both Trozny and Zotova. His sister Tixae was waiting at the dock where his ship would now begin to unload the goods that had been bought or traded in these other foreign ports. The North Ucellan merchant sailors were unloading the goods just as the sun came up. Redan helped for awhile, but then ceased when he saw his sister and another woman waiting for him. Another woman!

Linda Flannery was also there with Tixae. Spy Girl was dying to know if Redan had brought back any information for her. *Was he successful?* Linda thought. *Did Redan confirm if a Russian submarine was really on this planet? Better yet, did Redan take a picture?* Linda was anxious to say the least.

As he approached the two women on the dock, Redan naturally hugged his sister and gave her a kiss on the cheek. He likewise did the same with Linda. But Redan actually gave her a kiss closer to her mouth. Spy Girl was a bit surprised, yet she enjoyed the embrace and light kiss. "I have pictures for you," Redan said in broken English. He didn't know much of this new language to the Ucellans, but knew "picture" was very important.

The small house where Linda's office was located was nearby. When Tixae asked her brother whether he wished to go home first, he shook his head as if to say no. Linda, Tixae and Redan, carrying his two duffle bags, then made their way to the office.

Once inside Linda Flannery's humble intelligence agency office, Redan put his bags down and opened one. Buried deep under clothes and other items, Redan first presented the poloroid camera that belonged to Linda. Then, Redan took out four pictures that he had concealed in a book. The top picture was the one of Linda that had been taken of her over three months ago. Redan really treasured this picture of the American woman from Earth.

But what of these other pictures? When Redan handed them to Spy Girl, she studied them with a wide-open mouth and big eyes. *"I KNEW IT!"* Linda exclaimed. The painting of that submarine couldn't have been a coincidence. Like us, the Russians are also here on this planet. But how?" By now, Tixae was pretty good with her English and could comprehend what Linda was saying. However, Redan couldn't really understand much. Nevertheless, he was pleased that Linda appeared to be happy with the photos that he had brought her.

Two of the pictures did indeed reveal a submarine. It wasn't a close-up shot, as Redan had to take the photo from the cargo ship he was on. And he had to take the picture without anyone on his ship seeing him do this. No one would know what a camera was. In one of the pictures, Redan attempted to focus just on the conning tower of the boat. This was where a large, red star was visible. For being an amateur, Redan did remarkably well with the camera.

The third picture, though, was both interesting and mysterious. Once ashore on the docks, in Tannsisi-New Moscow, Redan, hiding between some crates to be loaded onto other ships, saw something interesting. A young, attractive woman with brown hair was being escorted by sailors in strange uniforms. That is, strange to Redan. Spy Girl recognized right away that these were Soviet sailors. No doubt from the submarine.

But who was this woman? It wasn't the same woman from the other painting that originated in the Port of Tellovaci. The woman in that painting was Valeria Rostova. Spy Girl had both the paintings of the submarine and the first mystery woman in her office.

"Great Samhain," Rowena spoke up," this picture that this Ucellan sailor took is none other than Kikimora."

"It sure is," Michaela affirmed.

"The Americans have no idea who these women are on the other side of this world," Cuca added.

"This is all unbelievable," Amaresh now said.

"And the Russians have no knowledge of the Americans," Lin concluded. "But this is all going to change in the near future."

The Time Maidens, for now, decided to fast-forward on the time scanner and see what the next plan of the Americans for the Ucellan Islands involved. For the time being, Linda Flannery told Redan and his sister to return home to see their parents. Along with the pictures of the submarine and another mysterious woman that appeared to be in charge of several Soviet sailors, were some other interesting items that Redan brought back. These included pamphlets, a four-page newspaper and, of all things, a comicbook. All in what appeared to be written in the Russian language. But more about that later.

Unknown to the Americans, the Russians on the other side of this world had already begun a full-scale modernization program in their sphere of influence. The Americans also had a plan to provide better housing for the Ucellans and bring industries up to date. As the Russians were finding out, these projects could be daunting, yet possible. And like the Zotovans, the Ucellans were eager to take part in improving their lives and culture under the direction of the people from another world. The Americans called these programs and projects, *OPERATION JUMP-START.*

As noted earlier, many cities in the Ucellan Islands were made up of buildings that were business centers. Most of these buildings were not very safe. Outside these business centers were marketplaces where goods were bought, sold or traded. The majority of the population lived in a type of housing for workers, or row homes. Depending on the size of the city, there were miles and miles of these structures. Although made from a type of brick, these row homes were dark and damp. There was no indoor lighting or plumbing. The Americans intended on changing that.

The Vanagians of the northern hemisphere also burned coal. Buring coal made the cities dark, sooty and very unhealthy for the inhabitants. Many cities on Earth still burned coal even in the 1980's. However, the leaders and people realized that a safer and cleaner form of energy was needed. The Earth was gradually finding alternative energy sources. North Ucella had a good number of coal mines. And the North Pole of Vanag had rich deposits of both coal and oil. Both of these resources would still have their place on Vanag. Many products could be made from oil.

There were very few stand-alone houses in the Ucellan Islands. And only the rich and powerful owned one. And these so-called stately homes were nearly one hundred years behind Earth. Even so, the new American planners intended to change that as well.

After World War Two, and with the emergence of what came to be called the Baby Boomers generation, the United States of America changed drastically in many ways. One of these changes involved housing. Suburbia America was born. Families should be entitled to their own home. Subdivisions began to spring up all across America during the late 1940's and into the 1960's. The same could be accomplished here outside every Ucellan city and town. But how?

The young Americans on the USS Tampa were a very energetic group. Being young, they were full of zeal and ideas. Captain Albritton and the other executive officers were already amazed at the results of some of the contributions of the young people to this new world. Linda Flannery, Miss Tampa, Sci-Fi Guy and Robert Newell, to name a few. And there would be more. Perhaps this was a diversion from thinking too much about Earth. Many still thought or dreamed about going home. But in the meantime, the senior staff agreed that it was best to keep the crew busy.

Two very innovative members of the crew were Lee Graver and Steve Litten. Lee was twenty-one years old and was born in Yreka, California, a small town near the Oregon state border. Lee's parents were hippies and pretty much lived off the land. His mother taught kindergarten at the local school. His father was a handyman, but also quite the builder and inventor.

Lee's father built their house and made it solar-powered way before this means of energy caught on. Mr. Graver also constructed a windmill that provided most of the power for several generators. Thus, the Graver household had their own electricity. Lee of course picked up his father's talents and inventive mind.

Like many of the crew on the Tampa, Lee joined the U.S. Navy, so that after his four yeas of duty were up, he could use the G.I. Bill and further his education. Lee wanted to become a builder and architect. Seaman Recruit Graver, which was Lee's rank in the navy, made friends with North Ucellan carpenters and builders in Torama. Some of these tradesmen of Lee's age were picking up the English language at remarkable speed. The comicbooks and movies still being featured at the dock contributed to this.

Lee first constructed a small model of what a solar-powered house would look like. The model had the features down to the last detail. Lee's plan was to start an industry of prefabricated homes, or simply prefabs. The boy from northern California called this soon-to-be company *Renee Industries*, named after his mother's first name.

Lee took his model to Captain Albritton and the two Lt. Commanders. After explaining everything about this future home, the captain said, "Very impressive, Seaman Graver."

"But can you actually build a real structure like this, with what's available on this planet?" Lt. Buchanan had to ask.

"Yes, Sir," the seaman replied. Lee then began to explain that everything needed to build these prefab homes could indeed be found on this planet, from plenty of wood to glass for the solar panels on the roof. True, the Americans would have to improvise on some materials, but they could nevertheless build inexpensive, comfortable homes for themselves and Ucellans. There was also plenty of ore in both North and West Ucella to extract and produce aluminum. Concrete could also be obtained.

The next phase of Renee Industries was to build an actual prototype of a prefab solar-powered home. Lee with his new Toraman friends, set out to do just that. A few obstacles aside, this new type of home on Vanag was completed. Both Lee's fellow Americans and North Ucellans were in awe of it. This prefab home actually had indoor plumbing with toilets and a shower. There was even a twenty-foot windmill with this house that could pump up water from a nearby lake and provide electricity from a solar battery. This young seaman had learned a lot from his father.

Captain Albritton gave Lee the green light to start building more of these prefab energy-efficent homes. Renee Industries, a joint American-Ucellan company was founded. "One could say that this was a joint Earth-Vanag alien company," Cuca had to state during the viewing.

Hundreds of North Ucellan workers were employed. Later, Ucellan men and women from the other two main Ucellan Islands would join this work force. In addition, Tiffany Ash had founded her clothing line business with young Toraman women. The housing and light industry business on Vanag was rapidly changing and being brought up to speed. With American backing, other industries would follow. Including the military.

"GOOD GOLIATH," Michaela exclaimed as she jumped up from her seat during this part of the viewing. "The military. I just knew it. Just like the Russians in Zotova." The other four Time Maidens simply reacted by raising one hand and then slowly lowering it down, as if to say to the Hebrew Time Maiden, *Calm down. Let's finish this part of the viewing.*

Similar to what the Russians were doing on their side of the world, Lee Graver, with a few other Americans who had construction skills, set up to train a group of North Ucellans as tradesmen and laborers. They in turn would train others. Renee Industries concentrated on one block at a time in Torama. Most of the rowhomes were demolished. The workers would save and use what was worth using again for the new housing. Families, of course, were placed in temporary housing, namely tents. But the prefab homes were being constructed at a fast pace. And well-built at that.

There was plenty of lumber from trees in North Ucella alone. Not to mention in forests on smaller islands off the coast of this large island nation. With the exception of a few hermits or nomads, these islands were fairly uninhabited. Many of the trees on Vanag were similar to cedar, pine and oak trees found on Earth. In a way, Vanag was Earth's twin, or Planet B, as astrophysicsts from Earth would later call another Earth-like world.

Regarding these trees, though, Lee, being raised by environmentalist parents, had a strict policy enforced. For every tree cut down, anywhere, a new one had to be planted to take its place. This new housing bonanza started in Torama where the Americans were still based. But the plan was to build houses for the Ucellans on all three islands. Almost simultaneously, when this building boom started in Torama, Renee Industries went westward to the other side of North Ucella. This was the other important port city of Cakovica. Suburbia Ucella was born.

While setting up operations in Cakovica, Lee was approached by a local builder. That is, a builder that constructed the famous Ucellan rowhomes. This North Ucellan wanted in on the action of this new building boom. He told the young American sailor that, if he could be a part of this new building program, that he would give his oldest daughter to him. Lee didn't even have to marry her. She was simply his for the taking. It was if the girl was just an object or piece of property.

Well now, when a translator explained to Lee what the builder offered him he replied, *"WHAT!"* The thought of this shocked the young American. Due to their cultural and religious belifs, the Vanagians had different morals. This was the way of life on Vanag. Lee informed the builder that there was plenty of work for all. After all, Renee Industries wasn't going to be building just houses, but had other projects on the drawing board as well.

Meanwhile, when Lee finally did see and meet this young lady from Cakovica, she caught his eye to put it mildly. Her name was Leilani. She was about the same age as Lee, and was a typical North Ucellan girl. Long blonde hair and legs, along with unique, aqua-blue eyes. Leilani was a real beauty. And was an excellent artist. Lee hired Leilani and put her to work drawing houses and other types of future buildings. Lee could have just taken Leilani, but decided for now to just court her while she worked for the company and started learning English.

The three main Ucellan Islands were in the perimeter of a great sea. After Doctor Sylvia Rizzo changed the name of this Vanagian sea to the *American Sea,* the name was official. The

American Sea had strong winds similar to the North Sea and Sea of Japan on Earth. And these winds could be harnessed. In what way? Again, Lee Graver had the answer: Windmills. Or better yet, solarmills.

Windmills had been used to pump water and provide energy on Earth for centuries. For whatever reason, the Vanagians had never invented windmills. Lee had helped his father build a windmill to provide energy for this home. Renee Industries was about to branch off into another direction: Constructing windmills for the new subdivisions and building much larger ones for the coastlines of the Ucellan Islands. The continuous strong winds from the American Sea would work well to harness this energy.

Wind Farms were constructed all throughout the Ucellan Islands. In the beginning, these mammoth structures were made of wood, including the large windmill vanes. Eventually, though, the windmills would be constructed of steel and aluminum as existing Ucellan industries could be brought up-to-date to produce these new materials. And with the help from the Americans, many industries did indeed receive a jump-start. And new industries came into being.

The other inspiring young sailor that the Time Maidens focused on during this viewing was Steve Litten. Steve is the electronics expert. He was one of those nerdy kids that grew up making radios out of cigar boxes. Although Steve wasn't old enough to be a journeyman electrician, he did attend a trade high school in his native Indiana and took every electronics course available. Steve was also the lead seamen onboard the Tampa when it came to electrical and electronic matters.

The field of electronics was still a theory on Vanag at this present time. So, with Steve taking the lead in this field, the Americans would have to start from scratch. But the materials were there on this planet, and the existing industries could be adapted to make and produce electricity. And recall, the so-called

Baghad Battery on Earth was about two thousand years old. This ancient battery was made up of three components: A ceramic pot, a tube of copper, and a rod of iron. Steve had even more than that to start with. With this in mind, though, Steve Litten called his new American-Ucellan company on Vanag, *Baghad Electronics.*

Before too long, between the windmills generating hydro-electric power along with Baghad Electronics, all of the new houses and buildings on the Ucellan Islands would have electricity. Not to be overlooked were the many young Ucellans that were eager to work and learn about this new technology. At least new for them. Many of these great minds also contributed to bringing this part of the world up to speed with 20th century Earth. The Ucellans just needed a little jump-start from the Americans, and they got it.

Comparable to Tatiana Semorova-Red Queen, in Soviet Zotova, the American journalist Terri Eden was covering all of these changes on the Ucellan Islands and writing about them. *This will make a great story, or even book when I get back to Earth,* Terri thought. *Once again if we get back to Earth.* Tatiana helped found the Zotovan Tass and Pravda news outlets. Under the direction of Captain Albritton, Terri set up an English language American-Ucellan newspaper. For the time being, the newspaper was called *The Toraman Times.* Because the three Ucellan Islands had a primitive telegraph service, the newspaper had an office on the other two island countries. Under Terri's oversight, a number of Ucellans that had mastered the English language worked and reported for this newspaper. *I've gone from reporter to editor on this world,* Terri again thought. *Anything is possible on this new planet.*

"Dear me," Amaresh stated, "Events are transpiring so rapidly on this world."

"I'll say," Cuca confirmed. "But with this outside influence from Earth, that is with help from the Americans and Russians, should we be surprised?"

"I sure would love to make a time-jump at this time period in the Ucellan Islands," Rowena said. "If anything, just to be an observer and have boots on the ground as it were."

"We can observe everything we need to know from the time scanner, Rowena," Michaela added. "And certainly a lot safer."

"I don't know, Michaela," Rowena replied. "Sooner or later, if we are going to keep studying this world, we will be planning and making time-jumps."

"About the only two Time Maidens that could safely blend in on a time-jump, Rowena, "Lin now said, "Would be you and Michaela. An Asian race doesn't exist on this world. That pretty much leaves me out. And there is no nationality even remotely similar to Cuca's people. Amaresh could possibly blend in to be a black, African-American woman. But I wouldn't recommend it. At least not in this early stage of Earth influence."

"Well, then," Rowena responded as she looked directy at the Hebrew Time Maiden. "perhaps Michaela and myself had better start planning a time-jump." Michaela felt uneasy, as Rowena displayed a serious and determined look on her face.

"But back to these developments with the Americans on Vanag," Amaresh said, "It appears to me that with this start, technology on this world is going to jump by leaps and bounds every five years."

"And they haven't even reached the first five years," Cuca affirmed.

"Very true, my sisters," Lin concluded. "Look what took place and how life changed on Earth from the years 1900 to 2000 A.D. It's still hard to comprehend how from the first airplane flight by the Wright brothers to man landing on the moon took place within only sixty six years."

It was now year 3 A.E. With both the Russians in Zotova and the Americans in the Ucellan Islands jumpstarting Vanagian technology, life was rapidly changing on this world.

"I don't believe what I think is going to happen next for the Ucellans," Michaela commented from the conference-planning room in the kingdom. Now that they were somewhat involved with this other planet, the Time Maidens just had to learn more. One must remember that time moved slower for the Time Maidens in their domain. For this reason, they could take time away from their own missions on Earth.

"Neither the Americans nor the Russians are going to sit still on this world," Rowena added. "And yet, with the exception of Linda Flannery's little spy agency, neither side really knows that their former Earth rival is even here."

As Operation Jump-Start continued to update Ucellan industry and technology, the Americans had another plan for the Ucellan Islands. Or at least the senior staff on the Tampa. Captain Albritton had been discussing this new plan with his fellow officers and chiefs. What was the plan?

Although the three large islands in this part of the world were made up of the same people and language, they were still three separate nations. The plan, or at least the suggestion, was to unite the three islands under one country or government. Since coming by accident to Vanag, the USS Tampa had been involved in dealings with all three of the Ucellan Islands.

First the Americans sailed into Torama, North Ucella. Unlike the Russians in Tannsisi, Zotova, the Americans were able to avoid a confrontation with the Ucellans. They then got in good with Benatta, the current leader of North Ucella, and his lovely wife, Kureyri. Doctors Caldwell and Rizzo had saved their daughter, Messina, from certain death.

This was followed by developing a vaccine for the deadly Ruteni Influenza in West Ucella. In order to manfacture the vaccine, the Americans enlisted the aid of the people of East Ucella who again, felt partially responsible for being the cause of this deadly pandemic.

By now, the Americans had a relationship with all three of the Ucellan Islands. They felt that the this was the time to recommend to the leaders to unite under one country. For one, West Ucella was virtually leaderless after a civil war with East Ucella and the Ruteni Influenza. As for East Ucella, a new moderate government was now in control. And North Ucella, the largest of the islands, wanted to have the Americans as an ally.

"Well ladies and gentlemen," Captain Albritton asked from a conference room on the Tampa, "Do we all agree then that we should go forward with the plan to unite these three island nations?" Lt. Commanders Cordova and Buchanan were present along with Doctor Caldwell and Sylvia Rizzo. They both held the rank of Lt. Commander as well. The two chiefs were also present.

"Captain," Lieutenant Buchanan, replied. "Just what kind of government are we attempting to set up here in this part of the world?"

"The only one that we know best, Lieutenant," the captain answered. "A democracy for the good, but not always perfect, democracy like our United States of America." No one could really dispute that the Ucellan Islands needed a single, strong central government. Especially East and West Ucella. And why not model this new government for these large island nations after their own American government.

Captain Albritton then began to explain to the others how they should proceed with this new Ucellan government. The captain had asked the journalist, Terri Eden, to join in this discussion. She was encouraged to take notes. The Toraman Times would be reporting on this possible new government. The newspaper would be published in both Ucellan and English. And more and more Ucellans were learning English.

Captain Albritton had also enlisted help from others on the Tampa. One was Christina Salter from Lincoln, Nebraska. Along with Linda Flannery, Christina was the other white girl that was part of the U.S. Navy's experiment of allowing women to be part of a nuclear submarine crew. She was barely out of high school when she joined the navy. Nevertheless, Christina came from a very political family and knew a lot about American history.

The other young woman that the captain enlisted was Cindy Henderson from Oklahoma. Cindy was the government intern that was the senator's aide from her state. The Time Maidens already knew that Cindy was not in the navy and was only allowed on the USS Tampa because of the senator's connections. As noted before regarding Cindy, when first coming aboard this new Los Angeles class submarine, she looked like a "Plain Jane." But once coming through the vortex to Vanag, and now having lived for almost three years in North Ucella, her appearance and farm girl personality began to change. The blonde-haired, blue-eyed Oklahoman started to dress and act in a provocative manner. Even most of the male crew of the Tampa that gave the nickname "Plain Jane," were shocked at this change.

This new government for the Ucellans was also an experiment at best. No one knew for certain if a democracy would work for these "alien people," but this was all the Americans had to offer. The Ucellans seemed like they wanted to be led, and the Americans were willing to take them by the hand for now. Besides, the senior staff of the Tampa thought that the more the young crew and others were involved with this world, the less that they would be thinking about getting back to Earth.

As Christina Salter and now Cindy Henderson were both attractive women, Captain Albritton had several young submariners accompany them in their new assignments. Some of these young men were also interested in spreading the word about American democracy.

The first means that were used were pamphlets. Tens of thousands were printed. Christina and Cindy quickly learned that there were quite a number of Ucellan volunteers that wished to take part in distributing this new information. Like the Toraman newspaper, one side of the message was written in Ucellan, and the other side in English. The pamphlet explained some brief points on how a democracy worked.

Steve Litten, the electronics expert, was able to set up a somewhat primitive radio station in Torama, North Ucella, Gosalia, East Ucella and Ruteni, West Ucella. For now, all that Steve could do was set up several large homemade speakers and little stations in the main town squares. However, hundreds, then a thousand or two, gathered around the town squares to hear the American broadcast in both languages. Christina and Cindy employed both male and female young Ucellans to present these broadcast.

The more the Ucellans were involved the better. Ultimately, this was all about their new government. It didn't take long for the pamphlets to reach every city and major town of the Ucellan Islands. Classes were even set up in the capital cities for Ucellans to learn more about a democratic government. Christina, Cindy and some of the crew of the Tampa taught these crash program classes.

The U.S. Constitution states that the U.S. Senate be made up of two senators from each state. At least for the senate on Earth. On Vanag, in Ucella, there would be more senators to represent each of the three islands. The Americans reasoned that six from each island would be necessary for the government to function properly. The same would hold true for a congress. The senate and congress would be made up of an equal number of both men and women. A small senate and congress compared to the one in the real United States, but this one for the Ucellans would suffice for now.

But now for a president. How would these Ucellan leaders be elected? The Ucellans were too new to properly understand the American election process. For this first and only time, the Americans would appoint a president and the members that would make up the senate and congress. Like in the United States, the president, would only serve for two four-year terms. Elections for the senate and congress would take place every six years.

Hopefully, by the time of the next presidential election in four years, the Ucellans would understand the election process better. The same for congress and the senate in six years. And this would also mean that the president and other officials would have to learn how to campaign. Again, the Americans would teach them how to do this.

For the first Ucellan president, the Americans unanimously appointed Benatta, the current leader of North Ucella. At least for this first four-year term. Kureyri, of course, would be the First Lady. By now, the English of Benatta, Kureyri, and their daughter, Messina was quite good. The Americans chose Benatta as the first president, as they knew this Toraman the best. He was the first leader the Americans encountered when coming to this world. And of the three Ucellan Islands, North Ucella was the most stable and powerful.

Once the wheels were set in motion in this region of the world, other changes began to transpire very rapidly. More name changes were in order. It was Doctor Sylvia Rizzo that renamed the strange-sounding name of the sea in which the three Ucellan Islands were located. It was now officially known as the *American Sea.*

Torama, the capital of North Ucella, was renamed *Great Columbia.* Columbia is the poetic name of the United States, in the feminine form. As in Washington, D.C. (The District of

Columbia.) Construction immediately commenced on an actual White House and Capital Building. These buildings weren't as large as the ones in America on Earth, but the design and interior were the same. Starting with Benatta, all Ucellan presidents would live and work in this White House. The Ucellan senate and congress would meet and pass laws in the Capital Building.

Gosalia, East Ucella, would also have a name change. As Christina Salter was so instrumental in setting up this new form of government for the Ucellans, she came up with the new name. Christina, being from Lincoln, Nebraska, suggested that Gosalia now be called *New Lincoln*. And in keeping with American names, Abraham Lincoln was the 16th president of the United States. The name was accepted by the East Ucellans.

As a result of the Ucellan Civil War and the Ruteni Influenza, the capital of West Ucella definitely was in need of a new name. A dark shadow hung over the city of Ruteni in more ways than one. Several names were suggested. Los Angeles II, Liberty and even New Tampa, in honor of the American city in Florida, and the name of the powerful submarine now on Vanag. However, none of these names were adopted. The new name would be chosen later. But for the time being, Ruteni and other Ucellan cities were undergoing a massive rebuilding and modernization process.

Similar to the United States, more than one political party needed to be established. The Americans came up with some new names for the political parties of Ucella. The crew of the USS Tampa was mostly made up of Democrats and Republicans. But with a few from the Independent Party.

One party was known as the *Ucellan National Party. (UNP.)* The party was very similar to the *GOP*, or Republican Party. Another was the *Democratic Party of Ucella. (DPU.)* As part of the name implies, it was modeled after the U.S. Democratic Party. The third was the *United Ucellan* Party. *(UUP.)* The Independents on the Tampa set up this party after the American

Independent Party. Other parties could come later as long as they followed the now new Ucellan Constitution.

At present none of the Americans would join these new American-inspired parties for the Ucellans. After studying and being tutored in all three political parties, President Benatta chose to be in the Ucellan National Party. As more and more Ucellans learned about these political parties, they, too could choose what one to join. Or even change affiliations at any time if they so desired. Many Ucellans, eighteen years or older were excited to have three parties to choose from. This was all new for Ucellans on the planet Vanag. Zotova was strictly a one-party communist state.

What about a flag for this new democracy? Comparable to the flag of the United States of America, the flag of Ucella would also be red, white, and blue. There were fifty states that made up the United States. However, there were only three large islands making up this new Ucella. North, East and West Ucella. On the American flag the stars were white. Thus, on the flag of Ucella would be three large white stars. These would be positioned on the top left section of the flag. The same place where the fifty stars could be found on the American flag. The thirteen red and white stripes on the Ucellan flag were identical and in the same place as the American flag. This Ucellan flag looked pretty much the same as the flag of the United States, except for the three large, white stars, instead of the fifty smaller ones.

Situated around each of the three main Ucellan Islands, were quite a few smaller islands and atolls. As noted before, some of these islands were inhabited by hermits and nomads. And many of these islands were made up of lush forests with a variety of fruits and animal life. A few primitive fishing villages were located on some of these islands. The people that lived on these islands appeared to be even more backward than the urban Ucellans. At least to the Americans.

Of the larger islands, future cities, industries and fishing centers could be incorporated. Yes, according to the Americans, the capitalist system had great potential in this region of Vanag. One larger island in the middle of the American Sea had great future possibilties. All of these islands, large or small, would be a part of this new "one' Ucella. No longer would there be three. At least as far as the political system was concerned.

"Well, now," Michaela stated at the end of this viewing, "like the Russians, the Americans are definitely getting a piece of the pie. At least in the region they now control."

"And in a relatively short time," Rowena added. "I've never seen anything like this."

"Yes," the Americans are creating another United States on Vanag," Lin concluded. "This is the birth of the United Islands of Ucella. Or *UIU*."

The appearance of a comet on two separate worlds at the same time, that caused them to be sucked through a vortex into a distant galaxy onto an Earth-like planet is what happened to a group of Americans and Russians. The humanoid inhabitants of this strange world one hundred years behind Earth were similar to earthlings, yet different in many ways.

It has now been over four-years since this disruptive event took place involving these people of Earth from two different, opposing nations and militaries. And both in two powerful nuclear submarines now on an alien world.

Naturally, most of the Americans and Russians longed to return to their homeworld. They may have all been busy with their duties and new assignment, but even silently they would think about Earth from time to time. In the meantime, many reasoned that they may as well make the best of these new circumstances. This included being in love.

"Isn't there a saying, 'love is in the air?' Cuca asked as she and the other Time Maidens viewed this next occurrence on Vanag.

"I believe there are many phrases, poems and songs regarding 'love is in the air," Rowena pointed out. "And it appears to be in the air on Vanag at present with some very interesting people."

"The Americans and Russians may not be Vanagians," Michaela added, "but they are humanoids, and so are the Vanagians."

"Not to mention," Amaresh stated, "that love is a necessary and powerful emotion. And most of these Earth people are very young."

"Well," Rowena also said. "it will certainly be interesting to see who the Americans and Russians will pair off with. Will it be their own people, or Vanagians?"

"Vanagians will certainly come into the equation," Lin concluded, "as there are very few women from Earth to choose from."

The majority of the crew were under thirty years of age. What would happen with this powerful emotion on the planet Vanag? Especially now, that a similar, yet alien, race existed on this world. The aliens being the Americans and Russians.

The USS Tampa and the Vodyanoy would normally be made up of an all-male crew. However, as a result of a pilot program involving the Tampa, and a secret, unusual mission with the Vodyanoy, a small number of females were on these submarines. And now, here they were on an alien planet with quite a number of male submariners from their respective nations.

On the Tampa were six young female sailors, along with a journalist, doctor and marine biologist. Then there was a Miss Tampa, a beauty queen and a government intern. And all fairly attractive.

As for the Vodyanoy, it, too, had its share of young girls and women. Starting with the stern, yet striking, political officer Valeria Rostova. A bit older, yet not bad-looking, was Doctor Yelena Ivanova. Also a biologist like her husband was Chaya Nimrosensky. Tatiana Semerova, or Red Queen, was the reporter from Tass who was also secretly onboard the Vodyanoy. The last two young women on the submarine were the two Muscovite college girls, Svetlana Lebedev and Anastasia Macagonova. Although not from Earth or Russian, two Troznyan girls also became a part of the crew on the Vodyanoy. This of course were none other than Kikomora and Baba Yaga.

It would make sense that the American women onboard the Tampa, would marry one of the many U.S. navy sailors. And for the most part they would. But some would fall in love with Vanagians. The same with the Russians. In fact, the majority of the Russian submariners would find Zotovan or Troznyan women as wives.

Starting with the Americans that got married were the following: Lt. Commander Cordova had become close to the new doctor on the Tampa. Namely, Sylvia Rizzo. The other Lt. Commander, Jeff Buchanan, married the marine biologist, Brenda Hutt. Recall that the crew had given Brenda the nickname Miss Vampire or Morticia, because of her long, dark hair and white complexion. But this couple seemed to click and go well together. As Captain of the USS Tampa, Captain Albritton could perform marriages, and did so with quite a few from the crew.

Terri Eden, the cute redheaded journalist, ended up falling in love with Chief Petty Officer Douglas Mathis. The petty officer was ten years older than Terri, but she felt close and safe with him. Perhaps this was the man she needed on this alien world.

Doctor Larry Caldwell, the Tampa's main doctor, would eventually take an East Ucellan woman as a wife. Her name was Aneese. She was what would be considered a healer, or doctor, on Vanag. Like everything else on Vanag, medicine was over a hundred years behind Earth. But along with love and marriage, this was a good match. A 20th century doctor from Earth, teaching and bringing up to speed an Ucellan-Vanagian medical woman.

The second Chief Petty Officer, that is Thomas Prescott, would end up marrying a North Ucellan woman named Zea. She was from Torama/Great Columbia, and the sister of Kureyri, now the first lady of the *UIU*. In this early time period of American-Ucellan relations, the inner circle of the two nationalties was still small and limited. Thus, the Americans and Ucellans were just beginning to intermingle with each other. But this would gradually change with Earth people and Vanagians.

But what about the enlisted men and women from the Tampa? And the other two young civilian girls? Being Miss Tampa and Cynthia Henderson. Sometimes opposites attract. This was the case of Miss Tampa and Sci-Fi Guy, aka Tim Spivey. Tiffany Ash, wearing the crown of Miss Tampa, was a socialite from the start. Yet, her track record already on Vanag revealed that she was not only beautiful, but brillant. Tiffany knew a lot about Earth history and proved to be a smart business woman.

Tiffany Ash's clothing company was an ever-growing business. She named it *San Fernando Manufacturing.* This had no connection with the San Fernando Valley in California, USA. San Fernando was the original Spanish name of what became Tiffany's native city. And the Tampa Bay area.

Tiffany was not really a big fan of science fiction or comicbooks. Although Miss Tampa and many others probably felt as if they were in a science-fiction movie. Especially, after having been transported to this alien world. Except this was not a movie but reality. As for comicbooks, Tiffany did have to admit that Tim Spivey and the other comicbook guy, Robert Newell, proved to be brillant in using comicbooks to teach the Ucellan youth English. Tiffany still marveled at how the comicbook concepts took root and rapidly worked in getting the English language out there in this alien culture.

Who knows if a relationship back on Earth would have worked for Miss Tampa and Sci-Fi Guy? But here on Vanag, it was working for Tiffany and Tim. As everyone thought that they were the perfect match, the Florida girl and Ohio boy got married. As Tiffany Ash had been influential in guiding the East Ucellans regarding the American political system, she had spent a lot of time on this Ucellan island.

As the main Ucellan currency had been coverted to U.S. dollars, Tiffany, with her clothing manfacturing company, and

Tim, with his comicbooks, had accumlated a lot of money. American-type banks were also now functioning in the *UIU.* Tiffany desired to build an exact duplicate of her parents' house, which was an old colonial-style home on Bayshore Boulevard in Tampa. This was a very influential area of mostly wealthy people, like Tiffany's parents.

Miss Tampa and Sci-Fi Guy hired Lee Graver's Renee Industries for the project. Tiffany even had a picture of her Earth home with her when she came aboard the Tampa over four years ago. Tiffany had a great memory, so she could recall every detail about the house. Lee Graver could build this house for the couple and make it more energy efficent than the original. The house would be located in New Lincoln, formerly Gosalia, East Ucella. The Spiveys, as they were now called, had done remarkably well on this new planet. And they were barely in their twenties.

As things stand at present, many of the enlisted crew of the Tampa had already served their four required years in the U.S. Navy. Still, they agreed to remain a part of the crew and checked in with Captain Albritton on a regular basis. In addition, the Americans were training young Ucellans to become part of the crew while the USS Tampa was in port. In this way, the Tampa had two crews. American and Ucellan.

Ron Willaims was the sailor that had been escorting and assisting Spy Girl, or Linda Flannery. Along with his duties on the Tampa, he would also help with Spy Girl's growing intelligence agency. Once the *UIU* was established, this new agency became known as the *UIA.* (*Ucellan Intelligence Agency.*)

Ron, now in his mid-twenties being an African-American, became tight and fell in love with the black girl, Leah Jordan. She was one of the female, trial sailors on the Tampa. Leah had broken away from working with Troy Cunnigham and his Bible comicbooks. She couldn't put her finger on it, but something wasn't quite right with this son of the preacher. Ron and Leah also got married. Captain Albritton performed the wedding ceremony.

Robert Newell, aka Comicbook Boy married the Toraman girl, Alya. She was one of the girls that assisted Robert and Sc-Fi Guy in their comicbook publishing company. And, Alya was the inspiration for The Rhea Girls. She continued to draw and make appearances promoting this concept. Like Red Queen in Zotova, dolls and action firgures were being made of The Rhea Girls. That is, of Alya and her sidekick, Palas.

Speaking of Palas, she ended up marrying David Hartford, the amateur astronomer from Arizona. Not all of the Americans would be married by Captain Albritton. Some chose to be married by a religious representative of either the Mozdoks or Aelianans. These ceremonies were considered legal and binding on Vanag. Whether these marriages would be considered legal in the United States on Earth was another matter. But at present no one cared.

Lee Graver, the founder of Renee Industries, did indeed marry the girl from Cakovica, now called *Port Angeles.* After Los Angeles. This was Leilani. "At least this sailor decided to marry this Ucellan girl," Michaela interrupted during the viewing.

"True, and good for him, " Amaresh stated. "Her father just wanted to give her to this Earth boy like she was some kind of livestock to be traded."

Tony Miller, the African-American on the Tampa, was the submariner that took the pictures of the two moons and stars at the North Pole on Vanag when the submarine first came through the vortex to this planet. Tony married the other young African-American girl, Cecila Rice, also one of the young, female crew members.

Another young American couple to get married were Steve Litten, the founder of Baghad Electronics, and Christina

Salter. Christina was the young female sailor that was heavily involved with the new government of the *UIU.*

Then there were the two young Latino, female sailors from the American submarine. These were Rosa Garcia and Jennifer Perez. Rosa married another one of the African-American crew members of the Tampa. His name was Adrian Reynolds. He was also quite the musician. Adrian, David Hartford and Tony Miller would have a future role to play involving music with Cecila Rice, Leah Jordan, and along with Rosa Garcia. But more about that later in another viewing.

With respect to Jennifer Perez, the cute girl from Miami, she would marry a young man from North Ucella, named Tafoya. As the Tampa was mostly docked in Torama, now Great Columbia, some North Ucellans were being trained as sailors in the manner of the U.S. Navy. Jennifer Perez worked in the supply section on the huge submarine. As Jennifer was responsible for training this new Ucellan sailor, they got close within a short time and were married.

And then there was the interesting relationship of Spy Girl with Redan. They, too, got married. Linda insisted that Captain Albritton perform the ceremony. Linda Flannery, along with her husband and new sister-in-law, Tixae, were the founders of the Ucellan Intelligence Agency. (*UIA.*) Even the fast-growing little girl, Scandie, was considered one of the founding members. Scandie would have an important role to play in the near future, as she had pretty much mastered the Russian language. Redan really loved Spy Girl and treated her like a princess. Many years from now, Linda would reflect back at this time and think, *I went from being a cashier at a* supermarket, *to becoming the director of the UIA.*

However, there was one other single woman left from the Tampa. Who was this? It was none other than Cynthia "Cindy" Henderson. The government intern for a senator from Oklahoma. Cindy helped in creating the United Islands of Ucella. As Cindy was very political, she continued to have a share in shaping this new democracy for the Ucellans.

Nonetheless, this woman, now in her late twenties, behind the scenes was less than virtuous or honest. In time, Cindy would become more corrupt and ambitious. Mostly in secret of course. Some of the crew had briefly dated Cindy. As mentioned, the crew initally called Cindy a "Plain Jane," but now couldn't help but notice her transformation. Eventually, the crew realized that there was something scary and kinky about this Oklahoman girl.

It was during this viewing that Rowena gave the woman a new name by saying, "This Cindy Henderson is nothing more than an American-Vanagian Vixen. In fact, that's what I'm going to start calling her. Vixen."

Cindy would never marry. After burning her bridges with most of the single crew members on the Tampa, she moved on to Vanagians. Actually, Cindy had simultaneous relationships with three Ucellan men. One from each island. And all three were married.

The first man for Cindy was a fast-becoming millionaire industrialist in North Ucella. The Americans had helped jump-start this Toraman's factory. When he started manufacturing new, modern goods, he became wealthy. This lover of Cindy built her a nice home in the now-renamed city of Great Columbia. Cindy wanted to be near the new capital of this new country, as she was deeply involved in its politics. Cindy joined and had a say in the new Ucellan National Party. (*UNP.*)

The next man that Cindy took up with was one of the new senators in the bustling, rebuilt island of West Ucella. With her influence, Cindy was able to aquire a new spacious apartment in Ruteni. This senator would come back and forth between Cindy and his actual family. Cindy didn't care, but the senator's family did.

The third man was also a senator from East Ucella. Once again, Cindy had another nice apartment in New Lincoln. Cindy was able to accumulate her own wealth. No one knew for sure how, but no doubt not always by legal means. In these early stages of development in the *UIU*, it was hard to track everything or anybody down. Cindy bought the best clothes and accessories from Miss Tampa's San Fernando clothing line.

Some of the crew of the Tampa had actually gone to Captain Albritton, telling him that Cindy Henderson may be up to no good and was an opportunist. The captain had already heard a few negative reports about this young woman from the midwest, but there was little he could do about it. Cindy was a civilian, and the only person that could do anything about her right now was the senator that she worked for back on Earth. Until there was proof that Cindy actually broke a law in the new *UIU*, nothing could be done. Besides, Cindy Henderson wasn't the first or last American to be an opportunist, politically or otherwise, on Earth and now Vanag.

As for the rest of the male crew on the Tampa, they would find lovely Ucellan girls to marry. A young sailor from the Tampa, married Tixae, the now sister-in-law to Linda Flannery. The USS Tampa would leave its home port now in Great Columbia, and make brief ports of calls in East and West Ucella. The Los Angeles class nuclear submarine was always quite impressive to the Ucellans. And thet knew that the Tampa was a powerful vessel and could ptotect them. Protect them from what? This would all come into play later.

When quite a few Americans began marrying Ucellans, the captain informed them that if a way was discovered to get back to Earth, not all of these Vanagian marriage mates may be able to come to Earth with their partners. At least not at first. Hopefully, if a way was discovered, then perhaps the vortex would allow traveling back and forth from both worlds. As this was all too mind-boggling for now, the Earth people went on with their lives. No doubt children would be born from these unions. There was no reason why this wasn't possible. Thus, a new race came into being. Earthlings and Vanagians.

By far, the strangest of marriages involved the now-controversial American Troy Cunnigham. Troy's tour of duty in the navy was up, and he chose not to enlist. In fact, he had pretty much distanced himself from the Tampa and crew.

Troy went so far as to take two wives for himself. Recall that when he first set up his religious comicbooks, he found two fifteen-year old Toroman girls to draw for him. Their names were Donya and Lipari. By *4 A.E.*, they were nearly twenty years old. Even though the Mozdok religion allowed multiple wives, and these two Ucellan girls were Mozdoks, Captain Albtitton and the rest of the senior staff on the Tampa were disturbed over these unions involving Troy. Besides, Troy claimed to be a Christian. Even this claim, though, was gradually changing.

When Troy presented his resignation letter to Captain Albritton, the captain tried to make sense out of this young man, but discovered that this boy from Arkansas had changed drastically since coming through the vortex. No wonder Leah Jordon broke off contact with this son of a preacher. One of the things the captain tried to explain to Troy was that he at least should stay in contact with his fellow Americans. There was still hope that the crew of the Tampa would find a way back to Earth.

"My home now, Captain, is on Vanag," Troy replied. "And this is just the beginning. There are higher beings from another realm communicating with me. I must prepare my followers to get ready to leave for this next realm."

Beings from another realm, the captain thought. *And just what is this realm?*

Having said that Troy Cunnigham departed and broke off all contact with his fellow sailors and the U.S. Navy. Troy with his two wives, Donya and Lipari, relocated to West Ucella. But this would not be the last the Americans would hear about Troy. These are the love stories involving the Americans and Ucellans on this world of Vanag. But who was falling in love in Soviet Zotova?

In the beginning, Valeria Rostova was against young Russians becoming close with Zotovans and Troznyans. She believed that the Russians should be above these two Vanagian nationalities. The political officer was of the opinion that they, that is the people of Earth, should be the rulers behind the scenes of Zotova. A puppet government had been set up in Zotova. Like the Americans, hopefully the Russians would find a way back to Earth. If they did and left this world, a new type of Soviet Union would have been set up on this planet. Furthermore, this government would be a lot better for the Zotovans than the chaos that existed under the crime bosses and warlords. *So why have serious relationships with these primitive aliens?* Valeria kept telling herself.

Yet, the rest of the crew didn't think like Valeria Rostova. What's more, by the third year on Vanag, the political officer fell in love herself. That's right. The beautiful, yet stern, Valeria ended up marrying a Zotovan named Tolari in now New Moscow. He was the son of Tefano, the former crime boss, and now leader of Soviet-Zotova. Tolari would also one day be the premier of this Vanagian-Soviet Union. Valeria Rostova wanted as much power as she could obtain. Valeria and Tolari were the same age.

Captain Starinov, ever loyal to the Soviet navy, also married one of the natives as it were. That is a Zotovan woman in her mid-forties, named Aina. Coming from Vladivostok, a city in the Soviet Far East, the captain had a love for fishing along the Sea of Japan. Aina came from a fishing family. Her family had a fishing business. By now, though, all industries were controlled by the state. As a result of being married to a Soviet captain, and an Earthman, Aina became a very prominent woman.

Chief Anatoly Poltav, married the young Troznyan woman Baba Yaga, now just called Baba. She was the sidekick of Kikimora. The chief was awestruck the first time he saw Baba on the Enaiman ship out in the middle of the Targu Ocean. It was Anatoly who saved Baba when the Russians first encountered a crime boss army in Tellovaci. After that, there was no stopping the romance between the chief and Baba. Anatoly, being from Kiev, was blonde with blue eyes, and so was Baba. Only her blue eyes had a slightly different tint, being a Trozny-Vanagian. Or should we say an alien girl as far as earthlings were concerned. Yet, Baba also looked similar to a White slavic or Nordic woman. They would later produce some beautiful children

The other chief from the Vodyanoy, Matis Gaida, a Lithuanian, married a Zotovan woman named Opeta. The chief would eventually be promoted to a Lieutenant Commander. He loved the Vodyanoy and, being a submariner, would always be a part of the crew. Matis would also have a share in forming the early Zotovan navy. Including future submarines.

Nikola Grodno, a Lt. Commander, chose Doctor Yelena Ivanova to be his wife. The two of them decided that they would rather marry a fellow Russian. And someone from Earth. Doctor Ivanova was instrumental in curing many preventable diseases in Zotova. She set up a state-of-the-art hospital in New Moscow. It was eventually called *Mother Zotova Hospital*. Although also remaining in the navy, Lt. Gordno assisted his wife with medical projects.

Pavel Tupolev, now in his late twenties, was Doctor Ivanova's, medical assistant on the Vodyanoy. He would in the near future be considered a doctor, as his experience was so much more advanced than the doctors and healers on Vanag. Pavel, too, was assisting Doctor Ivanova in setting up the new hospital in New Moscow. The doctor and Pavel found it rewarding that they could cure many of the diseases afflicting the

Zotovans. Especially with the children. Pavel, also married what was once a Troznyan brothel girl. Her name was Lismora.

The Time Maidens learned from a previous viewing that, for over two centuries, Zotovan pirates had raided the coast of Trozny and captured young girls and women to become sex slaves. When this new Soviet Union was established in Zotova, this all ceased.

One good thing about Valeria Rostova and Kikimora was that they put a stop to this sex slave business. All of the Troznyan girls were freed and cared for by Soviet Zotova. Any sex slave trader caught by this new regime in the country was promptly executed by hanging. These criminals weren't worth the bullets that were in precious demand at that time. And as for the pirates, the Soviet Zotovan navy would eventually hunt them down and destroy their ships.

The Time Maidens, especially Rowena, were disturbed about this sex slave trade from the start. During this part of the viewing, as Pavel Tupolev had taken a former brothel girl for a wife, the Celtic Time Maiden commented, "I for one would love to go on a mission to rescue some of these poor Troznyan girls. And take out some of these worthless, good-for-nothing pirates."

"I understand how you feel," Lin also stated. "But right now our missions are to gather data on Vanag, and do a bit of fact-finding, as it were."

"Our missions on Earth are on hold for right now as we gather data on this planet," Cuca added. "If we attempt to start missions on Vanag, we will need a lot of help from Vix and the Aeduians."

"Obviously, the Aeduians didn't mind us rescuing over two hundred Troznyan children minutes before the city of Zelessio went up in a mushroom cloud," Rowena said. "I think a time-jump every so often is good and will keep us in practice.

And will give us a break from these viewings." The other four Time Maidens didn't say yes or no to Rowena's suggestion.

The Jewish biologist couple, that is the Nimrosenskys, being already married decided to have a baby. Chaya, was already in her late thirties. Deep down the couple realized that there may not be a chance that they would ever get back to Earth. As such, Issac and Chaya gave birth to a baby girl in 3 A.E. They gave her the Jewish name Tamar. This baby would now be considered a Vanagian-Zotovan. In actuality, Tamar was a Russian-Earth girl. And a full-blooded Jewess.

Naturally, Michaela took an interest in Tamar, and stated, "I must follow this what could be considered a Vanagian Jew closely. Just think! There are only three Jews on this world." Tamar would indeed prove to be an important young woman in the future. In the meantime, the Hebrew Time Maiden would keep an eye on Tamar via the time scanner.

What about Tatiana Semerova, or Red Queen? The pale-skinned girl from Archangel led a busy life running Tass and Pravda, along with her portraying a now-popular comicbook character. Tatiana had her share of dates with many of the crew from the Vodyanoy. She also dated a good number of now-prominent, young Zotovan communists. For now, though, Tatiana wasn't interested in marriage. The Time Maidens would eventually discover she would get married. And from an unlikely source.

What about the two Soviet princesses, Svetlana Lebedev and Anastasia Macagonova? Svetlana married a young, upcoming Zotovan soldier named Tarzillai. He was made a captain in the new Zotovan Red Army. (*ZRA.*) Tarzillai would rise up in the ranks of this Soviet-made army. Svetlana would continue to teach at various schools in New Moscow. On Earth, Svetlana was related to a member of the politburo. On Vanag, she would be the wife of a soon-to-be prominent Zotovan army officer.

And what of the other Soviet princess, Anastasia? As red hair was rare on this world, Anastasia was considered to be very stunning. Being Svetlana's cousin, she also had connections in Moscow. But what of her new life in New Moscow? Anastasia became what she was trained for: Teaching. Like her cousin, she helped establish several schools, first in the new capital, then in other major cities of Zotova. Zotovan children would be well-educated. They had to be. The future and progress of Soviet Zotova depended on it.

There were obviously many young Russian sailors that would have loved to have Anastasia as a wife. Would she marry a Russian boy from Earth on the Vodyanoy? Hardly. Anastasia also married a Zotovan. His name was Kubov. The Russians were doing the same thing that the Americans were doing. Just as the Americans were training Ucellans to become part of an alternate crew on the Tampa, correspondingly, the Russians were training Zotovans to serve on the Vodyanoy.

Kubov wanted to be a submariner and would be one of the early sailors to make up the Zotovan navy. The young Zotovan would play a future role in building up this spin-off of the Russian navy. Whenever Kubov, was away at sea on the Vodyanoy, or on future submarines and ships that would be built, Anastasia would go on education tours throughout the country to monitor the progress of schools. The two Soviet princesses lived in a modern, spacious apartment in New Moscow. They, along with their husbands who were prominent communists, were also given nice dachas outside the capital city.

Like the American vixen, Cindy Henderson, the mysterious, yet sinister Kikimora would also never marry. She had no time for a family. Kikimora loved her new career more, being second in charge of the Zotovan *KGB*. Besides, Kikimora had several Russian sailors and prominent Zotovans to have a brief fling with.

"So these are the love stories involving the Americans and Russians," Cuca commented toward the end of this viewing. "Amazing how these Earth people found mates on this faraway alien planet."

"And what are the odds that these two humanoid life forms could find each other," Amaresh added. "I suppose only the Aeduians really know how many humanoid worlds are out there in the countless galaxies."

"Following these relationships is like reading the chronicles of my people in ancient Israel," Michaela now said.

"Many nations on Earth had a chronicle of their people and history," Lin stated. "But now we have the beginning of the *Earth-Vanag Chronicles*." This is eventually what the Time Maidens would call this epoch.

"And I still say," Rowena had to emphasize again, "that we need to plan another mission." That being said, this viewing officially came to an end.

Linda Flannery, as Spy Girl, and now the director of the *UIA*, may have thought that she and her fellow Americans knew about the presence of the Russians on Vanag, but that the Russians didn't know about them. This, however, was not the case.

Just as Ucellans would trade by ship with Trozny and Zotova, likewise Zotovan and Troznyan merchant sailors came to the Ucellan Islands. At least in the past. Zotova as a now-communist state, was working on becoming a self-sufficient country. The Soviet Union on Earth always desired to be self-sufficient, yet never seemed to be able to accomplish this goal. Although, Soviet Zotova on Vanag was able to achieve this in a little under five years. And the Zotovans appeared to be prospering.

For the most part, when Zotova was under the rule of the crime bosses and warlords, the people suffered. Yet, under Soviet rule, as long as the people were loyal to the state, they had protection and everything they needed. To the Zotovans it was indeed a "workers paradise." As Zotova was now a centralized economy, shipping and trade was regulated by the state. For several years very few ships from Zotova sailed to the Ucellan Islands. But ships from Trozny and Enaim continued to trade with the Ucellans. Above all, the United Islands of Ucella were now a thriving, capitalist country.

Futermore, Kikimora, being from Trozny, kept up with her contacts and what was taking place in her country. Kikimora hated the monarchy and provincial governors. She would also love to see a socialist revolution happen in Trozny. But, first things first. Soviet Zotova was still in its infancy of socialism and needed to get stronger.

Reports were coming back from Trozynan seamen regarding a huge, metal vessel that could travel underwater at great speeds. Generally, this vessel stayed in Torama, now with a new name: Great Columbia. When word of this account reached the desk of Valeria Rostova, in New Moscow, the *KGB* director had to think, *"Is this a coincidence? Another submarine on this world? Or is this just a rumor and made-up story by drunken Trozynan seamen?"*

Kikimora also heard the stories. Before sending Redan to get an actual picture of the Russian submarine in now New Moscow, Linda Flannery had a Ucellan sailor draw what he saw while in Zotova. Including the red star on the submarine. Using her contacts in Trozny and Zotova, Kikimora was also able to obtain a few drawings. Although crude, the drawings did reveal a type of submarine. And these Trozynan seamen had never seen the Russian submarine. What's more, it could be proven that these seamen had indeed been to the capital city of North Ucella. What next?

Kikimora approached her now-boss of the Zotovan *KGB*. As she was second-in-command of the spy agency, Kikimora had a plan. And a daring one at that. "We are not alone," Kikimora said to Valeria. "What I mean, Comrade Rostova, is that you Russians are not the only ones on our planet from somewhere else. There is another submarine different, yet similar to the Vodyanoy on the other side of the world."

Valeria pretended not to know of reports that she had heard already. The political officer wanted to see first what Kikimora knew. But Valeria was totally caught off guard when her second-in-command presented her with a folder containing several drawings of a modern submarine. Standing up from behind her desk, she asked Kikimora, "Where did yo get these drawings?"

"Now we're getting somewhere," Rowena stated from the conference room during this latest viewing. "The Russians are going to discover that someone else from Earth came through the vortex."

"And wait until they find out that it is the Americans," Michaela now said. "They will probably think that their rival from Earth is responsible for bringing them to Vanag."

"Along with this, the Americans will think the same thing," Lin affirmed. "As this was some type of advanced, staged wargame."

Back to the viewing, the Time Maidens observed with great interest. Kikimora answered her superior how she obtained these drawings. Her next comment also caught Valeria by surprise. "Comrade Rostova, I wish to go to this land of North Ucella, and see this other submarine for myself."

"*WHAT!*" Valeria exclaimed. "You can't go to a Ucellan Island. We have no idea about these islands or what they are like. You are too valuable, Kikimora, to go there. Send some of your Troznyan operatives." But then, the political officer began to ponder: *This girl had sometimes been a thorn in my side since we plucked her out of the ocean. Futhermore, I don't know if I even trust her. Would it be the end of the world if something did happen to this Troznyan girl? It's almost as if I can't live with her or without her. She is important to our new KGB on this planet.* "All right, Kikimora," Valeria spoke up, "tell me how you plan to go about this journey."

Kikimora was a crafty young woman, and had survived by her wits. She may have been a peasant girl from a village in Trozny, but Kikimora was tough and a fast learner. And besides being very attractive, she was also able to escape being taken as a sex slave in her native land and on the dangerous high seas. Not to mention her gift of learning several languages.

Kikimora's plan was to sail on a Troznyan steamer to North Ucella. The ship would be delivering simple goods to sell. Industry and manufacturing was producing goods by leaps and bounds in the Ucellan Islands thanks to help from the Americans. However, the open marketplaces in port cities still had a market for crafts, paintings, wooden utensils, wine and some fruits and vegetables.

As Kikimora went on with her plan to scope out the capital of North Ucella, Valeria listened intently. A political officer in the *KGB* was trained to listen, then analyze later. Kikimora was sailing on this steamer westward to the Ucellan Islands as a simple galley girl. At least this was her guise. She would have several Troznyan girls with her. These former brothel girls were now operatives in the Zotovan *KGB*.

"This will be an interesting spy mission for this Kikimora," Cuca interrupted during the viewing. "I'm not sure who she is trying to impress, but there seems to be no stopping this Troznyan girl."

"Maybe she is trying to impress herself," Amaresh added.

In the interim, Kikimora made preparations for her secret mission to North Ucella. After she departed from *KGB* headquarters, Valeria contemplated another possible problem with Kikimora: *Suppose this strong-witted Troznyan girl proves to be what she's not portraying.* That is, a true communist and *KGB* agent. *This girl could possibly defect to whoever is ruling North Ucella,* the political officer further considered. *If Kikimora did defect, she could reveal everything she knows about us.* Valeria hoped that this would not be the case. Not to mention that Kikimora had a lot going for her here in Soviet Zotova. Overnight she had become a powerful young woman.

"One thing is certain for right now," Rowena spoke up again during the viewing. "The Russians have no idea just yet that the Americans are on the other side of this world."

"But in the near future they will," Lin also stated. "And how will the Russians react when they discover that their Earth rival is also on Vanag and set up an American-like government in the Ucellan Islands."

"You can't help but wonder if they could or would cooperate with each other." Michaela stated.

"Well, the record of these two Earth nations hasn't been very good on their own world," Cuca added. "What makes us think they would do any better on Vanag. The Americans and Russians have way too many rivalries and suspicions."

"I'm sure we will find out soon," Amaresh deduced. "And they will both be shocked when they conclude that there are two governments like their own on this distant world."

Linda Flannery, or Spy Girl had not been idle either. The *UIA,* which she had founded, knew much more about the Russians at present. Under the direction of her husband, Redan, he took a deep interest in the agency. Perhaps it was a dedication to his new country, or he wanted to make an impression on his attractive "alien wife." Being a former merchant sailor, Redan still had connections on ships. Some of his former shipmates could be his eyes and ears when Ucellan ships were allowed to various, limited ports in Zotova. Especially in New Moscow. Even though Soviet Zotova was becoming self-sufficent, the new country still needed certain goods from the outside world.

Spy Girl and Redan recruited a few North Ucellan sailors as operatives for the *UIA.* The agency had the funds to reward or get them at the top of the list for new housing that was booming as a result of Renee Industries. Most of these young sailors still lived at home, so access to a new house would be a great gift for their parents and families.

Redan mastered the English language swiftly. As one of the key people in the *UIA*, he knew exactly what his wife wanted. To Redan, he observed how his country, and the other two Ucellan Islands, had benefited with the arrival of the Americans. If there was an outside threat to its survival, then he was going to do his best to protect it. From now on, Redan's warfare would involve espionage.

Spy Girl and Redan had instructed their operatives when they entered the port of New Moscow, to just casually look around. Actually, Linda still believed that this Zotovan city was called Tannsisi. A lot was changing and taking place on both sides of the world. Linda didn't need anymore pictures. The ones that Redan had taken on his visit would suffice for now. She and Redan did inform their operatives to buy or pick up anything unusual or of interest. And the Ucellan sailor-operatives did just that.

After arriving in New Moscow, the Ucellan operatives, and there were three, performed their duties on the ship and docks. They then fanned out in different directions in this new, renamed capital city. The port and city had strict rules. Identification papers had to be presented. Soldiers were everywhere. This of course was reminiscent of the Soviet Union on faraway Earth. The papers that the Ucellan sailors carried did reveal that they were from a country called the United Islands of Ucella. But thus far, the Soviet Zotovans didn't comprehend what this meant. Even though English was fast becoming the official language on all three islands, Spy Girl thought it was best to have the papers in the Ucellan language. Kikimora would figure this out very soon, though, when she went on her own spying mission.

The operatives visited several restaurants and bars. These establishments were clean and well-organized. There were no longer any starving children or beggers in the streets. The days of the crime bosses and warlords were gone. The Russians and Soviet Zotovans had made good on their promise to take care of the people.

New building projects were everywhere as this new city was being transformed overnight. Also evident throughout the city were huge, colorful posters and billboards proclaiming the achievements of communism in this new land. This, too, was a throwback to Soviet communism on Earth. The Ucellan sailors couldn't read or speak this new language being spoken in Zotova, but that didn't matter. They had printed material that they could take back with them for their bosses. Specifically, for Linda Flannery and Redan.

The operatives had money from Trozny, that was exchanged to what was called a Zotovan Ruble, so they purchaed several items. Soviet-inspired comicbooks that were still geared for Zotovan youth and teaching the Russian language, and several issues of the newspaper *Pravda.* Similar to The Great Columbia Times, Ucellan newspaper in English, this Russian paper was still basic with only four pages. The Americans and Russians were both working on improving the printing industry. The printed page was very important for the Earth people on this world. Other forms of media would come later.

As instructed, the Ucellan sailors also purchased some other unusual items. Toys. One was of a handcrafted doll with red hair. The doll, eight inches tall was dressed in a jumpsuit, red boots and matching cape. On the front of the yellow jumpsuit was a large red star. Another toy was of a young man dressed in a silver spacesuit. This figure was also eight inches tall. Zotovan youth now knew about space and this type of suits from other comicbooks that the Russians were continuing to print. The comicbooks were still only in black and white. The same with the ones printed in Ucella. Nevertheless, the imaginations of Vanagian youth were running wild. And at the same time were learning either English or Russian. Which was the goal anyway.

The doll and other character were none other than Red Queen and Takoda: The Time Traveler. These were the early stages of the toys. Better dolls and action figures would come later when the Russians developed and manufactured rubber and plastic. While studying the doll, one operative commented to his fellow operatives, "This doll reminds me of the two comicbook characters, Palas and Alya. My little sister is a fan ot them." He was of course referring to The Rhea Girls created by the Americans.

The other "unusal" items were again from the new ever-growing toy industry in Zotova. These were hand-carved out of wood. Very detailed and excellent craftsmanship. One was ten inches long. It was a submarine painted black. Also painted in red on the conning tower was a star on both sides. And in red on both sides of the submarine in the Cyrillic letters was the name Vodyanoy. By now everyone in Zotova knew about this powerful ship from another world, whether they had seen it firsthand or not. In addition on the bottom of each submarine were the carved Cyrillic letters, that read *UZSR*. The Americans would soon find out that this stood for Union Of The Zotovan Socialist Republic.

The last toy, once again hand-carved in wood was interesting. This piece of woodwork eight inches tall like Takoda, was a robot. A robot was like nothing found on the planet Vanag. How could there be at this point in time on this world? The Zotovan children, mostly boys, marveled over this character found in the comicbooks. They had already learned that Red Queen had an army of flying robots at her command. These toy robots were painted silver, but also had a red star across their chests. Along with the red star, on the helmetlike head was a hammer and sickle.

What was amazing regarding the wooden submarines and robots was that they all looked as if they had been carved by the same woodcarver. But this would be impossible, as there were tens of thousands of these wooden toys being made. A woodcarving factory had been set up in New Moscow and in another city in the western part of Zotova. This city was now called New Leningrad.

The Ucellan seamen-*UIA* operatives had gathered up enough items and information from Zotova. They had a few copies of Pravda, comicbooks and toys. Plus what they had observed firsthand in New Moscow. Their ship would be leaving the next day. After one port of call to the Troznyan city of Tellovaci, to pick up more goods, the ship would be sailing back to Great Columbia.

Before leaving New Moscow, the Soviet Zotovans did not check to see what the foreigners were taking back with them, at least of a personal nature. They were only interested in checking cargo coming off and on ships. It didn't matter to them about newspapers, comicbooks or toys.

In eleven days the Ucellan operatives were back in Great Columbia. They immediately reported to Linda Flannery and Redan. The three seamen gave the directors of the *UIA* everything that they had purchased in New Moscow. By now, Linda Flannery was no longer operating in a small wooden house near the docks. A new building had been constructed for the *UIA*. This building would be one of many as the spy agency grew in this new country, or *UIU*.

The Ucellan operatives also wrote down from memory everything they saw and heard while in their travels. Including a strange, new unknown language sweeping Zotova. The three seamen were rewarded for their efforts and, as promised, were put on the top of the list for new housing. One seaman hoped to be married soon and desired a decent house so as to start a family. The American dream was still being promoted as the Ucellan dream. As for the other two seamen, they informed Spy Girl and Redan that, if needed, they would continue to be operatives for the agency if any other missions should arise. Linda thanked and informed the two Ucellans by concluding, "I am sure the *UIA* can use your services again. And in the near future."

Spy Girl was both elated and alarmed with this latest information coming out of Zotova. Along with the printed material and toys the seamen brought back. Linda knew by now that the newspapers and comicbooks were written in Russian

Cyrillic. As for the toys, the wooden submarine obviously represented the one from the pictures Redan had taken when he sailed to Zotova. And the toy robot clearly had a hammer and sickle painted on its head. Next on the list, get these newspapers and comicbooks translated.

As noted earlier, there were two Americans on the USS Tampa that spoke Russian. Back on Earth, as radio transmissions could be picked up, a translator was needed. And there was always someone on the Russian ships and submarines that spoke English. Including the Vodyanoy. This was a reality of the Cold War.

One of the American submariners on the Tampa that spoke Russian was Nathan Berry. And in just a little over two years, little Scandie, now almost a preteen, had mastered the Russian language with help from the two Americans. This North Ucellan girl had a gift for picking up languages. She could fluently read and speak Ucellan, English and now Russian. No wonder Scandie was so valuable to the *UIA*.

Nathan and Scandie got to work in translating the newspaper and comicbooks. Nathan pointed out to Linda that the newspaper was called Pravda. "Oh, wow!" Linda acknowledged, "This is the official newspaper of the Communist Party of the Soviet Union."

"From what I can read," Nathan explained, "this Pravda, is the official journal for another Soviet Union. Soviet Zotova." Nathan translated for Linda some of the articles being featured. A Five Year Plan. Hospitals and medical centers being built, along with housing. Free education for both boys and girls. Equal distribution of food and clothing. And finally, all insurgences put down. According to Pravda, crime bosses and warlords were a thing of the past in Zotova.

"*HOLY COW!*" Linda exclaimed. "These Russians, have obviously been busy on the other side of this world. I need to take all of this information to the captain. We have suspected that the Russians were also on this planet, but now this confirms it."

Scandie's translation of one comicbook revealed that this issue was none other than The Night Witches. Spy Girl knew that the real Night Witches were female Russian pilots during World War II. And now here these heroines were being celebrated in Zotova. Spy Girl, pretty much figured out that the main purpose of these comicbooks, had the same intent of American comicbooks. To teach Vanagian children an Earth language.

Regarding the wooden submarine, clearly a model of one from the Soviet Union, Spy Girl, through the articles in Pravda, figured out what the Cyrillic letters *C3CP* represented: Union of Zotovan Socialist Republic. Yes, there was now another Soviet Union, but on Vanag.

Linda immediately made her way to the Tampa to inform Captain Albritton of her new discoveries. Until a house was built for himself and his new Ucellan wife, the captain still lived aboard the Tampa. With great enthusiam, Linda Flannery presented her information to the captain. He listened intently to his new spy chief. *I don't know if I should rejoice over this discovery that there are other people from Earth on this world,* the captain thought, *or be alarmed that our rival, the Russians, are the ones here with us.*

Linda then said, "Captain, we had a suspicion that a nuclear weapon was used in Zotova. We detected it from our submarine almost four years ago." She then added, "Nothing is mentioned in the Russian language newspapers regarding a nuclear weapon, but, clearly, with the Russians on Vanag, it had to be them."

"Good work, Ensign Flannery," the captain replied. "This appears to be the case."

"Sooner or later, Captain," Linda stated, "the Russians will find out about us. Then what?"

"That's a very good question, Ensign," the captain replied. "But for now, just keep on gathering any information that you can find. It's not like we can pull up anchor, as it were, and just sail into the port of this New Moscow."

Being dismissed, Spy Girl carried on with her intelligence gathering. Linda had the two Ucellan sailors from the previous mission at her disposal if she needed them. In addition, there were other Ucellan seamen that were recruited as operatives for the *UIA*. A few young women, were recruited as well. Like the young men, they were mostly from West Ucella. After years of civil war and then a deadly pandemic, these West Ucellans were eager to serve the Americans for all of the good deeds that had been done for them. The Americans had lifted them from poverty and death, brought them back from the dead so to speak, and were modernizing their land.

With help from the captain, Linda was able to purchase a new steamship from East Ucella, for her loyal crew of operatives. But this steamer was no ordinary ship. Steamships on both Earth and Vanag were used for the international transportation of people and cargo. This steamer, owned and operated by the *UIA*, was also used as a guise. In reality, though, this ship was a spy vessel.

Very few people, Americans or Ucellans knew the real purpose of this ship. Spy Girl gave this steamer a name. *USS Pueblo.* The original Pueblo was a U.S. Navy spy ship seized by North Korea in 1968. The crew was later released, but the ship remained in communist North Korea. This second USS Pueblo would be very active and busy on Vanag, gathering information for the *UIA*. The Americans would continue to call any future ship under their command first using the letters *USS*. (United States Ship.) Any Ucellan ships were an extension of the U.S. Navy.

Captain Albritton had already promoted Linda Flannery once. Like all the other sailors from the Tampa, Spy Girl still considered herself in the navy. Even if their four years were up.

They considered themselves in the reserves and would take part in training exercises while helping to train Ucellans. The captain decided to promote Linda again This time her title, or rank, was *Director of the UIA.* The spy agency would continue to grow.

With this latest information from Spy Girl, the captain couldn't help but think, *Could we possibly cooperate with the Russians to find a way back to Earth? We were allies during World War Two. And how did the Russians find their way to this world?* Then the captain further thought, *Are the Russians responsible for us being here? Is this some kind of psychological weapon? Does the Soviet Union on Earth have the means to transport people to another planet?* For now, there were more questions than answers.

Lin concluded by saying, "Kikimora is right, we are not alone. That is, they are not alone, regarding the Americans and Russians."

Around the third month of *4 A.E.*, Kikimora had her plan ready to sail to North Ucella. She would sail first on a Zotovan ship leaving New Moscow, and then make her way to Tellovaci, in Trozny. From there it was best that Kikimora, and a few of her fellow Troznyan girl operatives, sail to North Ucella on a ship from Trozny.

Even though Kikimora was second in charge of the Zotovan *KGB*, for this secret mission she would be nothing like her usual flashy self. The young Troznyan woman would dress down. She and the other girls would be portraying lowly galley workers. They would be pretending to cook for the Troznyan seamen on the ship. However, Kikimora was tough. She had held her own on the high seas of the Targu Ocean working on Enaimen ships.

The freighter ship that Kikimora was taking would be going to Torama, North Ucella. Although Kikimora had already received reports that the city was no longer called Torama. It had a strange-sounding name. Great Columbia. This didn't sound like a Vanagian-Ucellan name at all. Like the new Russian-named cities of Zotova, to Kikimora Great Columbia sounded otherworldly. And it was. This was another reason why Kikimora wanted to sneak into North Ucella. To find out about this newly-named city and another possible submarine.

Once arriving in North Ucella, Kikimora and her girls were going to stay in the shadows, or keep a low profile. They would pretend to be dumb, Troznyan farm girls. It was actually Michaela that gave Kikimora the nickname *Shadow Girl* by saying, "This Troznyan spy girl really is crafty and sneaky. Hiding in the shadows so to speak. For now I'm going to call her Shadow Girl."

"She hasn't really brought a whole lot with her," Cuca added. "I suppose sometimes the simple disguise works the best."

"Ah," Rowena now said, "Kikimora does have a small camera that the Russians gave her. Not if, but when, this Shadow Girl sees the American submarine, she will take a picture."

Departing from Tellovaci, Trozny while sailing across the Kovda Ocean to North Ucella, would be an eleven-day journey. Kikimora and her three female operatives carried on with their guise. They prepared meals for the seamen delivering goods and cargo from the freighter they were employed with. When the freighter reached Great Columbia, though, the *KGB* girls disappeared into the city for the next five days.

Kikimora, along with the three other Troznyan girls, found lodging at a refurbished hotel near the docks. Kikimora was impressed with what the Americans were doing with many of the older buildings in this city. Although, at this early stage of coming to North Ucella, Kikimora didn't know who the Americans were. While it was true, that Kikimora knew several languages, Ucellan was not one of them. Yet, one of the Troznyan *KGB* girls did. Pretending to be awestruck by everything she heard or saw, this spy girl asked many questions. All of this information would later be written down in great detail.

Just as the Ucellan sailors did when being sent to Zotova by the *UIA*, the *KGB* girls followed their example. They, too, bought several newspapers of the *Great Columbia Times*, and comicbooks written in an unknown language. At least unknown to these Troznyan girls. Kikimora and her operatives had been given quite a bit of Troznyan currency. The *UIU* was beginning to trade somewhat with Trozny. For this reason, the Troznyan currency could be exchanged for Ucellan dollars.

The next day, the *KGB* operatives hit the streets of the city, acting like sightseers, but, in actuality, spying. The first thing Kikimora wanted to investigate was this other so-called submarine. The operative that spoke Ucellan asked several people regarding this vessel. The Ucellans directed the "sightseers" to the dock of the "metal vessel from beyong this world." When the four *KGB* spies saw the USS Tampa, they froze in their tracks.

"It's true," Kikimora stated in Troznyan to her operatives. "There is another submarine on our world from some other planet."

Kikimora had become somewhat of an expert of the Vodyanoy. She knew that this other submarine before their eyes was similar, yet different from the Russian submarine back in Zotova. Why wouldn't it be? They were constructed by two separate nations from the other planet, Earth. *Or is this submarine even from the same planet as the Russians? Perhaps there is another world involved. Until recently, we didn't think that there was life beyond Vanag,* Kikimora thought. This was even more reason to keep spying. Kikimora wanted to know more about the people from this submarine, who were obviously in control of North Ucella. *Who are these people, and where do they come from?* She further thought.

When Kikimora got closer to the USS Tampa, she went down on her knees. The other three Troznyan girls surrounded her. Very discreetly, she was able to take two photographs of the submarine with the small camera provided for her by the Russians. One picture included a shot of an unknown flag flying above the conning tower. The American flag, which meant nothing to Kikimora.

Kikimora and her spy girls continued to roam around Great Columbia portraying themselves as tourists. In one section of a remodeled downtown were large models of what some buildings would look like in the near future. There were three such models behind glass enclosures.

The first one was of a rather unusual building. At least unusual in regards to Vanagian-Ucellan structures. In the middle of the model-building was a large dome or rotundra. This building was none other than a replica of the United States Capital Building in Washington, D.C. The newly-established *UIU* congress and senate would be meeting to pass laws and legislations in this future building.

The next model structure was of an obelisk tower that would be five hundred and fifty feet tall. It would be constructed of white marble. This would be a second Washington Monument. The Americans wanted the people of Ucella to know about one of their founding fathers and first president.

The final model structure was none other than the White House. Starting with Benatta, this is where all future presidents from the United Islands of Ucella would live. Great Columbia would somewhat resemble Washington, D.C. of the United States on Earth.

Needless to say, Kikimora had no idea what these model structures represented or where they came from. Similar to what she did when taking pictures of the submarine, Kikimora had her operatives huddle close to her so as to take a picture of these three models. These pictures and printed material that the *KGB* operatives purchased would be handed over to Valeria Rostova when they returned to New Moscow. Valeria, and the other Russians would know who was behind these structures: The Americans.

There were several Russian sailors that spoke English on the Vodyanoy. All of the printed journals would be turned over to them for translation. Just as the Ucellan *UIA* operatives had done with the printed material they had picked up in New Moscow. But Kikimora was by no means through with her espionage. There was much more intelligence to gather.

The *KGB* girls couldn't help but notice that there were men and women in white uniforms throughout the city. These were none other than U.S. sailors from the USS Tampa. In addition, quite a few young Ucellans had also joined the

American-inspired navy of the *UIU*. They, too, wore these uniforms. Military ships previously from the Ucellan Islands were now under the command of the navy representing the new *UIU,* no matter how old and outdated these ships were.

But the ever-perceptive Kikomora, knew that some of these sailors were not Ucellans. Especially the black, African-American sailors. This race didn't exist on her planet. They were humanoid and looked somewhat like Vanagians, but yet stood out by the way they talked as being different. Just as the Russians stood out as being different in Zotova. Kikimora's plan was to get closer to one of these "different" people now dwelling in North Ucella.

As most of the sailors that the *KGB* girls encountered were in passing, it was not possible to get a picture. But Kikimora was anxious to take a picture of at least the top part of these white uniforms. Being the Shadow Girl, Kikimora had a plan. She noticed one of the popular taverns near the docks. The establishment appeared to be a popular spot for these white-uniformed sailors. As noted, some of these sailors were Ucellans.

Kikimora and her "girls" did bring a fancy dress to wear. Modern clothes for both men and women were now also being manufactured in Zotova as a result of the Earth-Russian influence. They planned to visit this tavern for a night out, so to speak. The Troznyan girls strolled into this tavern like they were used to this environment. They went to the bar first, then made their way around various tables to try and pick up a conversation. Thus far, everyone was speaking Ucellan, according to the operative that spoke the language.

All of a sudden, though, at a table located in a far corner of the tavern, this operative heard another language being spoken. This was of course English, but none of the Troznyan girls could comprehend this tongue. At this table were two sailors: One Ucellan and the other American. This was the opportunity that Kikimora was looking for. To be able and get up close to a person speaking this unknown language. At least unknown to her.

The four spy girls stood around the table smiling and giggling. They were acting more curious than flirtatious. This was part of Kikimora's plan. Pretend to be nothing more than backward farm girls that just got off a boat from Trozny, visiting one of the Ucellan Islands.

After a moment, the Ucellan sailor asked in his language, "Do you girls want something? Would you like to sit down?"

"Yes, we would," one of the Troznyan girls replied. "But I am the only one that speaks Ucellan."

"I see," the Ucellan sailor replied back. "But that's good enough for myself and American friend."

As there were only two other empty chairs at this table, Kikimora and the girl that spoke Ucellan quickly sat down. The other two *KGB* girls would mingle around the bar and before long find two other sailors to drink with. Kikimora had to get to know this "different" sailor better.

The Ucellan sailor ordered another round of a type of Vanagian beer. Including two for the pretty Troznyan girls. Kikimora and her girls got purposely "dolled up" for this night. After sipping her beer, the *KGB* girl again spoke in Ucellan, saying, "Tell us about yourselves. What is your job as sailors?" The Ucellan and American sailors didn't think that anything that they did was really top secret. Especially to these two backward Troznyan girls. However, Kikimora and her other spy girls were far from backward.

Seeing how the American sailor didn't speak the language, the Ucellan sailor took the lead. It was no secret regarding the Americans being from another planet over one hundred years ahead of Vanag. The story was in all of the newspapers and comicbooks. The *KGB* spy girl listened intently.

Kikimora was dying to know what was being said, but she could debrief her operative later.

The Ucellan now began to brag about how he was in the new Ucellan navy that was an extension of the navy the Americans were a part of on their planet. And he was now pretty fluent in their language, known as English. And this American with him was his friend as he patted him on the back. It was clearly evident that both the Ucellan and American were feeling good as they had already had several rounds of beers before the Troznyan girls arrived.

The Ucellan sailor went on to explain the ongoing plans regarding the Americans and his new country known as the United Islands of Ucella. This, too, was in all of the newspapers of the three islands. And, the Americans were helping to build an army and navy for the Ucellans. This sailor informed the Troznyan girl that the present ships in the Ucellan navy were being modernized, and new ships would also be forthcoming. Proudly beating his chest with his left fist, the Ucellan boasted, "I am a part of this new powerful navy."

The Ucellan sailor said something in English to the American. The American sailor then looked directly at the Troznyan girls and said, "My name is Nathan Berry."

"Ask my friend, Nathan, anything you want," the Ucellan sailor added, "and then I will translate his language back to you in Ucellan."

Now we're getting somewhere, Kikimora thought. The first thing she asked was, "What is the name of the planet that you originally came from?" (Now, Kikimora already knew the answer, as this was brought out in the Great Columbia Times newspaper printed in the Ucellan language. The Troznyan *KGB* girl with her at this moment would later translate everything to her back at the hotel or on the return voyage home.)

"Earth," the American replied.

Next, Kikimora asked her operative to tell the Ucellan to ask the American to tell them about his country on Earth. That is, the United States of America. Nathan rambled on something in English to the Ucellan about his country being the greatest and most powerful nation on his planet. And soon, the *UIU* would be the greatest and most powerful nation on Vanag. The Troznyan girls feigned being awestruck.

Then the American Earthman was asked about the powerful, metal monster from the sea. That is, the USS Tampa. Nathan answered by bragging about the American submarine and what all it could do. Once this was translated back into Ucellan, the *KGB* girl just said, "Amazing."

When asked how his people, the Americans, came to Vanag, Nathan replied, "A comet. We were sucked through a vortex from our planet's North Pole."

Kikimora knew that the same thing happened to the Russians on the Vodyanoy, only at the South Pole on Earth. They then came through a votex and ended up at Vanag's South Pole. All of this was still very mind-boggling for the Americans, Russians and Vanagians. The Ucellan sailor and Nathan Berry clearly had a lot to drink, but, as Kikimora and the other Troznyan girl had Ucellan dollars, they continued to order more rounds of beer. The two women simply sipped on their glass as the Ucellan and American gulped theirs down.

Then, the conversation took a twist. As Nathan Berry could speak Russian, he started mumbling something in the language. As it was loud in the tavern, and the American was slurring in his speech, Kikimora couldn't quite understand what Nathan said. But it was in Russian. *This has taken a new turn,* Kikimora thought. This American speaks Russian. Quickly, Kikimora said in Troznyan to her operative, "Inform the Ucellan sailor that we wish for this American to speak in this other language. We can say that we are curious about other languages." The *KGB* girl did as instructed.

After the Ucellan sailor translated from Ucellan to English to the American, he smiled and nodded his head. Perhaps Nathan wanted to show off how smart he was to the Troznyan girls. As he began to speak in the Russian language, the two girls listened intently. Especially Kikimora, as this was now her main language.

Nathan started out by talking about how when his people first came through the vortex to this world, then to North Ucella. The Ucellans viewed the Americans as a powerful race from beyond. He even quoted Troy Cunningham by saying that they were like gods.

"That's the way many view the Russians." Kikimora muttered in Troznyan to her operative. Nathan didn't skip a beat and continued to speak more in Russian.

The American bragged more about the USS Tampa, and the powerful nuclear weapons that the submarine was armed with. Next, Nathan explained how his people helped unite the three Ucellan Islands, and how these islands became the United Islands of Ucella. Kikimora also already knew this from the newspapers. "So, you see girls," Nathan boasted, "we have set up another type of United States of America on Vanag. This Ucellan America will become the most powerful nation on this planet."

And the Russians say the same thing about Zotova, Kikimora thought. She then called out to a tavern girl, "More drinks for our sailor friends." Her operative then translated in Ucellan for her. Kikimora wanted to keep this American talking.

Nathan Berry also had to brag that he was one of three that actually knew the Russian language. The other two were another sailor and now Scandie. But what Nathan said next really got Kikimora's attention. Nathan said that he had been translating newspapers, comics and pamphlets into English from Russian, that had been obtained by Ucellan spies who had gone to this city now called New Moscow. The American had no idea that he was spilling out state secrets to the woman that was second in command of the the Zotovan *KGB*.

Futhermore, Nathan revealed that the Americans knew that their Earth rival, the Soviet Union, had used a nuclear weapon against a city on the other side of the world. Namely, Zelessio, Zotova.

WHAT! Kikimora thought. *The Americans know about a cruise missile being launched from the Vodyanoy to destroy the criminal stronghold Zelessio? Wait until we report back to Comrade Rostova with all of this valuable information. She will be surprised, yet grateful. Why, the Russians may award me the Order of Lenin.* Kikimora then chuckled outloud.

The night was getting on and Nathan Berry, along with the Ucellan sailor, were clearly drunk beyond comprehending anything. Kikimora knew that this was her move. She would call it a night. Kikimora had plenty of experience picking up sailors in the many ports she had frequented during her travels before joining up with the Russians. And the Troznyan girl had made the rounds with quite a few Russian sailors on the Vodyanoy. She was quite the voluptuous woman. And strong-willed and determined.

The Ucellan sailor had originally planned on taking the Troznyan *KGB* girl home for the night. However, as he was so drunk, he had passed out. His head was on the table. The tavern owner, when closing, would leave him there until the morning. The sailor would wake up not remembering much and with a terrible hangover.

Other sailors in the tavern had also planned on taking the two Troznyan *KGB* girls somewhere for the night. They had made the rounds at several tables and the bar throughout the night. But Kikimora had other plans. She ordered the other three opeartives to reurn back to their more posh hotel room nearby. Kikimora informed them that she would see them back at the hotel at dawn. And that was only several hours away.

In the meantime, Kikimora helped Nathan to his feet. He could walk with this beautiful "foreign" woman's help. Kikimora even whispered in his ear in Russian, "There, there, Nathan, let me help you." Again, as Nathan was so drunk, he didn't even realize that this girl from Trozny was speaking Russian to him.

Near the taverns by the docks were several cheap hotels. They were mostly used for foreign sailors to sometimes spend the night, or for one-night stands with local Ucellan women. One of these cheap hotels would work well for Kikimora's plan. After checking in with a middle-aged North Ucellan woman, Kikimora was given a key for a small room on the first floor. Kikimora still had plenty of Ucellan dollars. Helping Nathan to the room, the American sailor collapsed on the bed. Nathan muttered in Russian, "I'm valuable to the U.S. Navy and this new country, the United Islands of Ucella."

"Of course you are," Kikimora replied in Russian. Then, Nathan was out like a light. *Well at least I don't have to sleep with this American Earthman,* Kikimora thought.

Kikimora then got busy. As the American was laying face down on the bed, she rolled him over. Kikimora wanted to get a picture of the sailor's shirt with the insignia on it. It meant nothing to Kikimora, as she was unfamilar with this uniform. But her boss, Valeria Rostova, could most likely make sense of it all. The Americans and Russians were from the same planet, so they would both know about the uniforms of their enemies.

Taking a picture of the uniform, Kikimora then reached around to the back of Nathan and took out his wallet. She was not robbing him. Rather, Kikimora was looking for something else. She found it. It was Nathan's U.S. Navy identification card. She focused in close with the compact camera and took another picture. Kikimora put the wallet back into the American's back pocket. When she returned to New Moscow, the Russians could develop these pictures and blow them up if necessary.

As it was nearly dawn, Kikimora quietly left the old, run-down hotel. When Nathan woke up later, whether or not he would remember how he got to this hotel, or that he had been talking with a pretty Troznyan girl, didn't really matter. Kikimora and her *KGB* girls would change their appearance from the way they were dressed the night before. The four young women would go back to their galley girl image and return to the Troznyan freighter. By mid-day they would be departing from Great Columbia.

After taking baths at the better hotel, Kikimora and her three operatives checked out. As they were making their way to the port, who should walk by on one of the main streets? None other than Linda Flannery with her husband and sister-in-law, Tixae. They were on their way to the intelligence agency's building. Linda exchanged a glance at Kikimora.

What a homely group these Troznyan girls are, Linda thought.

And Kikimora thought, *Ucellan smugs.* Then further thought regarding Linda, *this one* woman *acts differently from the man and the other girl. She has a leisurly stroll to her walk. I wonder if she is one of the Americans from Earth.*

"Imagine that," Amaresh interrupted during the viewing. "The top spy of the *UIA*, that is Spy Girl, just walked past the second in command of the Zotovan *KGB*."

"And yet," Cuca affirmed, "neither Linda Flannery or Kikimora even know who the other person is." This would change in the near future."

The Troznyan ship then left North Ucella to return to New Moscow, Zotova. It would be the same eleven-day journey sailing home. But what a store of information awaited Valeria Rostova when Kikimora and her operatives returned.

Once back in Zotova, Kikimora wasted no time in reporting to her chief, Valeria. The political officer was somewhat surprised that Kikimora had returned. *She actually came back,* Valeria thought.

Kikimora turned over the newspapers, comicbooks and even the money and the film to be developed from the pictures that she had taken. Valeria Rostova was quite pleased, and would also be shocked that here was proof that Americans from Earth were also on Vanag. The political officer then said, "Well done, Comrade. But how is this even possible that the Americans are also here on this world?"

The second-in-command of the Zotovan *KGB* related to her chief what the American sailor had told her. And told her in Russian, that the Americans had come through a vortex similar to the one that the Russians had come through. Only at the North Pole. Kikimora also briefed Valeria about the American submarine, the USS Tampa. When the pictures were developed, more would be revealed. The political officer's eyes were nearly twice their regular size at what Kikimora had told her.

At present, Valeria called for one of the Soviet sailors from the Vodyanoy who spoke and read English to translate the written material that Kikimora had given her. The newspapers and comicbooks revealed quite a bit. After all, the Americans were doing a lot of boasting regarding the new country that they had formed. The *UIU* really was another United States on the planet Vanag. What's more, the Americans and Russians had only recently discovered that each other had found themselves together on this faraway world from their own. This of course would raise the stakes.

From the newspaper articles and pictures taken by Kikimora, Valeria learned how the city of Great Columbia was nothing more than another Washington, D.C. Just as the Russians now had a second Moscow. The pictures confirmed that the Americans also came to this world via a submarine. And a powerful one at that, as the Los Angeles class vessel would be an even match for the Vodyanoy. Captain Starinov was especially alarmed over this new discovery uncovered by the Zotovan *KGB.*

The pictures of Nathan Berry's uniform and identification card also proved that the American sailors were here and active on the other side of the world. Kikimora also had some of the strange-looking paper money she brought back with her. Being a Vanagian, she had no idea who the men were pictured on these paper notes.

One of the notes was a Ucellan dollar bill. The image was of an older man with long, white hair. The other note was the five dollar bill. The person on this paper note had black hair and a beard. Above the picture of each man on this money was printed, United Islands Of Ucella. Valeria Rostova recognized these two famous men in American history. They were none other than George Washington and Abraham Lincoln.

The Russians, too, had been printing rubles for the currency of Zotova. Karl Marx and Vladimir Lenin were some of the people featured on their money. *Like us,* Valeria thought as she placed the Ucellan money along with the other items in a file, *the Americans have also been busy. They have set up a government and are also printing money. This is not what we needed on this world.*

Valeria Rostova may have reasoned that eventually a red flag displaying the hammer and sickle, would one day be flying in every country on Vanag, but this had been thwarted for now. The Soviet Union's rival from Earth had also made their presence known on this planet. "Damn, Americans," Valeria said outloud.

The political officer next summoned Kikimora. The Troznyan woman asked, "Are you pleased with what I uncovered in the Ucellan Islands, Comrade Rostova?"

"Yes indeed Comrade Kikimora." Valeria replied. "Your good work has not gone unnoticed by the party."

Now that Valeria, as chief of the Zotovan *KGB*, had her own building in New Moscow, she rarely went onboard the Vodyanoy. Frankly, she was tired of life on a submarine. But it was necessary for Valeria to report to Captain Starinov, and show him the pictures her second-in-command had brought back from her spy mission. Especially the ones of the American submarine.

After studying the pictures, the captain stated to Valeria, "This is alarming, Comrade Rostova." Then added, "The Americans have also established a country in their image, and have built up an army and navy. Similar to the Zotovan ships that we also use for our coastal navy, these Ucellan ships are like antiques, but yet menacing. However, this submarine, the Tampa is a Los Angeles-class submarine. And an equal match for the Vodyanoy. The American missiles on this submarine could easily destroy major cities in our Soviet Zotova. Including New Moscow."

Nodding in agreement, the political officer further stated, "Who would believe that when we came to this world, we would also find the Americans here? It appears that this could be the beginning of a Cold War on Vanag?" It was clearly evident that both the Americans and Russians knew that they were not alone. That is, people from two rival nations on Earth were now on the planet Vanag. By the expressions on their faces, both the captain and the political officer were worried.

"Well now, "Michaela spoke up, "this was certainly an interesting, yet frightening viewing. As a result of their espionage missions, the Americans and Russians now know what the other has been doing for the last four years."

"For sure, Israelite Girl," Rowena replied. "And both have set up puppet countries on Vanag, along with building up the Zotovan and Ucellan militaries."

"You would still think,' Amaresh said, "that both the Americans and Russians would work together and attempt to find a way back to Earth. I wonder if they will set up a meeting together at some point?"

"Of course they will," Cuca added. "I'm sure a future viewing will reveal that."

"For now though, I think that Valeria Rostova, has it right,' Lin concluded. "The Cold War from Earth, has now moved to Vanag."

Between viewings, Rowena was growing restless. The Celtic Time Maiden was always the impetuous one. Or, as Michaela the Jewish Time Maiden called Rowena, "a woman of action."

All of the Time Maidens had access to the planet-time scanners orbiting both Earth and Vanag. When all five of The Time Maidens weren't watching viewings of what was unfolding on Vanag at either the conference room or one of their palaces, some of the former Earth girls did their own private research. This was the case with Rowena and Amaresh.

For instance, Amaresh, while searching through the Vanagian time scanner, stumbled across something interesting involving the American David Hartford. David would naturally be considered an amateur astronomer on Earth, but on Vanag this would not be the case. Why?

Part of the reason would be that, as already noted, Earth was one hundred years ahead of Vanag. Even though Vanag's telescopes were equivalent to ones found on Earth back in the late 1800's, David Hartford knew how to look up into the Vanagian night sky and calculate the distance and positions of other planets and stars. After graduating from high school and before joining the navy, David attended a junior college for one semister in his native Prescott, Arizona. He majored in science and math. All of his life David excelled in math and was considered quite the mathematician. David would use his knowledge of math to map out the solar system that Vanag was a part of, as well as the other visible stars in this galaxy.

But more about that later. What intrigued Amaresh was a name that David Hartford came up with. Another name for the planet Vanag. It may be that while doing his mapping of this new solar system. (At least new to the Earth people), he gave the planet Vanag the name *Tellus Two*.

What did this mean? Tellus is a Latin word that means Earth. Such as *Tellus Mater* or *Terra Mater*. The ancient Roman earth-mother goddess was also called *Terra Mater*. Seeing how *Tellus* means *Earth*, David Hartford may have inadvertently started calling Vanag, *Tellus*. Then he added *Two*. *Tellus Two*, meaning *Earth Two*.

The Great Columbia Times, the main newspaper for the *UIU* began to publish articles of David Hartford's discoveries and calculations of outer space. The newspaper also started referring to Vanag as Tellus Two. Eventually, the planet would be called Tellus Two. First in the *UIU*, then the whole world.

In her research, Rowena, along with Justinian and Rebecca, also discovered some interesting situations through the time scanner. Specifically, possible missions or time-jumps. Rowena reasoned that many of these missions could be similar to the ones on Earth during the year 1968. On this new planet, Vanag, or Tellus Two, the Time Maidens could again make quick, yet very productive time-jumps. "In and out," as Rowena stated before.

After inviting the other four Time Maidens to her palace, Rowena took the floor to explain why she asked the others for this meeting. "As you know," Rowena started off by saying, "I've grown a bit weary of these viewings regarding this planet, Vanag or, should I now say, Tellus Two according to Amaresh's findings. I realize, my sisters, that these viewings are necessary, yet I feel that we have to do more than just monitor."

"You've told us several times, Rowena, how you feel," Michaela said. "But this is what Vix and the Aeduians requested from us. Study and become familiar with this world."

"It's true what Michaela says," Lin now said. "This Vanag-Tellus Two is a very complex planet. Finding this planet by accident has put us in a unique situation."

"And what makes this world even more complex," Amaresh added, "is the fact that the Americans and Russians also ended up on this planet. As they are a hundred years ahead of the people of Tellus Two, the Earth people are bringing their technology up to speed. Even changing the name of this planet."

"Viewing, fine. Monitoring, also fine," Rowena replied. "But there is no reason why we can't go on missions. Some of us can keep viewing, while others of us can make time-jumps. If I must, I will go on missions by myself. Or take Justinian and Rebecca with me." The married couple had also been invited to this meeting, and were always eager to go on a mission."

"Rowena," Cuca stated, "We're not about to let you go on any missions by yourself. Tell us what you have in mind."

"Yes, Celtic Girl," Michaela said, "tell us."

Rowena proceeded to do just that. She informed the other Time Maidens that Justinian and Rebecca had assisted her in viewing the time scanner now orbiting Tellus Two. After all, the married couple were Time Maidens' assistants. They kept a record of their discoveries for future reference, but Rowena had a certain mission in mind for this next time-jump.

This time-jump would take place fifty-six years before the Americans and Russians came through the vortex to this world. The Vanagians had a different calendar before the Earth people arrived. The Time Maidens wouldn't attempt to figure that way of measuring time, except counting backwards to the year 1 *A.E.* (After Earth.)

This proposed mission by Rowena would take place in the other great landmass, Trozny, separated by the Acco Channel opposite Zotova. For many centuries Trozny had been ruled by a monarchy. Mostly kings. There were many provinces throughout

Trozny. Some large, others small. Each province was ruled by a governor, satrap, or whatever they wanted to be called. As long as these local rulers were loyal to the King or Queen of Trozny and paid tribute, they could pretty much do what they wanted. Which was not always good. In reality, some of these Troznyan governors were no better than the warlords and crime bosses in Zotova.

Rowena and her assistants also uncovered the fact that some of these governors in various provinces had brief mini-wars or conflicts with one another. The reasons for these wars varied. It could be over having more land for resources. It may be over a lake, river or coastline. Although most of the people were Troznyans, many times, depending on who won the conflict, some in Trozny were mistreated. This could include forced military conscription, slave labor, and even sex slaves in the case of captured women.

The mission Rowena was planning involved twenty-three Troznyan women taken captive in a recent border war between two governors. When a certain village had been overrun by the opposing army, the young women and girls were rounded up. These captured females would fetch a high price when sold to Zotovan pirates and slave traders. The pirates sometimes kept a few for themselves, but most of the time the girls and young women were resold to crime bosses or warlords in Zotova.

When the captured Troznyan women got to be too old to be sex slaves, they then were used for domestic duties or slave labor. The Time Maidens had already observed that the sex slave trade had been taking place for a long time. This is how many Troznyan women ended up in Zotova. They had to admit that one good thing the Russians accomplished on Tellus Two was to put an end to the sex-slave trade in Zotova.

Of these twenty-three women that Rowena wanted to rescue, four of them were over eighteen years old. The oldest woman being twenty-four. Of the other Troznyan girls, their ages ranged from fourteen to seventeen years old. Any adults involved in a rescue mission by the Time Maidens could be relocated to the planet Texacos. It was during this briefing that Rowena suggested to Amaresh that, as Ambassador to Texacos, she contact President Dinah Yates concerning these possible new arrivals. The Time Maidens had already rescued and sent adults from Earth to Texacos. If they did this from missions on Earth, they could likewise do the same thing on Tellus Two. This was how Texacos was founded in the first palce. That is, when the former Confederate-Americans from mission thriteen were rescued.

During Rowena's presentation, Lin politely interrupted by asking, "Rowena, how do you plan to enter this time period, and what kind of attire did you have in mind?"

The Celtic Time Maiden had it all figured out. "There was a saying in the old American west," Rowena replied, "to go in with guns blazing. Some of our most successful missions were when we came through a time ring with the weapons the Aeduians gave us. If we plan this mission right, we can have the element of surprise."

Rowena continued on with the plans for this mission. She made it apparent that input from the other Time Maidens would be appreciated. "Michaela," Rowena said, "you are fascinated with the indigenous peoples of the arctic regions. See if you can come up with a frightening mask from one of the cultures. We've worn masks in the past on previous missions. We will need something for this next mission." Michaela nodded and would do just what Rowena asked of her.

"Cuca," Rowena now asked, "can you come up with an interesting-colored jumpsuit for us? Then perhaps a cape of a different color and matching boots. We always throw our opponents off guard whenever we wear jumpsuits, capes and masks." Cuca would come up with something.

As Michaela and Cuca followed through with the attire, Rowena filled in Lin and Amaresh about how and where this next time-jump would take place. The other two Time Maidens could be briefed later.

For this rescue of the twenty-three women and young girls, the captives had already been rounded up and were being held in a cell. Or more like a pit with bars over it, dug out of the ground near the shoreline in the northeasten part of Trozny. This part of Trozny was located along the body of water known as the Umea Ocean.

There were three ruthless Zotovan pirates that would be transportating the captives who had been handed over to them by the governor who had captured them to begin with. The crime bosses and warlords in Zotova would pay a good price for each of these Troznyan women and girls. There was no shortage of sex slaves and brothel girls in this lawless land, as this trade was in great demand.

Pirate ships used in the slave trade were only about thirty feet long. Below the deck was where booty from raids could be stored, along with human cargo. That is, slave girls. It would be easy for only three pirates to keep these young women and girls at bay. Besides, the slave girls would be chained below. When all of the Time Maidens saw this on the time scanner, it made them sick to their stomachs and angry. In a way, this was a good thing as it made them more determined to be successful on this mission. And they would be.

This time-jump would actually involve two phases during this mission. Rowena had planned this mission well. All five Time Maidens assembled in the ring operations complex. They would all be taking part in this mission. Justinian and three of the Time Maidens' personal androids would also be involved, but only in phase two.

Cuca found the perfect attire for this time-jump. The Time Maidens would be dressed in glistering, gold jumpsuits. They would also have a red cape with matching red boots. Any clothes worn by the Time Maidens on a mission were both fire resistant and bulletproof. The Aeduians provided these clothes and wanted the Earth girls to be protected. In this latest attire, the young women appeared exotic, mysterious and once again otherworldly. Not being from Vanag-Tellus Two, they were indeed aliens.

Regarding the masks, Michaela came up with a frightening one. And one from an arctic culture. It was a replica of a wooden dance mask. The mask had two half faces, one on top of the other. A man and a seal. Dancing aside, the mask was horrorifying. Which was what the Time Maidens wanted. As the mask had two sets of eyes, the wearers would see through the bottom face. That is the seal. Concerning the top face of the mask, the man, the eyes would blink on and off in red. If a Time Maiden spoke through the mask, her voice would be amplified, and in a deep, scary manner. Again, what the Time Maidens desired. These masks and clothes would be unlike anything the Zotovan pirates had ever encountered. And this was just the beginning.

"All right, my sisters," Rowena said as a time ring was activated, "let's go and rescue some Troznyan girls." The androids Illapu and Akan would send and recover the time ring.

Reminiscent of previous missions, Rowena went through the ring first. Then Lin and Cuca came through the ring and took up a posistion to Rowena's right. Michaela and Amaresh next came through the ring and stood to the Celtic Time Maiden's left. They appeared on a beach. It was now dark. The three pirates were huddled around a fire.

"LOOK OUT, YOU GOOD-FOR-NOTHING PIRATES," Rowena screamed, *"WE ARE HERE TO FREE YOUR SLAVES."* Rowena's voice sounded frightening as a result of the amplification through the mask.

Now four of the Time Maidens had their weapons. Rowena, Michaela and Cuca were armed with their special Aeduian-made staffs. A time ring out of nowhere had already startled the pirates. But now five strange-looking beings that came out of the glowing ring stood in their midst. To the pirates, these beings were dressed in the most unusual clothes they had ever seen. And what of these faces? The masks that the Time Maidens were wearing did indeed appear to be real faces. And yet, as the jumpsuits that the Earth girls were wearing were always very form-fitting, their female bodies stood out. But were these beings even females? And where did they come from?

"TAKE HEED, YOU PIRATE WORMS," Michaela shouted. The Hebrew Time Maiden then kicked back her right leg and aimed her laser staff towards the ship anchored about forty feet from the shore. A green laser beam emitted from her staff. Instantly, starting with the sail, the ship was engulfed in flames. Michaela did likewise to a small rowboat on the shore that would be used to transport the slave girls to the larger ship.

The pirates were aghast at seeing their ship going up in flames. This ship was their livelihood. But an evil, corrupt livelihood. Just then, one of the pirates reached for a crude pistol strapped to his belt. Cuca had been keeping her eyes on the pirates. *"OH, NO, YOU DON"T,"* Cuca also shouted. Her voice, too, was amplified and sounded frightening. The other set of eyes on the mask blinked red. The Incan princess now aimed her golden staff at the pirate attempting to fire his pistol. The staff emitted a stream of ice. The pirate's hand and gun were at once frozen. The pirate screamed, and then appeared to be in shock at the sight of his frozen hand.

Next, it was Amaresh's move, *"OBSERVE, YOU VILE ZOTOVANS,"* she stated as she held up her shield and activated it so that it lit up like an exploding mini-sun. As the pirates were looking directly at the Time Maidens, they were now blinded. The rest of the Time Maidens were standing behind Amaresh when she activated her shield. Nevertheless, all of the Time Maidens wore special contact lenses for protection.

The Zotovan pirates screamed in terror over their blindness. One pirate accidently got too close to the campfire and his trousers caught fire. He screamed even more, but realized that there was water at the nearby beach. The pirate dove into the shallow water and rolled over several times to extinguish the flames. After a moment he crawled back towards the beach.

"I'll take it from here, my sisters," Rowena stated. She then sprang into action. Starting out with the pirate crawling on the beach, Rowena struck him across his back and knocked him out. As her Aeduian-made quarterstaff's blows were five times more powerful than an average staff, and it didn't take much for Rowena to render the blind pirate unconscious, he was taken out of the equation in no time. The Celtic Time Maiden then moved on to the other blind pirates groping in the darkness.

With a strike on the head, Rowena took out the second pirate. "*OUCH,*" the pirate said as he fell face down in the sand.

Rowena then approached the third pirate and gave him a whack across the chest. "*UGH,*" he cried out, and then fell to his knees. Rowena struck him on the head. He, too, fell face down. And was out cold. All three of the pirates had been taken out and were now unconscious. When they regained consciousness later, they would be somewhere else. But that would be phase two of the mission.

Lin now took the lead as she sprinted over to the caged pit where the Troznyan girls and young women were being held captive. "Troznyan women," Lin called out from above the pit in their language, "We are here to rescue you." Once the pirates had been taken out, the Time Maidens had removed their frightening masks. There was no longer any need for them.

Cuca and Amaresh removed the thick, wooden pole latch that secured the caged door. The pirates had a roped ladder rolled up nearby that had been used to place the captives into the deep pit. Rowena lowered the ladder and she and Michaela stepped on one end of it to secure it for each of the Troznyan girls to climb out one at a time. Lin counted each girl as they climbed out so as to make sure that all twenty-three of the former captives were accounted for. The younger girls emerged first, followed by the four young women that were over eighteen years old.

Cuca and Amaresh assembled the now-freed girls into a group. The time ring had remained materialized the whole time during this mission. Naturally, the girls and women just stared at the glowing ring. These were all simple, peasant girls, so they had no idea what this strange object was.

"Come," Cuca also said in Troznyan. "Everything will be all right."

"Yes," Amaresh added, "Follow us through the ring." In fact, Cuca and Amaresh each took two of the Troznyan girls by the hand and led them through the time ring.

Lin, Rowena and Michaela then instructed the other girls what to do as they all entered through the ring. Following up in the rear, Rowena was the last one to go through the ring. The ring then vanished back to the kingdom.

Next, though, was phase two of the mission. What did this involve? As soon as the first time ring vanished after the Time Maidens rescued the Troznyan girls, another one materialized on the shore. For what purpose? This would involve the three unconscious Zotovan pirates.

The pirates did not see the actual faces of the Time Maidens. They observed only five women with frightening faces dressed in strange clothing and carrying powerful weapons. Whether anyone would ever believe the pirates, if they were allowed to tell their story, mattered little. The Time Maidens were going to see to it that they never got the chance.

Out of the second time ring came Justinian taking the lead, followed by the androids Golem, Taranis and Mao. The three androids knew what to do. Having been created by the Aeduians to possess much greater strength than an average man, each of them picked up a pirate and threw them over a shoulder. The androids then went back through the time ring with Justinian following behind. The time ring then disappeared.

The pirates lives had been spared and they would regain their sight. But where were they? They awoke on a beach, or shoreline. Nevertheless, not the same beach they had previously been on in Trozny. Under the direction of the Time Maidens, Justinian and the androids took the pirates to a small uninhabited isalnd in the middle of the Targu Ocean. The island, about three miles in diameter, was over one thousand miles away from the continent of Enaim. There were many uninhabited isalnds sprinkled throughout this ocean in the Southern Hemisphere of Vanag-Tellus Two.

These pirates were all in their late thirties. As noted, this mission took place fifty-six years before the new calendar of *1 A.E.* (After Earth.) was established. It would be over thirty more years after this new calendar before anyone else stumbled onto this unknown island where the pirates were sent.

There was an abudance of fruit, birds and small animals that the pirates could live off for food. One might say that this island was a paradise. But a boring paradise as the pirates only had each other. Their life of pillaging, taking sex slaves and drunken bouts had come to an end. They would remain on this island, as there was no way off, until their dying days.

After the first decade of the establishment of Soviet Zotova with Russian know-how, submarines were being constructed on Tellus Two. And the Americans were doing the same for the Ucellans. These submarines would not be nuclear-powered like the Tampa and Vodyanoy. The Earth designers reverted back to a simpler time in this business of submarine manufacturing. That is, post-World War Two, or the beginning of the Cold War.

By the first decade of when the Americans and Russians came to Tellus Two, both Zotova and Ucella were drilling for oil at the planet's North Pole. By the year *22 A.E.*, two polar wars would have been fought between these two new superpowers of Tellus Two. (But more about that later.)

Now having diesel fuel to operate electric motors, ships and submarines became a part of Zotova and Ucella's navies. The Soviet Zotovans constructed several classes of submarines previously used by the Soviet Union on Earth. One such class was the *Foxtrot.* The Zotovan navy would eventually have twelve Foxtrots as part of their fleet.

In *31 A.E.*, one such Foxtrot submarine stumbled upon this small island in the Targu Ocean where the pirates had been sent by the Time Maidens many years earlier. The last pirate had already been dead for five years. As they had been submerged for several weeks underwater, the Zotovan submariners on this submarine wanted to take turns relaxing on this island for a few hours.

It was at this time that the submariners discovered what was left of the pirates. Two of the pirates had been buried in shallow graves and covered over with small rocks found on the island. As the third and last pirate couldn't be buried, his remains were discovered in a nearby cave where the pirates had taken shelter.

It was what was carved into a larger rock near the cave that perplexed these now-modern Zotovan sailors. The last pirate, before dying, used a smaller rock to carve these words in Zotovan: *BEWARE OF THE SHE-DEVILS FROM BEYOND.* Or something to that effect in the Zotovan language.

This was obviously in reference to The Time Maidens. The Zotovan sailors had no idea what this meant, even though they could read the warning message. It mattered little, and the Time Maidens achieved their goal on this mission.

Once all of the rescued Troznyan girls and young women came through the time ring to the kingdom, Shako, along with Rebecca and Mary Collard saw to their needs. All three of these women were Time Maidens' assistants. The former captives were directed to the children's complex. There, the girls and women could take a hot bath, something that none of them had ever experienced before, and put on fresh clothes. When rescued, their clothes had been reduced to tattered rags. Next, a delicious meal had been provided for them.

As the four women over eighteen years old were to be relocated to the planet Texacos, arrangements had already been underway to take them there. Amaresh, the Time Maidens Ambassador to Texacos, had already contacted President Dinah Yates about the arrival of the four young women. By now, Amaresh knew how to pilot the Aeduian-made shuttle. She and Rebecca escorted the Troznyan women to the shuttle. A time ring was activated, then enlarged to accommodate the shuttle.

Once on the other side on the planet Texacos, Amaresh piloted the shuttle for a short, low flight, then landed the craft in a field near the Governmental House in New Richmond. As the President of Texacos, this was where Dinah Yates lived with her husband Thomas.

As usual, the Texacosians were eager to see Amaresh and Rebecca. Especially Rebecca, as she had once been one of their own. Amaresh briefly met with Dinah and explained to her about these young women from another Earth-like world. As the Troznyan women didn't speak the language of Texacos, that is, English, they would have to learn. And under the care of the Texascosians, it wouldn't take long. Others taken to Texacos were proof of that.

There were still quite a few eligible young men in Texacos. It wouldn't be long before these Troznyan women became the wives of some of these men. Before departing Texacos to return to the kingdom, Dinah Yates asked Amaresh, "Will there be more people from this other world coming to Texacos?"

"Who knows, President Yates," Amaresh replied. "Events are moving very fast on this other world. We don't know how we can keep up." Amaresh and Rebecca then returned to the kingdom.

Right after the Troznyan girls and women had been rescued on the beach, while Cuca and Amaresh were directing them through the time ring, Rowena helped herself to a few collectibles, or Vanagian booty. The Celtic Time Maiden gathered up a pistol, sword and two impressive daggers from the unconscious pirates. Michaela saw Rowena doing this out of the corner of her eye. Once they got back to the kingdom, the Hebrew Time Maiden intended to ask Rowena about this latest stunt.

Once Justinian and the three androids had returned through the other time ring and reported that the Zotovan pirates had been left on the obscure island, the ring operations complex became quiet. Lin had already departed to contact Vix and the other Aeduians that nineteen Troznyan girls would soon be coming through the master time ring for the planet Aedui.

"So, Rowena," Michaela stated, "I noticed that you helped yourself to some more Vanagian weapons. Are you going to start a collection of souvenirs from Vanag? Like you've done on Earth."

"By all means, Israelite Girl," Rowena replied.

"And where may I ask," Michaela further said, "are you going to put all of this war booty collection of yours?"

"Oh, I don't know for now," Rowena answered. "But there is plenty of room here in the kingdom. Better yet, Michaela, I could start sharing some of this booty with you."

"WHAT!" Michaela exclaimed. "You already gave me a dagger from one of your missions. And don't say that 'one never knows when a girl may need a knife.' Or something like that."

"But it's true, Israelite Girl," Rowena just had to add. "With the right dress or jumpsuit, a knife would be very becoming of you if strapped to the side of your hip."

"OH, ROWENA," Michaela screamed. "You're impossible." Then the Hebrew Time Maiden exited the ring operations complex. As she did so, Rowena howled with laughter.

In due course, the nineteen Troznyan girls needed to be sent off to Aedui. All five Time Maidens along with Shako, Justinian and Rebecca assembled in the ring operations complex. The future young Aeduian girls were clean and were dressed in cute, comfortable dresses. About half wore red dresses, while the rest were in yellow.

From the planet Aedui, the master time ring was activated. The Troznyan girls had been briefed about what to expect. Nevertheless, with the appearance of this huge ring with blinking lights and a humming noise, they were not sure what to expect. The Time Maidens' assistants assembled them into two rows for departure.

But then Rowena came forward and stood before them saying, "Troznyan girls. Your days of misery and harassment are over. You're about to enter a new world where you can live in peace for many, many years and all of your needs will be provided for you."

The three assistants then directed the girls to enter through the master ring. Once they had done so, the ring was deactivated from the other side by the Aeduians. These young girls only spoke Troznyan, but they would be given the device to implant in their ear. Then they would all be able to speak and comprehend Aeduian.

The next day, the Time Maidens met in the conference-planning room to discuss what they should do next regarding Tellus Two. The matters considered by the former Earth girls were as follows: *Should they keep viewing and monitoring what was taking place on Tellus Two? Would more missions be planned for that planet, or would it be best to forget about Tellus Two and resume their missions on Earth?* Vix and the Aeduians were silent about these matters. It was the Time Maidens' decision.

Previously, it had been brought up that some Time Maidens would resume missions on Earth, while others planned more on Tellus Two. However, every time they considered missions on both worlds, the Earth girls concluded that it may get too complicated or confusing. For now, it was decided to just concentrate on one planet. But which one? Earth or Tellus Two?

After a long discussion, and hearing all points of view, it was unanimously decided that for the time being, the Time Maidens would continue to monitor Tellus Two, and in all probability plan more missions. But eventually turn their attention back to their own planet Earth.

"If we eventually go back to missions on Earth," Michaela stated, "and continue to be involved with both worlds, then we are going to need help. And I don't think that we can count on the Aeduians to get directly involved. That is not part of their agenda."

"That's the key, Michaela," Lin concluded. "Help. And I think I know how and where we can obtain this help."

TO BE CONTINUED...

ABOUT THE AUTHOR

Evan F. Riley, Jr lives in St. Petersburg, Florida with his wife, Alice. He is a U.S. Army brat that traveled a lot as a child. Evan is deeply interested in all types of history, geography, astronomy, theology, mythology, science fiction, and is a long time fan of The Beatles. Evan is also the author of a series of books called The Time Maidens. And the books Visitor from a Distant Star and The Beatleologist Kid. He and his wife love to travel to different locations to this day.